I0629474

Powders To Microorganisms

Wallace Berry

Published by Wallace Berry, 2024.

POWDERS TO MICROORGANISMS

First edition. February 11, 2024.

Copyright © 2024 Wallace Berry.

ISBN: 979-8990123601

Written by Wallace Berry.

Table of Contents

Chapter 1
The Mysterious Chest

As the boys pull their jon boat up to the shadow-drenched shores of Bird Island, they immediately note a peculiar silence blanketing the area, an eerie hush apart from the gentle lap of waves against the hull. The usual cacophony of bird calls is conspicuously absent. Guided by their curiosity, they step onto the island, and their eyes are drawn to a strange, glinting object half-buried in the sand near the high-tide line.

It's a weathered, ornate chest, its metal aged by salt and time, with rusty iron bands clasping it shut. A large lock, nearly eroded away, suggest the chest may have once been a prized possession. The scene grips them—it's as if they've stepped through time, the chest a silent testament to voyages and storms past.

This discovery sets their hearts racing with endless questions. How did such an object come to rest here on Bird Island, known mostly to local fowl and fishermen? The chest could well be remnants from a shipwreck, concealed by tides and only now revealed by the shifting sands.

Bird Island, located off the southeastern side of East Matagorda Bay along the Texas Gulf Coast, is a flat, low-lying oasis of cordgrass, vines, bushes, and the occasional live oak tree. The island stretches one and one-half miles long and about one-half a mile across, running east to west. It harbors a variety of wildlife, including coyotes, rabbits, bobcats, alligators, rattlesnakes, water moccasins, nutria, and other unnamed creatures. A barely noticeable low ridge runs the length of the island, peaking at just 7 feet above the high tide level, concealing hidden and long-forgotten World War II underground structures.

The island's shoreline is predominantly mud flats interspersed with oyster beds and sporadic sandy beach areas, with chalky clay streaks and minor rock formations along the southwest tip. An old military bunker near the southeastern tip serves as a silent witness to the island's past. Bird Island is a remote natural haven with an air of mystery, where history and wildlife co-exist quietly away from the hum of civilization.

The boys, each echoing the other's wide-eyed exhilaration, approach the chest, a mixture of apprehension and excitement stirring in their chests. Richie, with his practical nature, cautions them to be wary of anything that might reside within—be it historic treasures or hidden dangers. Pug, ever the enthusiast, can barely contain his urge to wrench the chest open and unveil its secrets. Wally, practical and mechanical-minded, suggests they inspect it thoroughly before attempting to open it, ensuring it isn't booby-trapped or structurally unsound.

Together, they decide to investigate this mysterious chest, unaware that it will lead them on an adventure far bigger than they could have imagined. An adventure that will test their friendship, their courage, and their resolve as young men standing on the precipice of adulthood.

THE THREE BOYS GATHERED around the mysterious chest, awe and uncertainty etched on their faces. Pug's eyes shone with exhilaration as he envisioned the treasures that could lie within. "C'mon, let's open 'er up!" he exclaimed, rubbing his hands together in anticipation.

Pug, Richie, and Wally are three high school friends bound by their shared love for the great outdoors and the rugged landscapes of the Texas Gulf Coast. Their relationship is solidified through a mutual spirit of adventure and a brotherly bond that has formed over countless trips to Pug's family fishing cabin in Chinquapin, Texas.

Wally shook his head, his studious nature taking over. "We should make sure it's safe first. Could be boobytrapped." He knelt down, scrutinizing the chest for any signs of wires or triggers.

"I don't like this, guys," Richie said nervously, glancing around as if expecting someone to jump out at them. "We should put it back where we found it."

Pug scoffed. "And let someone else take it? No way!" He grabbed the lid, but Wally stayed his hand.

"Hold up. I gotta check it over real good before we open it. Don't wanna get blown sky high." Methodically, Wally inspected every inch, probing gently with his pocket knife. After several tense minutes, he leaned back on his heels. "Looks clean. No traps that I can see."

Pug whooped and reached for the lid again, but Richie blocked him this time. "We can't just leave it sitting here. What if someone comes along and takes it?" He chewed his lip worriedly.

"He's right," Wally conceded. "It ain't safe to go traipsing all over the island with this thing either. And we sure as heck can't lug it around the bunker."

Dejection flickered across Pug's face, but he rallied quickly. "I know, we can stow it under the stern bench in the boat for now. No one will spot it there."

Richie and Wally exchanged glances and nodded. Working together, they lifted the heavy chest and made their way carefully down the rocky shoreline toward the boat. Wally kept watch while Pug and Richie shoved their gear aside to make room, nestling the chest securely beneath the bench.

"There, that oughta do it," Pug said with satisfaction, dusting off his hands. "Let's get back to the cabin and figure out our next move."

Eagerness shone in his eyes once more at the promise of adventure. As the boys climbed aboard to head back, anticipation hung heavy in the air, mixing with their unease. The mysteries of Bird Island had only just begun.

THE BREEZE WAS BARELY a whisper, just enough to gently ripple the glassy surface of East Matagorda Bay. With the outboard motor on Pug's small aluminum jon boat purring smoothly, the three friends made excellent time returning from Bird Island to the fishing cabin. Pug stood at the motor's controls, expertly steering them along the shortest route across the shallow bay. Richie sat upright in the boat's bow, keeping an eye out for obstacles. Wally was amidships, one hand resting on the ancient chest they had discovered, as if protecting their unusual find.

Before long, the cabin's dock emerged into view. Pug reduced the throttle, angling the boat to align with the weathered wooden structure. He cut the engine and allowed their momentum to carry them forward, bumping gently against the dock's edge. Richie hopped out, rope in hand, and tied them off.

The fishing camp, owned by Pug's family, is a functional and versatile structure located on Live Oak Bayou, less than half a mile upstream from where the bayou meets the inter-coastal waterway and flows into the northeast end of East Matagorda Bay. Measuring 20 feet by 30 feet, the camp features an open-concept kitchen, dining, and living area, with an adjacent open sleeping space and a separate enclosed bathroom with a shower. The camp's design includes hinged exterior walls that can be lifted to create a breezy screened-in area or secured shut against bad weather. It stands about three feet off the ground with a walkway leading to a dock, and it is connected to a boat shed with a roller ramp winch system for a 16-foot jon boat. Additionally, wire mesh crab traps dangle from ropes off the sides of the walkway. All of this is accessed by a shell-covered driveway that weaves through the marsh to the main highway, making it a secluded but accessible spot for outdoor activities like fishing, hunting, shrimping, and crabbing.

Together, the three boys carefully lifted the chest, swaddled in an old crab trap to disguise it. They carried it down the dock, the boards creaking under their steps. At the shoreline, they paused to get a firmer grip before continuing up the crushed shell driveway to the boat shed.

Once inside, they set the chest down and caught their breath, scanning the space. After a moment, Richie spoke up. "I'll put on some coffee. You guys see what you can figure out about this thing." He gestured to the chest before heading up the ramp toward the cabin.

Pug's eyes lit up. He grabbed a screwdriver from the tool bench and set to work removing the crab trap wire. As the chest was revealed, he let out a low whistle. "Would you look at that engraving? This thing is fancy."

Wally nodded, leaning in for a closer inspection. "It definitely looks old. But it could still be dangerous. Better check it over carefully before we try to open it." Ever the pragmatic one, Wally began methodically searching for any sign of traps or triggers attached to the chest.

Soon Richie returned, three steaming mugs of coffee in hand. "Any luck?" he asked, passing the drinks around before joining them in examining the chest.

"Not yet," Pug replied. "But we'll get it figured out."

"Well, it just so happens I took a locksmithing course last summer," Richie said, a glint in his eye. "I might be able to pick the lock if you can't find the key."

The three exchanged excited looks, knowing they were one step closer to unlocking the chest's secrets. But they also felt the weight of this discovery, and the uncertainty of what lay ahead. For now, they drank their coffee, studying the weathered container. Then, with care and cunning, they would unravel its mysteries.

RICHIE RETURNED TO the cabin, scouring the cluttered shelves and dusty corners for anything that could aid in picking the ancient lock on the chest. After rummaging around the hot water heater, he found a small roll of bare wire that gave him an idea. Armed with his makeshift lockpicking tool, Richie headed back to rejoin Pug and Wally who were examining the chest's intricate engravings.

Kneeling down, Richie carefully inserted the end of the wire into the chest's keyhole. With practiced finesse, he maneuvered the wire around, searching for the locking mechanism inside. After a few minutes of diligent focus, a soft click sounded out as the internal pins aligned and the lock disengaged. However, as Richie tried to slide the locking bar, it refused to budge, rusted firmly in place.

"We just need something to loosen this up," Richie muttered, sitting back on his heels.

Pug sprang into action, scouring the boat shed and cabin for anything that could penetrate the thick rust. He soon returned triumphantly with a can of penetrating oil. After liberally applying it along the sliding bar, the trio waited with bated breath for the oil to work its magic. As the minutes ticked by, the excitement hanging in the air was palpable.

Finally, Pug gripped the bar and applied firm pressure. With a coarse screech, the rusted mechanism slowly began sliding backwards until, at last, the chest popped open. The three friends stared at each other wide-eyed, on the cusp of uncovering the chest's long-held secrets. What awaited them inside? They were about to find out.

THE ANCIENT CHEST CREAKED open with a groan, its hinges protesting against decades of disuse. The three friends gathered around, holding their breath in anticipation as dim light spilled over the contents within.

"Whoa," Pug murmured, reaching inside first. His hands brushed against coarse fabric, grasping onto a bundle of aged journals. Carefully, he lifted them out, noting the musty scent of old parchment mingling with pipe tobacco. The journals were bound in cracked leather, faded gold lettering visible on their spines labeling each volume with a Roman numeral.

Wally's eyes widened as he caught sight of what looked to be an antique compass and matching sextant. Gingerly, he retrieved the navigational tools, turning them over to inspect their craftsmanship. "These look really old," he remarked. "I bet they still work though."

Meanwhile, Richie sorted through a collection of black and white photographs depicting uniformed men and strange machinery. One figure in particular appeared frequently - a bespectacled man who Richie guessed must be the elusive Dr. Sinclair. Alongside the photos were military medals and ribbons, denoting service and achievement.

"Guys, check this out," Pug said suddenly, extracting what appeared to be a detailed map of the Texas coastline. Cryptic symbols marked certain areas, with Bird Island prominently circled in red ink. The three exchanged excited glances, realizing the true adventure was only just beginning. What secrets might the contents of this chest reveal? And did Dr. Sinclair intend for them to find it after all these years.

THE THREE FRIENDS GATHERED around the open chest, eyes widening as they took in the assortment of items within. Nestled on top was a weathered leather journal, its pages yellowed with age. Pug reached in and lifted it out, handling the fragile book as if it were a priceless artifact.

"Is that what I think it is?" breathed Wally.

Pug nodded, tracing his fingers over the embossed title on the cover: Journal Numeral I.

"It's one of the journals from the research expedition back in the 60s," Pug said in hushed awe. "The one led by Dr. Sinclair to study the weird stuff happening around Bird Island."

Richie peered over Pug's shoulder as he gently cracked open the journal's cover. The first page was filled with elegant cursive handwriting, detailing Dr. Sinclair's arrival on the island over 50 years prior. Pug turned the page, the sound of rustling paper filling the quiet room.

"This first entry describes unusual sightings the locals told him about," narrated Pug. "Ghosts in the water, lights beneath the waves."

Wally and Richie exchanged an uneasy glance. Pug continued reading Dr. Sinclair's clinical documentation of the unexplained phenomena surrounding Bird Island. One account stood out - his observation of a ghostly stingray illuminating the dawn waters.

Pug looked up, voice hushed. "Guys, remember those lights people have been seeing offshore lately? And the stories about shapes moving under the surface?"

"You don't think..." Wally trailed off, unsure how to even articulate the possibilities swirling through all their minds.

"Let's keep reading," suggested Richie. "We need more information before jumping to conclusions."

They pored over the remaining entries detailing Dr. Sinclair's early days on the island, including initial theories about the source of the bizarre events. The journal ended on an ominous note, with Dr. Sinclair expressing doubts about continuing the research.

A tense silence settled over the room. The three friends stared at the journal, grappling with the implications of what they had read. This was no longer just a quest for adventure - Dr. Sinclair's account hinted at forces beyond their comprehension. What had he uncovered? And what darker secrets remained buried on Bird Island?

THE BOYS HUDDLED AROUND the weathered journal, poring over the hastily scrawled pages. Dr. Sinclair's account of his expedition to Bird Island had sparked more questions than answers.

"How do you think this ended up in the bay?" Pug wondered aloud, flipping through the journal's dog-eared pages.

Richie furrowed his brow thoughtfully. "Hard to say. Could've been an accident, maybe the doctor dropped it overboard somehow."

"Or maybe someone dumped it to keep it hidden," Wally suggested. "To prevent it from being found."

Pug nodded. "You might be onto something. This sounds like pretty sensitive stuff, especially with the military involved."

"It could've been stolen too," Richie added. "Then lost or discarded by whoever took it."

The three boys fell silent, considering the implications. This journal contained explosive revelations about the inexplicable events at Bird Island. No wonder it had been locked away in that weathered chest, bound in oilskin - someone had wanted it concealed.

Wally flipped to the journal's abrupt ending, where Dr. Sinclair's rushed scrawl deteriorated into inky scratches. "What do you guys think we should do next? Keep digging into this, or just leave it be?"

Pug's eyes glinted with excitement. "Are you kidding? A mystery like this, we gotta keep investigating!"

Richie bit his lip uncertainly. "I dunno, this seems really serious. Messing with stuff we don't understand."

"But don't you wanna know the truth?" Pug pressed. "We can't just ignore it after reading all this."

Wally nodded. "I'm with Pug. We oughta see where this leads."

He sighed, then smiled wryly. "Alright, you've convinced me. But we've gotta be real careful."

Pug grinned and slapped Richie on the back. "Careful's my middle name! Let's get to the bottom of this thing."

The three friends hunched over the journal again, rereading key passages for clues about what sinister secrets still lurked on Bird Island. The afternoon sun dipped towards the horizon as they plotted their next move, ready to unravel the mysteries that Dr. Sinclair had only begun to uncover so many decades ago.

PUG, RICHIE, AND WALLY gathered around the ancient chest, still in awe at the mysterious artifacts they had uncovered. The journals, map, and equipment raised more questions than answers about the chest's origins and purpose.

"So what should we do now?" Pug asked, breaking the contemplative silence.

Richie furrowed his brow. "I think we need to be really careful with this stuff. We don't know who it belonged to or why it was hidden on the island."

"Oh come on, don't be such a worrywart," Pug said with a dismissive wave of his hand. "This is the discovery of a lifetime! I say we start figuring out what all these clues mean."

Wally chimed in. "I'm with Richie on this one. We shouldn't jump to conclusions. For all we know, these items could be dangerous or illegal."

Pug, Richie, and Wally gathered around the ancient chest, still in awe at the mysterious artifacts they had uncovered. The journals, map, and equipment raised more questions than answers about the chest's origins and purpose.

"So what should we do now?" Pug asked, breaking the contemplative silence.

Richie furrowed his brow. "I think we need to be really careful with this stuff. We don't know who it belonged to or why it was hidden on the island."

"Oh come on, don't be such a worrywart," Pug said with a dismissive wave of his hand. "This is the discovery of a lifetime! I say we start figuring out what all these clues mean."

Wally chimed in. "I'm with Richie on this one. We shouldn't jump to conclusions. For all we know, these items could be dangerous or illegal."

Pug rubbed his chin thoughtfully. "You both make valid arguments. However, we can't simply turn a blind eye to what we've found. It's like a siren call—you can't just walk away from it." He flicked a glance at the chest, feeling the gravity of their discovery. "What if we consult Old Man Barnes? With his wealth of local experience and wisdom, I'm sure he'd have a thing or two to say about this chest." The weight of their situation seemed less burdensome with the thought of Barnes' input.

Old Man Barnes was more than just a retired fisherman; he was a living archive of the area's history, especially the secrets of Bird Island. Having navigated the Gulf waters for half a century, his knowledge of the local geography and maritime conditions was unparalleled. Not to mention, his possession of lore and anecdotes from the war era—due in part to his brother's service on Bird Island—made him an invaluable resource.

The old man also had a knack for storytelling that turned dry historical facts into vivid pictures. This ability to make history come alive could potentially give them new perspectives on the origin and contents of the chest. Considering his experience with locating hidden things at sea, he could help the boys interpret the cryptic symbols on the maps they'd found. His keen understanding of the island's layout would be instrumental in deciphering Dr. Sinclair's intentions and perhaps even lead them to other hidden treasures or clues that were beyond the grasp of an untrained eye.

Yet, it wasn't just Barnes' encyclopedic knowledge that made him an ideal ally. His affection for imparting wisdom to younger generations meant that he would likely be eager to assist and guide them through their findings. After all, for Old Man Barnes, passing down the torch of knowledge was not just a pastime; it was a responsibility he carried with pride.

Pug knew that Barnes' physical presence on a possibly treacherous exploration might be limited due to his age, but his strategic insights, historical clues, and moral support could very well be the cornerstone of their success. So it didn't come as a surprise when Pug proposed seeking his aid; it was almost a natural recourse for the boys who had been plunged into the depths of a mystery that was part of Barnes' legacy.

Richie and Wally looked at each other and nodded. Pug's dad and Old Man Barnes went way back, having been fishing buddies for over 20 years. If anyone could shed light on their findings, it would be him.

"Alright, let's give Barnes a call," Wally said. "If he thinks it's safe, we'll show him what we found and get his take."

Pug grinned and grabbed the cabin's corded phone, dialing the number by heart. After a brief conversation, Old Man Barnes readily agreed to come first thing the next morning. Pug assured him it was quite the discovery, piquing the old man's curiosity.

With a plan in motion, the three friends felt a new wave of eager anticipation. Tomorrow, they just might uncover the truth behind the chest's mysteries. But they would let wisdom and caution guide their actions, heeding the advice of Old Man Barnes.

Chapter 2
Echoes from the Past

Harold "Old Man" Barnes pulled his dusty pickup truck alongside the fishing cabin just as the first rays of morning sunlight peeked above the horizon. Pug was manning the outdoor grill, frying up a hearty batch of bacon and eggs that sizzled and popped. The savory aroma mingled with the briny scent of the bayou.

Inside, Richie was busy preparing his famous buttermilk biscuits and sausage gravy. Richie hummed an upbeat tune as he worked, kneading the dough with well-practiced hands before cutting out perfect circles and arranging them on a baking sheet. Before long, the biscuits emerged from the oven, flaky on the outside and soft and steaming on the inside.

As Barnes climbed out of his truck, he was greeted enthusiastically by the three friends. "Mornin' Mr. Barnes! We're just sitting down to breakfast - have a seat and join us!" called out Wally, motioning to the outdoor picnic table situated at the edge of the fishing cabin's dock.

Barnes ambled over, the weathered planks creaking under his footsteps. "Well don't mind if I do!" he replied. "Can't think of a better way to start the day than with a hot meal and good company."

Soon the group was seated around the table, passing plates loaded with food as the bayou's waters lapped gently below. Richie, Pug, and Wally wasted no time filling Barnes in on the mysterious chest they had found on Bird Island, and the intriguing artifacts it contained.

"We found all kinds of strange things inside - old journals, antique navigation tools, military medals. But this map is the real head-scratcher," explained Pug, laying out the yellowed, cryptic map they had discovered.

Barnes adjusted his glasses and leaned in to inspect the map closely. His brows furrowed as he pored over the intricate symbols and markings. "Hmm, well this is mighty peculiar," he muttered. "Some of these landmarks look familiar, but others I just can't place. We may need to do some more digging to get to the bottom of this."

The boys' eyes lit up at the prospect of an adventure unfolding. But first, there was the rest of breakfast to enjoy amid lively conversation and speculation about what mysteries may lie ahead. The salt-tinged breeze and chirping gulls provided a fitting backdrop as the group sat together on the dock, fueled up for the day ahead.

THE MORNING SUN STREAMED in through the open windows of the fishing cabin, casting bright rectangles of light across the worn wooden table where the map lay spread out. Around it stood Pug, Wally, Richie and Old Man Barnes, each holding a magnifying glass over the yellowed paper as they inspected the cryptic symbols and grids that covered its surface.

Pug's gaze darted back and forth eagerly across the map, his magnifier swooping over the coastline as he searched for recognizable landmarks. "There's the cove entrance on Bird Island," he exclaimed, pointing to a tiny ink drawing in the upper left corner. "And that's got to be the old concrete pier over here."

Beside him, Wally nodded, leaning in close to trace his finger along a winding inlet marked with tiny x's. "This is the cove where we go redfishing. See how it opens up right where the old pier is?"

"Good find, Wally!" said Richie enthusiastically. Though quiet and thoughtful by nature, Richie shared the infectious excitement of discovery pulsing through the group. He pivoted the map slightly, aligning the known landmarks, before peering closer at the center.

"Now look here," he murmured. "There's a section that's been crossed out, where the grid gets real tight." He glanced up at Barnes with questioning eyes. "Any ideas what that might've been, sir?"

The old fisherman rubbed his grizzled chin, brow furrowing as he studied the obscured area. "Can't say I've seen markings like that before," he rumbled. "But the spacing reminds me of the old cattle guards we used to have out past the marsh fields."

"A cattle guard, way out here?" Pug looked doubtful.

"It's possible," Barnes nodded sagely. "Maybe there used to be a ranch on that island many years back. Long before your time or mine."

The boys mulled this over. Pug's eyes lit up first as a thought struck him. "Say, didn't that Dr. Sinclair mention something about livestock experiments in his journal? Top secret stuff?"

"He did!" Richie replied, snapping his fingers. He retrieved the journal from the counter behind them, flipping through the aged pages. "Here it is: 'The test subjects are responding well to the newest batch of serum. Appetites remain strong, no signs of aggression or distress. Will monitor closely for further developments.' It's gotta be linked!"

"Tampering with nature never ends well," Wally said grimly, gazing at the obscured section. "Whatever he was up to out there, it sounds like bad news."

"Too right, son," Barnes agreed, folding his arms across his chest. "I remember the stories my Pa told about that island. Folks always said it had a strange sort of energy to it. Unnatural-like. Wouldn't surprise me if Sinclair stirred up something best left alone."

The old man and the boys exchanged solemn looks. Though the promise of adventure beckoned, each of them sensed they stood upon the threshold of a darkness lurking beneath the island's tranquil surface. There was more to this mystery than missing livestock or peculiar experiments.

Pug broke the silence first, a determined glint flashing in his eye. "Well, I say we go check it out. Can't let a little bad energy scare us off! We'll take the boat over tomorrow at first light, see if we can figure out where this grid leads."

Richie looked uncertain, chewing his lip as he considered the dangers that might await them. But Wally nodded firmly, clapping a hand on Pug's shoulder. "I'm with you, buddy. We've got to follow this trail, no matter where it takes us."

Barnes gazed fondly down at the three boys who had become like grandsons to him over the years. "You stick together now, you hear?" he cautioned. "We don't know what Dr. Sinclair stirred up out there, but you boys are smart and brave. Trust each other and you'll get through this, just like all your other adventures."

Their course was set. As the sun dipped low over the bayou, the old map lay like a promise before them, its secrets beckoning to be unlocked come the morning light. Together they would unravel this mystery, guided by loyalty and determination no matter the challenges and perils that awaited.

THE FIRST RAYS OF DAWN bathed Bird Island in a warm golden glow as Pug, Richie, and Wally silently glided their boat along the eastern shoreline. Though the hour was early, the boys were wide awake, fueled by excitement and apprehension about the day's explorations ahead.

As the island's northern bank came into view, Pug cut the motor and drifted, squinting toward a disturbance up ahead. "Hey, check it out," he whispered, pointing toward three figures emerging from the tall cordgrass. The men hauled a flat-bottomed skiff onto the muddy bank with strained effort, concealing it within the reeds.

"Why are they hiding their boat?" Richie wondered aloud.

Wally furrowed his brow. "And what are they doing out here so early?"

The three friends exchanged uneasy glances as the possibilities swirled in their minds—none of them good. It was well known that Bird Island was uninhabited and seldom visited by boaters this far from the mainland. These men clearly did not want their presence known, adding an air of mystery and threat to the morning stillness.

"Should we turn back?" Richie asked nervously. As the youngest of the trio, his cautious nature always emerged in uncertain situations.

Pug pondered for a moment, then shook his head. "We need to see what they're up to. But we'll have to be real careful from here on out. Dead quiet."

Wally nodded in agreement, his expression serious. "Let's stick to the plan. We'll anchor on the southeast tip by the bunker. I can stealthily circle the west side and get a closer look at what these guys are doing."

"Good idea," Pug said. "I'll keep an eye on our boat while Richie watches the bunker entrance."

Richie bit his lip but nodded, knowing their best chance was sticking together.

They motored cautiously toward the familiar sandy spit of land jutting from Bird Island's southeastern corner, where the old WWII bunker was nestled in obscurity. Pug cut the engine and they drifted in, dropping anchor a safe distance from shore.

As the hull nudged against the soft bottom, Wally slipped over the side into knee-deep water, landing without a sound

WALLY MADE HIS WAY west along the shoreline, the morning sun glinting off the gentle waves lapping at the shoreline. In the distance, he could hear men's voices carrying on the breeze. He tread along the waters edge, moving from bush to bush to stay concealed. About thirty yards ahead, he spotted a gathering of tall cord grass that would provide cover to observe the men. Crouching low, he peered through the vegetation.

There in a small clearing were three tents arranged in a circle, military-style. The men had made camp, with packs, bedrolls, and cooking gear scattered around the site. Wally's eyes narrowed as he studied them: one stocky and bald, one lanky with a scraggly beard, the third of average height but broad-shouldered. Their voices drifted over to Wally's hiding spot as they bantered while preparing coffee over a small camp stove. From their conversation, Wally picked up their names: Jack, Alexei, and Harry.

Alexei's slight accent piqued Wally's interest. Russian? He filed the information away as he watched them ready their gear, packing tools into a large duffel bag. Soon the aroma of fresh coffee permeated the campsite. The men poured steaming cups into thermoses and secured the duffel bag. Leaving one tent erected, they headed off toward the old bunker, their voices fading into the distance.

Wally's mind raced, scenarios flashing through his head. What business did these men have here on this remote island? Whatever their purpose, it surely wasn't good. His instincts told him to retreat, to go back and confer with Pug and Richie about this development. But curiosity rooted him in place. If he could just get a look inside

that remaining tent, it might shed light on these mysterious
interlopers.

Steeling himself, Wally slipped from the clump of grass and crept
toward the campsite. The men were well out of sight, but still he
moved cautiously, senses alert for any sound of their return.
Reaching the tent, he steadied his nerves and unzipped the flap.
Peering inside, he saw an array of supplies: canned food, fuel
canisters, tools, and what looked to be radio equipment. Rifling
through, nothing jumped out as overtly suspicious. Until he spotted
a detailed map of the island with markings that appeared strategic.
His breath quickened. Were they planning something dangerous?

Wally hesitated, contemplating his next move. If he took the
map, they would surely notice and be put on guard. But leaving it
could make them harder to track later. As he deliberated, the sound
of approaching voices reached him, still faint but drawing nearer. He
had only seconds to decide. In a rush of impulse, he grabbed the map
and fled toward the vegetation.

Reaching the palms safely, he turned back in time to see the
men returning to the camp. Wally's heart pounded, clutching the
map tightly in his fist. The men showed no indication they suspected
an intruder. After a few moments, they headed down to the water's
edge, gear in hand. Wally let out a shaky breath, willing his pulse to
steady. When the men moved out of sight, he emerged from hiding
and approached the camp once more.

Inside the solitary tent, the camp stove still burned, its flame
languidly dancing. Wally hesitated only a moment before stepping
forward and tipping the stove onto its side. The flame leapt and
ignited the pile of supplies with a whump. Wally jumped back as
flames engulfed the tent's contents. The fire would distract the men,
buying him time to escape. Smoke plumed high into the sky as Wally
turned and sprinted back to the shoreline, his prize map secure in his
grasp.

THE MORNING SUN GLINTED off the tranquil waters surrounding the remote island as the three men made their way back to camp, oblivious to the chaos awaiting them. Alexei marched steadily ahead, eager to examine the old bunker's contents, while Harry and Jack trailed several paces behind, engaged in lighthearted conversation. Their casual chatter ceased abruptly as the acrid smell of smoke wafted towards them on the breeze. Breaking into a sprint, they crested the sandy rise to find their camp engulfed in flames, the roaring fire having already consumed two of the tents and spread to the third.

"Chyort voz'mi!" Alexei cursed in Russian, his eyes wide with shock and fury. He whirled to face Harry. "You left the stove burning again, didn't you, you idiot? I told you to be careful!"

Harry threw his hands up defensively. "Bullshit, I didn't start this! I made damn sure that stove was off before we left!"

The two men stood toe-to-toe, Alexei's face twisted in anger while Harry refused to back down. As tensions escalated, Jack attempted to intervene, wedging himself between them. "Hey, take it easy! I'm sure we can figure this out if we just-"

Alexei cut him off with a vicious backhand across the face, sending Jack reeling. "Get out of my way!" He turned back to Harry, shoving him forcefully. "This is the last time you pull this careless shit!"

As the scuffle intensified, Jack drew his pistol and leveled it at Alexei's back. Without hesitation, he pulled the trigger. The shot cracked loudly over the roar of the flames, and Alexei crumpled to the ground.

Harry froze, chest heaving. Jack lowered the gun. "Come on," he said gruffly, "let's grab what we can and get to the boat, help me drag him to the water."

In shocked silence, the two men gathered the few undamaged supplies scattered around the burning camp. With Alexei's body lying motionless in the sand, they hurried as they grabbed Alexei and dragged him to their skiff. They then cast off from the island, leaving behind billowing smoke that hinted at the violence that had transpired.

WALLY CREPT THROUGH the tall grasses, keeping low as the men loaded gear into their skiff. He clutched the stolen map tightly, his heart pounding. In the distance, the men's voices faded as their boat sputtered and pulled away.

Wasting no time, Wally scrambled to his feet and sprinted along the shoreline, vaulting over bushes and sinking into soft mud. He had to find Richie. Minutes later, he spotted his friend crouched behind a live oak tree, binoculars in hand.

"Richie!" Wally hissed, waving him over urgently.

Richie whipped around, eyes wide. "What happened?"

Wally explained the confrontation at the camp, the gunshot, the flaming tent. Richie listened, glancing back toward the billowing smoke across the island.

"We need to get out of here," Wally urged. "I got this from their tent." He unfolded the mysterious map, pointing to the markings.

Richie studied it and nodded. "Let's go."

They crept through the brush toward the bay where Pug kept watch from their boat, concealed in reeds. At the sight of his friends, his shoulders relaxed.

"Time to shove off," Wally said as they waded out and climbed in.

Once aboard, Wally and Richie rapidly explained the chaotic events as Pug prepped to cast off. His eyes widened at the mention of the gunshot.

"Just be thankful y'all are safe," Pug said, firing up the outboard motor. "We'll take the long way back to avoid any encounters."

They motored off, running along the far eastern shoreline, everyone processing the wild events of the morning. But an air of excitement lingered too. The strange map seemed to promise more adventure ahead.

THE EARLY MORNING SUN peeked above the horizon, casting its warm glow across the bayou as Pug expertly guided the boat back to the dock at the fishing cabin. He cut the engine and allowed their vessel to glide smoothly into place while Wally hopped out to tie them off. Richie helped unload their gear, including the mysterious map they had acquired, and the three friends made their way inside.

Pug filled the old percolator with water and coffee grounds, placing it on the stove to brew a fresh pot. The aromatic scent of coffee soon permeated the cabin, mingling with the salty bay air that drifted in through open windows. Meanwhile, Richie picked up the old rotary phone on the wall and dialed the number for Harold 'Old Man' Barnes.

Harold "Old Man" Barnes, a 75-year-old retired fisherman whose life is etched in the lines of his weathered face and the maritime tattoos that adorn his skin. Standing tall with a rugged, lean frame, Barnes is a local legend along the Texas coast with his white, thinning hair and a thick beard as markers of his seafaring past.

Friendly and sociable, Barnes is a font of stories, always willing to share a piece of history, especially about World War II and Bird Island, over a pint or a cup of coffee. His deep blue eyes carry the weight of wisdom and untold tales, which he generously imparts to anyone keen to learn from him.

"Morning Barnes, it's Richie," he said when the gruff voice answered. "We're back at the cabin and have something real interesting we'd like you to take a look at, an old map of some kind with strange markings. Any chance you can come by within the hour?"

Barnes readily agreed, his curiosity piqued. As they awaited his arrival, Pug and Wally cleared the wooden table and unrolled the map, peering closely at the intricate details. Faded lines and symbols marked the coastline in ways unfamiliar to them. What secrets might this map divulge if they could only decipher its code?

Precisely an hour later, the crunch of shells under tires announced Barnes' arrival. The wise old fisherman ambled up to the cabin, bushy white brows knit together in thought.

"Well let's have a look at this map then," he said, pulling up a chair. The three boys gathered around as Barnes studied the markings, recognition slowly dawning on his weathered face.

"This here's the north tip of Bird Island," he said, pointing to a spot. "And this symbol by the lagoon, that's one of them old cattle guards from when they used to graze livestock out here."

He continued identifying landmarks, referencing Dr. Sinclair's journal entries regarding animal experiments on the island. Though unable to interpret all of the map's secrets, Barnes surmised it indicated something important lay hidden out there, waiting to be discovered. The boys sat in rapt attention, knowing this map marked the beginning of a thrilling adventure awaiting them on the island.

AS THE MORNING SUN glinted off the gentle waves outside, Pug, Richie, Wally and Old Man Barnes hunched over the weathered table inside the fishing cabin, sipping steaming mugs of coffee. Spread before them lay the mysterious map they had recovered, its faded markings and inscrutable symbols concealing untold secrets.

Barnes traced his calloused fingers over the map, his bushy white brows furrowed in concentration. After several moments he sat back with a sigh, taking a long draught of coffee before speaking.

"I think we need to get my friend Jeff involved. He could be a big help with all this," Barnes said, glancing between the three boys.

Pug's eyes lit up with interest. He leaned forward eagerly, nearly sloshing coffee over the rim of his mug. "Ok, tell us about him, we are all interested in anyone that can help."

Barnes nodded, a smile crinkling the leathery skin around his eyes. "Jeff Mitchell, though most folks round here call him Seawings on account of him being the best seaplane pilot in these parts."

He went on to explain how he and Jeff went way back, having met during Barnes' time in the navy. Jeff had flown reconnaissance missions, earning a reputation for skill and bravery under fire. Since returning to civilian life, he had started a small seaplane charter service, providing tours and transportation up and down the coast.

"If anyone can help us cover ground and get an aerial view of things, it's Jeff," Barnes concluded, draining the last of his coffee.

The three boys glanced at each other, a new energy in the air. This was the break they needed.

"Let's ask him to help," Richie said. The others nodded, eager smiles breaking over their faces. This adventure was getting bigger by the minute.

Barnes fished his cell phone out of his pocket and stepped out onto the dock for better reception. The morning sun glittered on the bayou's rippled surface as he spoke with Jeff, laying out the basics of their discovery.

After several minutes, Barnes returned, grinning broadly. "He's just as curious as we are. Jeff will be here first thing tomorrow morning to look everything over."

A new day dawned, rich with promise and uncertainty in equal measure. But with Jeff on board, the mysteries of the map seemed a little less daunting. The pieces were coming together, although none could yet grasp the full picture.

AS THE SUN BEGAN ITS descent towards the horizon, the three friends settled into a relaxed evening at the cabin after their eventful day. With no pressing mysteries or maps to decipher for the moment, they decided to take the opportunity to unwind and enjoy the simple pleasures of their hideaway retreat.

Pug busied himself preparing an evening meal, firing up the propane burner on the dock to heat a cast iron pot filled with oil. He coated fresh shrimp in a light dusting of flour, then dropped them into the bubbling oil, the scent of frying seafood beginning to waft through the camp. Wally washed greens for a salad, tossing butter lettuce, grape tomatoes, cucumbers, and shredded carrots in a large wooden bowl. Richie put a pot of water on to boil, dumping in a mesh bag filled with freshly caught blue crabs.

Soon enough, Pug's golden fried shrimp were drained and piled high on paper plates, alongside Richie's bright red boiled crab claws, and Wally's crisp garden salad. The three carried their movable feast over to the weathered picnic table by the water's edge, poured up cold ice tea, and dug in with gusto.

As the sun sank lower, splashing the bayou with vivid hues of orange and pink, their old friend Harold 'Old Man' Barnes came ambling down the shell-strewn driveway in his dusty pickup truck. "Howdy boys," Barnes called out with a smile, taking a seat at the table. "Don't mind if I join you for a spell, do ya?" The elder man's eyes lit up when Wally dealt him into their ongoing game of spades, which carried on late into the evening amid joking insults and raucous laughter.

Full bellies, tired muscles, and the day's excitement soon had the boys yawning. As Barnes bid them goodnight and climbed back into his truck, the friends cleaned up their makeshift kitchen on the dock. Pug doused the burner while Wally boxed up the leftover salad. Richie gave the dishes a quick scrub in a bucket before leaving them to air dry.

Soon the camp was still and quiet, the lapping of water against the pilings the only sound. Safe within the cozy confines of the cabin, the boys drifted off to sleep, thoughts wandering to the mysteries that awaited them in the days ahead. But for now, they relished a simple evening together, strengthening their bond through camaraderie, food, and fun - resources they would surely need on the adventure that lay before them.

JEFF ARRIVED AT THE fishing cabin just as the first rays of dawn began peeking over the horizon. The crunch of shells under tires announced his arrival as he rolled down the driveway in a shiny new blue Ford F-150. He gave two short taps on the horn to alert the boys of his presence.

In the passenger seat rode Harold "Old Man" Barnes, who had recruited his longtime friend to aid in the investigation of the mysterious map. As Jeff parked the truck, Barnes extricated himself from the vehicle, his old joints creaking. Jeff followed at a measured pace, the two men making their way to the table on the pier where Richie had just finished pouring fresh coffee into tin mugs for everyone.

The three boys gathered around as Barnes made the introductions. "Fellas, I'd like you to meet my good buddy Jeff Mitchell, though most folks 'round here know him as Seawings." Jeff gave a smile and touched the brim of his worn leather pilot's cap in greeting.

"Pleased to make your acquaintances," Jeff said, his voice weathered like his sun-lined face. "Barnes tells me you boys found something peculiar out on Bird Island. I have to admit, you've raised my curiosity."

Jeff went on to give the boys a quick rundown of his background - his service as a Navy pilot, and his years operating a seaplane charter service up and down the coast. "I've flown over these waters more times than I can count, but I'm always game for a new adventure," he said with a twinkle in his steel blue eyes.

The boys took an instant liking to this adventurous spirit. Over coffee, Jeff and Barnes listened as the three friends recounted the strange tale of the artifact discoveries on Bird Island and their theories about the cryptic map. By the time the coffee pot was empty, they were all eager to unravel the mysteries that lay ahead.

JEFF AND BARNES HUDDLED over the stolen map as the morning sun climbed higher in the sky. Jeff took a long draw from his coffee mug, the bitter liquid helping to focus his mind on the task at hand.

"Alright, let's go through this again," Jeff said, gesturing to the cryptic symbols and landmarks scrawled across the weathered parchment.

Barnes nodded, leaning in closer. Over the next hour, they meticulously analyzed each feature of the map, debating possible meanings and matching terrain to places they knew around the island and bayou.

Jeff's calloused finger landed on one particular marking - SCR-520. "Now what in the world could this be referring to?" he muttered. Barnes furrowed his bushy brows, racking his memory but unable to place the reference.

After exhausting their ideas, Jeff rolled up the map. "I reckon it's about time we bring the boys up to speed on what we've uncovered so far. Maybe they'll have some fresh ideas."

Barnes nodded in agreement, rising with a grunt and following Jeff outside. They found Richie, Pug, and Wally chatting on the dock, skipping stones across the shimmering water.

"Boys, front and center," Jeff called out. "Barnes and I have gone over this map forwards and backwards. We've got some interesting theories to share."

The three friends joined Jeff and Barnes, their faces alight with curiosity. Jeff unfurled the map once more as all five huddled around it. The boys listened as Jeff and Barnes described their findings, ready to brainstorm their next steps in uncovering the full mystery that lay before them.

JEFF PONDERED THE MYSTERIOUS map, stroking his salt-and-pepper stubble. The cryptic SCR-520 marking nagged at him, stirring fragments of memory just out of reach. He glanced over at the three eager young explorers—Pug, Richie, and Wally—huddled together on the dock, deep in animated discussion about the map's hidden meanings. Jeff smiled, reminded of his own youthful adventures with his navy comrades long ago.

"I think this might indicate a hidden entrance to an underground bunker," Richie said, pointing to a small x near the shoreline.

Pug leaned over the map. "Hey, I think I recognize this shape here. Could it be that old concrete dock over on the southeast side? I've fished near there before."

Wally scratched his head. "No clue what SCR-520 could stand for. Radar of some kind?"

Jeff perked up. SCR-520 did sound familiar. "You know, I think that might ring a bell from my navy days. Give me a minute, let me call up an old seadog buddy of mine."

Jeff stepped away and dialed his friend Frank, another military pilot. After exchanging greetings, Jeff described the map markings. "SCR-520 you said? If I remember right, that was a WWII radar model - one of the first shipboard sets. Pretty cutting edge in its day."

Returning to the dock, Jeff shared what he'd uncovered. The three boys' eyes lit up with excitement. Clearly this map held more mysteries to unravel, perhaps even leading to long-forgotten relics of the past. Jeff smiled, happy to lend his knowledge to their quest for discovery.

Chapter 3
The Secret of Bird Island

J eff and Barnes departed the fishing cabin by mid-morning, leaving Pug, Wally, and Richie to ponder their next steps. The three friends lounged on the dock, gazing out at the shimmering bayou as they debated how to proceed with uncovering the secrets of the cryptic map.

Pug skipped oyster shells across the water's surface, restless with anticipation. "We need to get back out there. I say we take the boat and do some scouting around the island ourselves."

"I don't know," Richie said, shaking his head. "That could be dangerous, especially if those men are still lurking around." He sat cleaning his binoculars with a rag, his movements slow and methodical.

Wally leaned against a piling, arms crossed. "Richie's got a point. We should lay low until Jeff and Barnes get back to us."

The debate continued until noon, when the cabin's phone rang. Pug dashed up to answer it, returning a few minutes later with news. "That was Barnes. He and Jeff came up with a plan."

The three gathered around as Pug explained. Jeff proposed conducting an aerial reconnaissance flight around Bird Island in his seaplane. With his expert piloting skills, he could spot any terrain changes, unusual markings, or anomalies not visible from the shoreline. After completing a thorough sweep, Jeff and Barnes would return to the fishing cabin before nightfall to update the boys on their findings.

"Yes! Now we're getting somewhere," Pug exclaimed, pumping his fist.

Wally nodded, a glint in his eye. "Good thinking. Jeff will be able to cover a lot more ground from the air."

"I hope this sheds some light on the map's secrets," Richie added, looking relieved they weren't rushing into danger just yet.

As the afternoon sun dipped lower in the sky, the friends tidied up the cabin, anticipation building for the revelations the aerial search might reveal. Soon, the mysteries of Bird Island would unfold before them.

JEFF AND BARNES RETURNED to the fishing cabin late that afternoon, bursting with news from their aerial reconnaissance mission. The three boys—Pug, Richie, and Wally—rushed from the dock to greet them, faces alight with anticipation.

"Well, don't keep us in suspense! What did you find up there?" Pug asked eagerly.

Jeff grinned, holding up aerial photos. "Looks like there are some uncharted structures on the northeast tip of the island. And what appears to be remnants of an old landing strip, nearly hidden by the grass."

The boys crowded around to examine the photos. Richie traced his finger along faint lines in the grass. "That's definitely man-made. Any idea how old it is?"

Barnes shook his head. "No telling for sure without getting boots on the ground. But could be a relic from the war days. Maybe even tied to that SCR-520 radar site."

Wally nodded, gazing at the photos. "If we can find that landing strip, it might lead us right to whatever's hidden there. This is big!"

"Sure is, kid," Jeff agreed, clapping him on the back. "Up for a little exploring first thing tomorrow morning?"

The three friends looked at each other and grinned. "You bet!" Pug exclaimed. "We'll take my boat before sunrise. Get a jump on the day."

Barnes chuckled at their enthusiasm. "Now hold on. Before you go rushing into things, we need a plan."

The five of them moved to the cabin's dining table. Barnes spread out the photos while Jeff retrieved his navigation charts. Together they traced possible routes and access points, contingencies and risks.

As dusk fell over the bayou, their strategy was set. The boys could barely contain their anticipation for the morning's expedition. The lure of discovery called to their adventurous spirits. They would unravel this island's secrets once and for all.

THE PROMISE OF ADVENTURE made sleep impossible for Pug, Richie, and Wally. Long before the first hints of dawn, they were up and moving about the cabin, unable to contain their excitement. Pug brewed a pot of strong coffee while Wally checked their supplies and Richie prepared a hearty breakfast of eggs, bacon, and biscuits. The sizzling sounds and savory smells of the food mixed with their eager chatter about what the day might hold.

As the inky night sky softened to gray, they finished their meal and headed down the walkway to the boat shed. All their gear from the previous trip still lay stowed aboard their sturdy jon boat. Life vests, a first aid kit, flashlights, canteens of water, and rain ponchos were swiftly loaded beside rods, nets, and a cooler of sandwiches and drinks. Double-checking they had all they needed, the boys uncovered the boat and slid it down the ramp into the still waters of the bayou.

The faint morning light reflected off the ripples as they steered the boat out of the shelter of Live Oak Bayou into East Matagorda Bay. In the distance, the shadowy outline of Bird Island beckoned to them. Drawing nearer, their eyes scoured the shoreline, searching for any signs of life. All remained tranquil and undisturbed.

As the sky brightened, Pug maneuvered the boat to their usual landing spot on the southeastern tip of the island. Wally grabbed the anchor rope and hopped overboard, the water only reaching his knees this close to shore. He slogged through the wet mud to dry land, then dropped the anchor securely.

The island seemed to hold its breath, waiting. But at last they had arrived, ready to discover its secrets. Their pulse quickened as they surveyed the wilderness before them, then exchanged eager grins. Come what may, this time they would not turn back until they had searched every inch of Bird Island.

THE MORNING SUN BEAT down on the backs of the three friends as they traversed the tangled marsh grasses of Bird Island. Richie led the way, holding a compass and marking their path due east. Pug and Wally followed on either side, spaced thirty feet apart just as they had planned. It was not the most efficient way to search the island, but they were operating on enthusiasm rather than strategy.

As they crossed the island for the second time, the excitement of exploration was wearing thin. The grasses grasped at their clothes with dozens of tiny barbs, and mosquitoes buzzed incessantly around their heads. Rivulets of sweat dripped down their necks. They had been at it since daybreak, and the island was larger than it appeared from a distance.

"This is taking forever," Pug grumbled, swatting at a particularly persistent mosquitoes. "At this rate it'll be midnight before we cover the whole place."

Wally paused, leaning on a shovel he had brought to probe the ground. "There's got to be a better way than just walking back and forth." He looked to Richie expectantly.

Richie frowned down at the compass. As the most analytical of the three, the others often looked to him for direction. But this task had him flummoxed.

"I'm not sure," he admitted. "The island's too big to search thoroughly on foot." He wiped his brow and thought for a moment. "If only we had a bird's eye view, we could spot any structures or unusual landmarks."

Pug's face lit up. "A bird's eye view - that's it!" He pointed up with excitement. "We need to get some altitude. See if we can spot anything from higher ground."

Wally's eyes followed Pug's gesture. The island's interior was a flat expanse of grass, but along the northern edge, the shoreline rose into a low ridge about ten feet above sea level.

"Good thinking, Pug," said Richie. "That ridge could work. Let's head that way."

Reinvigorated by the new plan, the trio angled west, periodically consulting Richie's compass. The change of terrain was subtle, but soon they felt the ground rising under their feet. Cresting the top of the ridge, a refreshing breeze cooled their sweat-soaked shirts. They took deep breaths of the salty marsh air.

"Now this is more like it," said Wally, gazing out across the island and bay beyond.

Richie shaded his eyes with one hand, meticulously scanning the landscape. Pug put his fingers in his mouth and let out a loud, sharp whistle. Wally raised the shovel above his head like a flag. They stood there, looking for any indication of human influence on the island's natural state. But nothing caught their eye - no structures, no straight lines cutting through the flowing grasses.

Pug's shoulders slumped. "I don't see anything. Are you guys getting anything?"

Wally shook his head. "Nothing. It all looks the same from up here."

"Wait a minute, what's that?" Richie extended his arm, pointing toward the island's eastern tip. The other two followed his gaze. There was a small, rectangular clearing visible just at the water's edge.

"I can't tell for sure from here, but that could be something." Richie squinted against the glare.

"Only one way to find out!" said Pug. He was already scrambling his way down the ridge toward the suspicious spot, not waiting for the others.

Wally followed, trying not to turn an ankle on the uneven ground. "Pug, hold up!" he called. But Pug was locked on target, crashing heedlessly through the brush.

Richie picked his way down the slope more carefully, catching up to Wally.

"That kid's got no patience," Richie said, shaking his head. "But I think he's onto something here."

When they reached the eastern tip, Pug was already exploring the perimeter of the clearing. It measured approximately ten feet square, and was conspicuously free of vegetation. The ground surface was covered in a layer of crushed shells.

Pug gestured proudly. "Told you I saw something promising."

Wally had to admit he was right. This was clearly not a natural formation. "Good eye, Pug."

Richie paced the clearing methodically. "It's too small for a building foundation. But the shell layer is suspicious." He pointed to faint tire tracks in the crushed shells. "And it looks like vehicles have been through here."

"But where did they come from?" Pug mused. "And where did they go? There's no road, no structures..." He trailed off, perplexed.

Wally dug his shovel into the ground near one edge. About two feet down it clanked against something hard. "I've got something here," he called to the others. Scooping away more dirt, the dull metal shape of a large pipe emerged.

Richie examined it closely, running his hand along its length. "It's a storm drain outlet. And look-" he traced his finger along a nearly invisible seam in the shells "-it runs that way, toward the center of the island."

Pug's eyes lit up. "A secret road! Just like on the map!" The mysterious map they had found showed a dotted line crossing the island, but they had not discovered any road on the surface.

"You might be onto something," said Richie. "If it drains runoff from a road, it has to lead somewhere."

Wally was already following the path of the drain pipe, pushing through waist-high grasses. Pug and Richie hurried to catch up. The pipe remained barely visible, but its straight course was unmistakable.

After several hundred yards, they came to a cleared corridor through the vegetation. Tire ruts were visible in the soft earth. The drain pipe ran parallel to the makeshift road before curving out of sight.

"This is it!" Pug shouted. "The map was right!" He took off running down the roadway.

"Pug, wait up!" Wally called after him. "We need to stick together!"

But Pug was deaf to their warnings. The road fed his burning curiosity, drawing him swiftly toward whatever secrets lay hidden at its end. He had to know what they would find.

Richie and Wally raced after him, shoes pounding the hard earth. The road was not wide enough for them to run side by side. Wally's long legs allowed him to gain ground on Richie.

"Come...on!" Wally panted, glancing back. "We...can't...lose him!"

Richie nodded, face flushed with exertion. He pushed himself to keep up.

Meanwhile Pug charged on ahead. The road curved gently, obscuring his view of the destination. What sort of structure would they find? A secret lab? Abandoned military base? The possibilities spun through his adrenaline-fueled mind.

Rounding the last bend, the road ended abruptly at a small clearing. Pug skidded to a halt, shoes slipping in the soft dirt. "Whoa," he breathed.

Before him stood a rusting vehicle. Its bulky shape was shrouded with vines and grass, like the island was reclaiming it. A pair of sliding doors confirmed it as some sort of van or truck. The hood and front bumper were missing, giving it a prehistoric, skeletal look.

Pug was circling the vehicle in awe when Richie and Wally caught up to him, doubled over and gasping.

"Pug...you can't...run off...like that," Richie wheezed.

Pug barely heard him, entranced by the discovery. "Just look at this thing! It's like a dinosaur fossil."

As they caught their breath, Richie and Wally had to admit it was an incredible find. The vehicle looked decades old, yet it hinted at more recent human activity on the island. What was its purpose here?

Richie tried the driver's door. Unsurprisingly, it was locked tight. Cupping his hands to peer through the filthy window, he could make out a bare metal floor and a passenger seat, but no other details.

"I can't tell much from out here. We need to get inside and look for any documents or markings." He pulled a slim case from his pocket. It held his lock picking tools.

"Can you pop it open?" asked Wally eagerly. He had always been fascinated by Richie's quasi-criminal skills.

"I can try." Richie selected two hooked metal picks and inserted them into the keyhole, gently probing the mechanism inside. His brow furrowed in concentration. Pug and Wally watched over each shoulder.

After a few moments of maneuvering, they heard a faint click. "That did it," Richie said with satisfaction, turning the handle. The heavy door swung open with a creak.

The three crowded into the musty interior. It was stripped bare except for the two seats. The dash and steering column were gone, leaving only ragged wires.

"Strange for it to be so empty," said Wally. "

AS THE BOYS FOLLOW the hidden road, the dense coastal brush of Bird Island gives way to a subtle clearing, masked by the relentless gnarl of underbrush and weather-stunted trees. Nature has embroidered a shroud of greenery over this enigmatic place, as if intent on keeping it secret from prying eyes.

The leaden sky squeezes the light, casting the world in drab tones – a fitting prelude to a discovery that is anything but ordinary. Ahead, partially obscured by haphazard foliage, an unusual formation of stone and metal lies embedded within the island's ground – an outgrowth that seems at odds with its environment.

Pug's keen eyes pick up the oddity of the terrain; it's too symmetrical, to angular to be a trick of nature. Together, the three friends draw closer, pushing aside the long fingers of Spanish moss and tangles of bramble.

There, disguised under a veil of earth and overgrowth, is the rusted hatch of an underground bunker. The boys exchange a mix of puzzled looks and excitement. Richie, ever practically minded, inspects the hatch, scouring for any sign of a trap or caution. But the structure speaks only of age and abandonment, with smears of rust streaking the metal like old blood.

With effort, they force open the hatch, its hinges protesting with a groan that seems to resonate through the spine of the island itself. A rush of dank air, heavy with the earthy scent of mildew and forgotten time, wafts upward, and with it, a sense of foreboding.

Wally, with an uncharacteristic spark of bravery, shoulders a flashlight and is the first to descend. Dank concrete steps, slick with moisture, lead down into the bowels of the bunker. The walls, once purposefully built and smooth, now weep with moisture and the patter of seeping water echoes in the stale air.

The flashlight's beam slices through the gloom, revealing a long corridor lined with rooms – offices and operational quarters that once thrummed with strategic purpose. Papers, yellowed and curled, litter the floors. Decaying furniture molds into shapes almost unrecognizable, and on the walls, the shadows cast by the trio seem almost alive, dancing in the periphery of their vision.

The bunker spreads out beneath the island, more extensive than any of them anticipated – a relic testament to wartime activities that, until now, lay as dormant as the island's myths. The ever-practical Richie begins to document their findings with a camera, while Pug's eager eyes comb the liter for any significant objects – maps, journals, or leftover equipment that could shed light on what transpired here.

In the dim penumbra of history, the boys traverse the bunker, each room unraveling a bit more of the concealed narrative of Bird Island. They are explorers in a temporal maze, messengers for stories untold, and for each of them, the discovery of the bunker marks an indelible shift in their young lives, an initiation into the complexity of the adult world and the shadows of the past.

AFTER AN HOUR OR SO exploring the expansive underground bunker, Richie motioned for Pug and Wally to gather close.

"I think we should head out soon," Richie suggested in a hushed tone, glancing around the shadowy bunker interior. "This place is huge, and we're not equipped to fully search it today. We should come back another time with Old Man Barnes, Seawings, better lighting, and more supplies to really uncover its secrets."

Pug and Wally nodded in agreement, realizing the scope of their discovery exceeded their current resources. There was an unspoken understanding between the three friends that this would not be their last visit to the hidden wartime relic.

Exiting the rusty hatch, the boys took a moment to let their eyes adjust to the bright coastal sunlight. They lined up shoulder to shoulder, faces set with determination, and continued their methodical traversal of the island's terrain. Hours passed as they combed the landscape, finding little but brambles and biting insects to impede their progress.

Finally, on the southwestern curve of the island, their persistence paid off. Pushing through a snarl of cordgrass, the trio emerged onto a small, rocky cove no more than two hundred feet across. At its center sat a concrete dock, nearly swallowed by mud and vines. The boys approached it with care, inspecting the structure closely. It was unlike any dock they had seen before, and its presence in this remote place sparked more questions in their inquisitive young minds.

Satisfied with their discovery but exhausted from the day's efforts, the three friends agreed to mark the location and make their way back to the cabin. They would return to both sites with fresh eyes, eager to unravel the secrets that lay just beneath the surface. This was only the beginning of something bigger than any of them had imagined.

JEFF SAT IN THE COCKPIT of his seaplane, gazing out at the expanse of water below as he flew back from his meeting. His mind turned over the details his old navy friend had shared about the elusive Dr. Sinclair. According to the patrolman's account, Sinclair had grown up locally in Bay City before the war. Jeff made a mental note to follow up on that lead, hoping it might shed light on the cryptic map and other artifacts the boys had uncovered.

As the shoreline came into view, Jeff contemplated their next steps. Clearly there were more secrets hidden on Bird Island than met the eye. He would need to strategize with Harold to determine how best to proceed with the investigation. Jeff angled the plane downwards, beginning his descent towards the bay.

Back at the fishing cabin, Pug sat on the edge of the dock with his cell phone pressed to his ear. Harold's warm, gravelly voice emanated through the speaker as Pug recounted the day's events on Bird Island. He described the hidden bunker and dilapidated vehicle they had stumbled upon amidst the dense foliage. Harold listened, interjecting an occasional "hmm" or "is that so?"

When Pug finished, Harold shared the new details Jeff's navy friend had provided about Dr. Sinclair's local origins. Pug's excitement grew at this development, eager to find the connection between Sinclair, the artifacts, and the island's concealed areas. They agreed to convene again soon to analyze their collective findings. After exchanging enthusiastic goodbyes, Pug clicked off the call and stared out across the shimmering bayou, mind racing with possibilities.

AS DARKNESS OVERTOOK the camp, the boys were busy making plans for the next day. Pug spread out a map of Matagorda County across the wooden table as Wally set three empty mugs down with a thunk, the bitter aroma of coffee wafting up. Richie slid onto the bench beside Pug, clicking on a lantern and angling it over the wrinkled map.

"Alright, here's Bay City," Pug said, tapping a finger on the county seat. "We need to pick up more gear if we're gonna keep exploring that bunker."

Wally nodded, gazing down at the map while he poured coffee. "Rope, for sure. And flashlights."

"Don't forget breadcrumbs," Richie added wryly.

Pug snorted. "Good thinking, Hansel. But seriously, we should grab a few hundred feet of rope. Maybe some glow sticks too, to mark our path."

"Ooh, and chalk!" Wally said. "To label different tunnels."

Richie grinned. "My man, Wally, always keeping it practical."

They spent the next few minutes listing supplies, Pug jotting each item down in a small notebook. Rope, utility lights, batteries, non-perishable snacks, first-aid kit, canteens, paper and pencils for mapping, and walkie-talkies in case they got separated in the subterranean maze.

Pug tapped his pencil on the page. "Alright, that should do it for gear. But while we're in town, we should hit up the records office at the courthouse. See if we can dig up any info on this Dr. Sinclair and his family."

"Good idea," Wally said. "Maybe we can find Sinclair's relatives. Could help piece this whole thing together."

Richie nodded, taking a contemplative sip of coffee. "It's worth a shot. If Sinclair was local, there's gotta be some history on record."

They finalized plans as the hissing lantern cast flickering shadows across the weathered map. A quick breakfast at sunrise, then into town for supplies. Swing by the courthouse to investigate genealogical records, then grab a burger at Ann's Drive-In before heading back to camp.

Pug folded up the map with an air of satisfaction. "All right, boys. We've got a full day tomorrow. Let's turn in and get some shut-eye."

Richie yawned, stretching his arms overhead. "Sounds good to me. My brain is fried."

The trio cleaned up their mugs and shut off the lantern, moonlight filtering in through the screened windows. Crickets and frogs serenaded them as they unrolled sleeping bags and settled onto creaky cots. Despite the day's adventures, sleep came quickly for the worn-out friends.

At the crack of dawn, Pug's alarm jolted them awake. Bleary-eyed, they shuffled outside to splash cold bayou water on their faces and brush their teeth at the pump. Wally got a small fire going in the stone ring and brewed a pot of coffee. Richie mixed up pancake batter, and soon the smell of sizzling batter filled the camp.

After scarfing down stacks of pancakes and draining their mugs, the trio loaded into Pug's dusty pickup, bound for Bay City. Cool morning air rushed in through cracked windows as fields and marshland zipped past. Pulling into town just after 8am, they parked near the courthouse square and headed inside the stark brick building.

The records office was tucked in a quiet corner, with vaulted ceilings and rows of ancient filing cabinets. An older woman in cat-eye glasses looked up as they entered, raising her eyebrows at the gangly teenagers.

"Can I help you boys with something?" she asked in a dry, papery voice.

"Yes ma'am," Pug said politely. "We were hoping to look up some old genealogy records, for a Dr. Sinclair. He would've lived here back in the 60s."

"Dr. Sinclair, hmm?" The woman eyed them over her spectacles. "Research project for school?"

"Yes ma'am," Pug said again, offering an earnest smile.

With a soft hmph, she gestured to a row of cabinets in the corner. "Birth and death records are over there, filed alphabetically by year. Help yourselves. Holler if you need anything."

"Thank you, ma'am," Richie said, flashing his dimpled grin. "We appreciate it."

They got to work, pulling heavy drawers open with squeals of metal and riffling through yellowed certificates and microfilm reels. An hour passed in focused silence, punctuated by occasional murmurs and the scratch of pencils on notepads.

"Bingo," Wally muttered. "Found a John Sinclair, born here in 1924. Mother's maiden name Trask. Died...'67. Guess that's our guy."

Pug clapped him on the back. "Nice work, dude! Knew his roots had to be around here somewhere."

They dug a little deeper, uncovering details about Sinclair's family—a circuit court judge for a father, mother a schoolteacher, two younger sisters. Scholastic achievements at the local high school. A biology degree from Texas A&M.

"No wife or kids though," Richie mused as he flipped through military enlistment paperwork. "Apparently he shipped out in '43 for the Navy. Must've gotten into some serious research after the war."

"Man, can you imagine if he had descendants still living around here?" Pug said. "We gotta keep digging, see if we can connect with anyone who knew him back then."

Nodding, they wrapped up their search and headed for the hardware store, jotting down a few potential contacts. As they crossed the courthouse lawn, the morning sun shone down with gathering heat, raising beads of sweat on their necks. Adventure awaited back on Bird Island, but first—lunchtime.

THE BURGER JOINT'S neon lights flickered in the gathering dusk as Pug, Richie, and Wally sat in a weathered picnic table, pondering their next move. They had spent the morning combing through the Bay City archives for any mention of Dr. Sinclair or his mysterious experiments on Bird Island. The search had turned up Sinclair's roots in the area, but little else.

Now, as they bit into the savory burgers, the faint sound of light traffic mingling with oldies from the diner's crackling speaker, their focus turned to tracking down living relatives. They joked half-heartedly, fatigue from the day's research setting in.

A middle-aged waitress named Betty, her teased hair stiff with hairspray, sidled up to offer refills. "Couldn't help overhearing you boys mention the Sinclairs," she said, topping off their icy Cokes. "I used to babysit for an Emily Sinclair when she was just a little thing. Of course, her last name's Hillshear now."

The boys perked up at this revelation as Betty continued. "If it's the same Sinclairs you're looking for, I can get you her number. She's lived over in Victoria for ages now."

Pug's eyes lit up as he slid over a napkin for Betty to jot down the contact details. This felt like a breakthrough, exactly the lucky turn they needed. They thanked Betty profusely, excitement mounting at the prospect of connecting with someone who might hold the keys to unraveling the Bird Island enigma.

Bellies full, they piled into the pickup and headed back to camp as the pinks and oranges of sunset spilled across the sky. Pug grabbed his cell phone to give Old Man Barnes an update.

"Barnes, you're not gonna believe it, but we got a solid lead on a Sinclair. Betty from the diner used to babysit an Emily Hillshear, whose maiden name was Sinclair. We're headed back to camp now. Can't wait to see where this takes us!"

Pug imagined Barnes' eyes crinkling into a smile, pleased by their progress. Adventure awaited as they drove into the growing darkness, the phone crackling with Barnes' enthusiastic response as they hit a bad spot the cell phone went dead.

JEFF DIALED THE NUMBER Barnes had given him for Emily Sinclair Hillshear. As the phone rang, he thought back to his days in flight school with her father, Dr. Harold Sinclair. They had been good friends, but lost touch over the years as their careers diverged.

"Hello?" a woman's voice answered.

"Emily Sinclair?" Jeff asked. "This is Jeff Mitchell, an old friend of your father's from his navy days."

There was a pause on the line before Emily responded cautiously. "Jeff Mitchell? I don't believe I know you."

"No, you wouldn't," Jeff chuckled. "I was a few years behind your father in flight school. We became friends though, both being navy men. I haven't spoken to him in ages, but a mutual acquaintance passed along your number. I hope you don't mind the intrusion."

"Not at all," Emily replied, her tone warming. "Dad so rarely talked about his navy days. What can I do for you Mr. Mitchell?"

"Please, call me Jeff." He went on to explain about the artifacts the boys had discovered on Bird Island and their speculation that Emily's father may have been involved somehow based on the journals and medals.

"That does sound like Dad," Emily mused after hearing the story. "He was always taking off on one adventure or another. I want to help any way I can. When would you gentlemen like to meet?"

They decided on the upcoming Saturday morning at Emily's home. After finalizing the plans, Jeff hung up and immediately called Pug to share the good news.

"She's on board," he told the eager young man. "Emily's ready to help us get to the bottom of this Bird Island mystery. I've got a good feeling about where this is headed boys. I think we're on the verge of something big here."

THE LONG-AWAITED SATURDAY had at last come for the three eager boys, their excitement evident. Richie, Pug, and Wally had passed the previous days in restless expectation, ticking off the time until their next adventure could commence. This specific morning, they had gathered with Jeff "Seawings" Mitchell and Harold "Old Man" Barnes to embark on an interesting portion of their trip.

The united team loaded into Jeff's dependable F-150, leaving early to travel to Victoria, Texas. An unusual combination of thrill and inquisitiveness occupied the truck as it crossed the rousing scenery.

Navigating through Victoria presented its own challenges, with Emily's residence coyly tucked away from plain sight. Set adjacent to a nondescript country road, the property's entrance eluded them at first, causing them to drive past its camouflaged gateway more than once. However, their persistence was soon rewarded, as they discerned the correct entrance and guided the truck onto the winding driveway that led them several hundred yards away from the main road.

Time seemed of little concern as they arrived slightly behind schedule, the gravel beneath the tires crunching to a halt. Waiting for them, a picture of elegance and anticipation, stood Emily Sinclair Hillshear on her spacious front porch. The empty chairs around her implied the southern hospitality embedded in the home's very bones.

With formalities in the air, Jeff orchestrated the round of introductions with warmth and respect for Emily's willingness to entertain their assembly. The group settled into the comfortable seating, the boys looking on with keen interest.

Jeff began to explain the relevant facts about their trip: the puzzle of Bird Island and how their journeys had come together to uncover its past. As the outline of the mystery they were discussing took shape, Emily's face became thoughtful. She described her father's profound worry about what had happened on the island—a weight he carried quietly, admitting only his anxiety without revealing details.

Motivated by her dedication to exposing the truth—regardless of what it may reveal—Emily promised her help. The atmosphere was imbued with a shared determination as her accounts became intertwined with the fabric of their mission, signaling the merging of separate pursuits into a unified campaign.

Appreciation was reciprocal, and after voicing their thanks for her openness to lend a hand, the crew left the coziness of Emily's veranda. They bid their farewells, heartened by the newly forged partnership, and continued on their way with a bolstered objective.

THE DRIVE BACK TO CHINQUAPIN from Victoria was filled with animated discussion and eager planning for the next phase of the adventure. Pug, Wally, and Richie were invigorated by the progress made at their meeting with Emily Sinclair Hillshear, the daughter of the mysterious Dr. Sinclair. Though they had gained some valuable insights and an important ally, the core enigma surrounding Bird Island remained.

As Pug navigated the pickup truck down the coastal highway, the three friends talked over one another, tossing out ideas for how to approach further exploration of the island. Their main point of focus was the hidden bunker they had discovered on their initial foray onto the rugged terrain. That sprawling underground complex had yielded tantalizing clues but also seemed to contain many more secrets just waiting to be unearthed.

Wally was particularly excited to get back to the bunker. "There's just so much we barely got to see down there," he said. "All those offices and storage rooms looked untouched. I bet we could find all kinds of stuff that hasn't seen the light of day in decades."

"Yeah, but we'll need to be prepared this time," Richie chimed in, always the careful planner of the group. "We should go in with better gear - flashlights, tools, cameras. Last time we were just wandering around. We need a strategy."

Pug nodded along as he steered the truck. "You're both right. I think we should spend today getting equipped and then hit the island first thing tomorrow ready to do a systematic search."

The animated conversation continued as they pulled into the crushed shell driveway of the cabin. Jeff Mitchell's seaplane was docked nearby, and Harold "Old Man" Barnes sat smoking his pipe on the pier. Jeff and Harold had provided invaluable help so far, contributing their knowledge of the area's history and their analytical skills for deciphering clues.

As the boys shared their eagerness to re-explore the bunker, Jeff and Harold offered advice on how to safely and methodically investigate its mysteries. Jeff recommended they create a map of the interior spaces to get better oriented. Harold reminded them to watch for unstable structures and to mark their path so they didn't get lost. Their wisdom tempered the boys' zeal with prudent planning.

By the time Pug grilled up some fish for dinner, a solid strategy had taken shape. The next day they would gather supplies and tools in town and then launch an organized search of the bunker, this time ready to fully uncover its secrets. The thrill of discovery pulsed through them as they sat on the dock sipping ice tea, everyone eager to soon be unraveling the next layer in the mystery of Bird Island.

Chapter 4
Dr. Sinclair's Legacy

The morning sun cast its rays across the rippling waters surrounding Bird Island, illuminating the small jon boat as it made its way along the eastern shore. Anticipation hung thick in the air as Pug, Richie, and Wally approached the hidden concrete portal entrance to the island's mysterious WWII bunker.

Though they had discovered the bunker days before, this was to be their first thorough exploration of its depths. Questions brewed in their minds about what artifacts and secrets from the past might still remain undiscovered within its walls. Who had occupied this place, and what was its purpose so many decades ago? What clandestine activities had transpired here, so close to home yet somehow forgotten?

As their boat slid onto the sandy shore, the ghostly cries of seabirds echoed across the island, as if cautioning the boys against venturing forth. They secured the boat and gathered their gear, double-checking their flashlights, notebooks, and cameras. Wally had insisted on bringing a spool of orange surveyor's tape to mark their path. Though initially skeptical, Richie and Pug now appreciated his preparedness as they faced the reality of navigating the bunker's maze-like interior.

"Ready?" Pug asked, a hint of nerves in his voice. The others nodded, steeling themselves before plunging into the unknown.

They wound their way inland, picking through the dense thickets of cordgrass and live oaks that both concealed and guarded the bunker entrance. The concrete entrance "E3" soon emerged, its once gray surface mottled with splotches of rust. Vines snaked their way across its face, making it seem almost a part of the earth itself.

Reaching the low concrete entrance covered in vines, the boys descend the wide steps, coming to a wide steel door, Richie grasped the handle, pausing to share one last look with his friends. Then, with a firm tug, the door creaked open. Cool, damp air rushed out, carrying with it the musty scent of stillness and aged concrete.

One by one, they slipped through the narrow opening. Moving cautiously, eyes slowly adjusting to the dim interior, they felt along the weathered walls until they arrived at the top of a staircase. Five steps led down into inky darkness before disappearing from view.

"Here we go," Pug whispered. Flicking on their flashlights, the three boys descended into the belly of the bunker.

Their beams illuminated a sprawling chamber, its true dimensions difficult to ascertain in the shadows. Stepping forward, their footsteps reverberated through the space, announcing their presence. They swept their flashlights methodically across the room. In the crisscrossing shafts of light, they began to make out telltale signs of the room's purpose.

Against the far wall, steel file cabinets and wooden desks hinted at office work once conducted here. A pair of sturdy workbenches and scattered tool chests suggested some kind of workshop. And along the right side, cots, footlockers, and a kitchenette area revealed living quarters.

"Look at this place," Pug marveled. "It's like a whole underground base down here!"

"Yeah, and it doesn't seem like anyone's touched it in ages," Wally added.

Richie paused, shining his light on an opened locker door. Its contents remained perfectly preserved, as though hastily abandoned long ago. A prickle of unease passed through him, a sense that they were trespassing somewhere that time had forgotten.

"Let's drop our marker line here before going any further," he suggested, shaking off the feeling. "That way we can always find our way back."

They tied one end of the surveyor's tape to a leg of a heavy desk, feeding the line out as they ventured forth. Selecting a hallway that branched off from the central chamber, they were careful to keep the orange beacon in sight.

The passage narrowed as they delved deeper into the bunker's interior. Doorways appeared intermittently, each opening onto small offices and storage rooms. The boys took turns choosing which ones to explore, shining their lights over the contents.

In one room, they found shelves lined with ration tins and equipment boxes stenciled with cryptic military abbreviations. Another held a ham radio setup, headphones dangling as if recently abandoned mid-transmission.

"Man, what do you think went on in this place?" Pug wondered aloud. The others just shook their heads, equally bewildered.

They continued onward, tracing the often circuitous paths laid out by the bunker's original architects. Some passages led to dead ends, while others looped back unexpectedly. The deeper they traveled, the thicker the air seemed to grow, weighted by the sediment of years.

Strangely, their flashlights began to dim and waver, despite fresh batteries. Shadows danced at the edge of their vision, playing tricks on their eyes. A mild claustrophobia crept up their spines, urging them to turn back.

"Let's keep moving forward," Pug said, shaking off the oppressive ambience. "We can't stop now, we have to see what else is down here."

The others agreed reluctantly. Pushing ahead, they arrived at a wider passage terminating in a sealed metal hatch. Trading glances, they knew this could mark a threshold to a major discovery.

Gripping the wheel, they heaved in unison until the hatch creaked open.

Beyond lay an expansive laboratory, filled with rows of exam tables, glass-fronted cabinets, and mysterious equipment. Charts and diagrams adorned the walls, many featuring cryptic scientific sketches and equations. At the back, heavy blackout curtains concealed an unknown space.

"This must have been where they conducted all their secret research," Wally said. "Remember those experiments Dr. Sinclair mentioned in his journal?"

Pug nodded. "Let's look around. If we find any reports or notes, it could help piece together what happened here."

Moving amidst the lab equipment, they opened drawers and cabinets in search of documents. Most held inscrutable medical tools and specimen bottles, eliciting uneasy curiosity.

UPON EXPLORING THE lab area of the bunker, the boys discover a well-preserved but dust-covered journal buried under a pile of decaying maps. The cover is embossed with a mysterious insignia, neither military nor recognized by the boys as anything related to their known history. The pages inside are filled with meticulous handwriting, diagrams, and formulae.

As they leaf through the journal, they realize it belonged to a scientist or engineer from the World War II era, who was perhaps conducting top-secret research within the bunker. Some of the notes pertain to the natural ecosystems around Bird Island, suggesting that there may have been an effort to harness the local wildlife or plants for some kind of strategic advantage during the war.

Further exploration reveals a hidden compartment in the lab. Within this hollow, they find an unusual artifact – a partially assembled device made of brass and glass, reminiscent of some sort of navigational tool, but with an inexplicable complexity that does not fit any known instrument from the period.

Richie brushes dust off the journal cover, revealing an emblem of an owl perched on an anchor. "I don't recognize this symbol at all," he murmurs. Wally examines the insignia closely. "It's definitely not any military branch I know of," he concludes.

Pug eagerly flips through the delicate pages, scanning the handwritten notes and sketches. "This journal must be from some kind of scientist back in the forties," he deduces. "Look at these drawings of local plants and animals. It seems like they were studying the island's ecosystems."

Wally points at a diagram of a marsh plant. "Maybe they were trying to develop some new wartime technology using stuff they found here on Bird Island?" he suggests.

Invigorated by these mysterious finds, the three friends continue to explore the abandoned lab, driven to unravel its obscure history. The journal and strange device offer tantalizing clues, compelling the amateur sleuths deeper into the island's forgotten past.

AS THEY VENTURED DEEPER into the maze of corridors and rooms within the bunker, Pug paused and turned to face his two friends. "Guys, we're trying to find anything related to 'Shadow Masking' - focus on that," he reminded them. The mysterious term had appeared several times in Dr. Sinclair's journal, but its meaning still eluded them.

Richie nodded, pushing his glasses up on his nose as he replied, "Remember 'SCR-520' scribbled on the map too, watch for that as well." The cryptic label had directed them here, to this hidden island bunker, and remained a pivotal clue.

Wally rubbed his chin thoughtfully as they walked, musing aloud to the others. "You know, all those supplies stacked up in the main room at the entrance - do you think that's what they had gathered up to take, but then just left behind?" The large front chamber had contained rows of crates, boxes, and equipment, covered in decades of dust.

"Yeah, maybe the war ended, or maybe someone killed the funds for the research here," Richie suggested. It was clear the site had been abruptly abandoned, years ago.

Glancing at his watch, Pug noted the time. "It's getting to be mid-afternoon already - we don't have a ton of time left before we'll need to head back." Their daylight exploration window was closing. "Let's swing back around to that main room and search it before we go. There could be some useful stuff there."

His two companions readily agreed, and the trio shifted course down the gloomy concrete corridors, retracing their steps. Soon they arrived back at the expansive front chamber, their flashlights cutting through the musty dimness. Moving purposefully now, the boys began sorting methodically through the contents, seeking anything related to Shadow Masking, radar models, or other clues.

Crouching down to sift through one stack of wooden crates, Richie coughed as a plume of dust erupted. Waving it away, he examined the faded stenciled lettering on the sides - ordnance designations and part numbers. "I think these are just spare radar components," he called over to the others. It seemed like a dead end.

Across the room, Pug was digging into a large crate filled with neatly packed folders, pulling them out one by one to inspect. "Hey, these are personnel files!" he exclaimed. "We need to go through every one of these."

As he began sorting through the exhaustive collection of documents, Pug glimpsed personnel photos, project assignments, payroll forms, and handwritten notes. One name kept appearing over and over - Dr. Harold Sinclair. The same man from the journal they had found. "Guys, Dr. Sinclair definitely worked here," Pug announced. "He must've been in charge of whatever they were doing."

Meanwhile, Wally had discovered a smaller side room off the main chamber. It appeared to be some kind of workshop or laboratory. Stepping cautiously inside, his flashlight revealed shelves lined with glass beakers, jars, and scientific instruments. A large metal table dominated the center of the room, its surface scarred and stained from years of use. Approaching closer, Wally noted the remnants of mechanical parts and tools scattered across the tabletop. He reached down and picked up a strange brass object, turning it over in his hands. It almost resembled some kind of antique compass or navigational device, but far more complex.

As Wally puzzled over the unusual object, he caught sight of a large cabinet along the back wall. Walking over, he grasped the handle and tugged it open, the old hinges squeaking in protest. Inside sat rows of binders, stacked neatly from floor to ceiling. Pulling one out, Wally blew dust from the cover and opened it. Diagrams, schematics, and pages of handwritten notes met his gaze. The depth of mathematical calculations and technical details was staggering. "This looks like some kind of engineering archive," Wally murmured aloud. Based on the dates, it seemed much of the research had occurred in the months leading up to the end of World War II. Replacing the binder, Wally scanned the organized rows, looking for anything related to their investigation. Suddenly, one title leaped out - 'Project Shadow Masking - Radar Refraction Analysis.' This was it. Hands trembling slightly, Wally retrieved the binder and brought it into the light. Flipping it open, he began to skim the contents. Formulas, charts, and terminology he did not understand covered each page. But interspersed were fragments he could grasp - references to radar, to 'bending' radio waves, and to experiments conducted along the shoreline of Bird Island. "Guys, you need to see this!" Wally called out excitedly to his friends. This vital clue appeared to unlock at least some of the secrets surrounding Dr. Sinclair's cryptic journal entries. The revelations within this binder might just confirm their theories about what had taken place here decades ago.

THE BOYS EMERGED FROM the vine-covered bunker entrance, blinking against the harsh sunlight. In Pug's hands was a worn manila folder, labeled "Shadow Masking" in faded type. He clutched it tightly as they descended the rocky slope to where their jon boat was moored.

Wally untied the boat and hopped in, securing their gear while Richie and Pug climbed aboard. As the small outboard motor sputtered to life, Pug stowed the folder containing their precious find underneath his seat. The three friends were bursting with excitement, eager to return to camp and pore over the mysterious documents.

The journey back across East Matagorda Bay proved more treacherous than expected. A strong southeasterly wind had whipped the water into a churning froth of whitecaps and swells. Wally grimly navigated the jon boat through the turbulent waters, fighting to keep their heading straight. More than once, the bow crashed down hard into an oncoming wave, drenching them in spray.

Finally, the familiar outline of their fishing cabin came into view. Wally guided the boat expertly against the dock, while Richie leapt ashore to secure the mooring lines. As soon as the engine cut off, Pug retrieved the "Shadow Masking" folder and hustled up to the cabin, shielding it from the elements.

Inside, Pug called Harold Barnes, eager to update him on their discovery. Meanwhile, Richie and Wally began preparing dinner - fresh speckled trout cooked over an open fire in the stone-lined pit outside. The tantalizing aroma of fish sizzling in cast iron soon filled the camp.

Just as they were sitting down to eat, Barnes' truck pulled up outside. The old man's eyes were alight with interest as Pug handed him the folder. "Well now, let's just see what secrets are hidden in here," he murmured, settling into a chair. The boys grinned, ready to unravel another piece of the Bird Island puzzle.

AS THE BOYS FINISHED up preparations for the evening meal, Barnes poured over the folder labeled "Shadow Masking" that they had recovered from the bunker on Bird Island. He turned page after page, his attention unbroken, occasionally jotting down notes in a small pocket notebook. Excitement and intrigue were evident on the old man's weathered face.

At last, Barnes looked up from the documents and exclaimed, "Unbelievable! Who would have ever thought secret experiments like this happened way back in the 40s on little Bird Island?"

He continued, "From the looks of it, the beginnings of our military's radar-evading stealth technology may have started right here along this stretch of the Texas coast." Barnes shook his head in amazement. He made a mental note to show these findings to his friend Jeff Mitchell, knowing the former naval aviator would be just as surprised.

Despite the chill and steady breeze coming off the bayou, the group moved their dinner preparations outside to the cabin's screened-in outdoor kitchen. The three boys cooked up a meal of fried fish, potatoes, and hushpuppies as Barnes set the picnic table with plates and utensils. They all gathered around the table, the tantalizing smell of fresh fried seafood whetting their appetites. As they ate, Barnes continued to pore over the mysterious folder, hungry to devour its secrets.

JEFF MITCHELL WAS WASHING down his seaplane when he received the call from Harold Barnes.

"Jeff my friend, you're not going to believe what we uncovered today," Barnes said, barely containing his enthusiasm. Jeff could hear clattering dishes in the background as the boys cleaned up after dinner.

Barnes went on to describe the mysterious folder labeled "Shadow Masking" that the boys had discovered in an abandoned bunker on Bird Island. He detailed the references to experimental radar stealth technology and maritime reconnaissance operations during WWII.

Jeff's mind raced as he pictured the implications. "This could be huge, Harold," he said. "It sounds like Dr. Sinclair and his team were decades ahead of their time."

They speculated back and forth about what "Shadow Masking" might have entailed before Barnes had to hang up to help the boys. But not before securing a promise from Jeff to come see the documents for himself first thing in the morning.

Jeff barely slept that night, tossing and turning with anticipation. At the first light of dawn, he jumped out of bed and headed straight for his seaplane. The short flight to the fishing cabin gave his mind time to run wild with possibilities.

Landing smoothly, Jeff strode down the dock to find Barnes and the boys waiting. Barnes wore a knowing smile as he handed Jeff the folder. Jeff's eyes lit up as he rapidly scanned the pages, taking in words like "anomalous propagation," "knife-edge diffraction," and "radar countermeasures."

"You were right, Harold," Jeff said after a long silence, "This changes everything we thought we knew about Sinclair, the navy, and Bird Island." He couldn't wait to delve into every detail with the team. This cryptic folder seemed to be just the beginning of a much larger mystery.

THE MORNING SUN FILTERED through the windows of the cozy fishing cabin, casting shafts of light across the worn wooden table where Harold "Old Man" Barnes and Jeff "Seawings" Mitchell sat with steaming mugs of coffee. Richie, Pug, and Wally occupied the surrounding chairs, their own drinks in hand, as an air of contemplation settled over the group.

Barnes set down his mug, brow furrowed in thought. "I can't figure out where to go with this from here," he mused. "Is this knowledge still important? Would it still be considered 'top secret'?"

Jeff took a slow sip of coffee, carefully considering his response. "I've been thinking about that too," he said. "First off, I think we should keep exploring that bunker, mapping it out, seeing what else can be found. Once outsiders get involved, whether military or not, we may get locked out and lose access to everything we've uncovered so far."

The three boys listened, exchanging glances between themselves. Though the adults carried an air of solemnity, excitement glinted in the eyes of Pug, Wally, and Richie at the prospect of further mysteries awaiting them on Bird Island.

"I agree," Barnes said with a firm nod. "We keep this between us for now. No sense in stirring up trouble before we understand the full scope of our findings."

Murmurs of assent rippled around the table. The path forward was clear: continue their exploration of the abandoned bunker's secrets, piecing together the fragments of history hidden within its depths. For now, its mysteries belonged solely to them.

PUG, RICHIE, AND WALLY sat around the wooden table on the dock of the fishing cabin, looking over some faded documents and photographs they had found in the abandoned bunker on Bird Island. Across from them sat Jeff and Harold, the elder explorers who had been helping the boys unravel the island's mysteries.

As Jeff and Harold debated keeping the discoveries amongst themselves, Pug suddenly spoke up.

"Jeff, Harold," he began, "can you help with the exploration, seeing what we see first hand is better than being told about it. Besides, we may not realize something's importance even when seeing it."

Jeff and Harold glanced at each other. They had not considered joining the physical exploration itself.

"The boy's got a point," said Harold, stroking his gray beard. "We can't rightly assess all this just by looking at their finds second-hand."

Jeff nodded. "Too true. And an extra pair of eyes never hurts in a place like that bunker. Who knows what we might uncover."

"Exactly!" said Pug, smiling. "With all of us searching, we're bound to find something key."

Richie and Wally voiced their agreement.

"We'd be happy to have you along," said Richie. "We can handle the legwork, digging through all those documents and storage crates. But your expertise would be invaluable in realizing the importance of what we find."

"And an extra set of hands is always useful for moving debris and clearing areas," Wally added.

Jeff grinned. "Well, when you young'uns put it that way, me and Harold would be honored to join the exploration."

He extended his hand. Pug eagerly shook it, Richie and Wally joining in.

"It's settled then," said Harold. "We'll organize a thorough sweep of every room, passage, and crevice. Together we're sure to uncover whatever secrets still lie hidden on that island."

The group smiled, invigorated by the promise of new discoveries and the strength of their intergenerational bond. They spent the rest of the morning planning their approach, eager to embark on the next leg of their adventure.

JEFF AND BARNES DEPARTED the fishing cabin as dusk settled over the bayou, the sounds of insects and frogs rising in a nocturnal chorus. A long day of poring over maps, journals, and schematics had left them weary but invigorated by the promise of revelation soon at hand.

"See you boys at first light," Jeff said, clapping a hand on Pug's shoulder. "We'll take my plane over and scout it out from the air before you follow in the boat."

The three friends nodded, minds racing with questions about what the coming day might bring. After quick handshakes, Jeff and Barnes headed out into the creeping night.

Pug latched the screen door and turned to his companions. "Well, we better get our gear squared away so we're ready to shove off at sunrise."

They worked efficiently, checking their flashlights and packing the boat with supplies—rope, carabiners, energy bars, and rain slickers. By the time the task was finished, weariness had settled into their bones. They triple-checked everything was in order before collapsing into their cots.

As he drifted off, Pug's thoughts swirled with imaginings of long-buried secrets soon to be unearthed on Bird Island. He glanced over at Wally and Richie, their faces relaxed in sleep, then closed his eyes and surrendered to his own fatigue. Morning would arrive sooner than they knew.

RICHIE WAS THE FIRST one up, already preparing a hearty breakfast of shrimp and grits on the stove. The savory aroma of sautéed shrimp, cheesy grits, and sizzling bacon filled the cabin, rousing Pug and Wally from their slumber. They stumbled into the kitchen, lured by the mouthwatering smell, their excitement for the day's adventure overcoming any remaining grogginess.

The three friends hurriedly shoveled down spoonfuls of the rich, creamy grits studded with plump shrimp, crispy bacon adding a smoky contrast. They knew they would need the sustenance for the trials ahead. As soon as their plates were cleared, they sprang into action, loading up their gear and supplies into the jon boat moored at the dock. All the while, their eyes frequently glanced at the phone, anxiously awaiting the call from Jeff that would set their mission into motion.

Right on cue, the phone jangled, piercing the morning quiet. Pug lunged for it, immediately recognizing Jeff's gravelly voice on the other end of the line. "Morning boys, Seawings here. I've just completed an aerial pass over the island and all looks clear from above. I spotted some promising sites along the eastern ridge through my binoculars that are worth investigating further. Meet me at the usual rendezvous point on the southern tip when you arrive and I'll go over the plan. Good luck and take care out there, over and out." Pug nodded along, absorbing the instructions.

After Pug relayed Jeff's message, the three cast off, motoring out of the bayou toward open water. As the fishing cabin receded from view, swallowed by the marsh grasses, a sense of anticipation hung thick in the air. Today was the day they would uncover Bird Island's secrets once and for all.

JEFF MANEUVERED THE boat skillfully across the calm bay, the light southeasterly breeze barely rippling the surface. Here and there, seabirds dove for shad in slick patches on the water. In no time, they reached the shore of Bird Island.

Wally leapt out, rope in hand, and hauled the boat high up onto the sandy beach, anchoring it securely. The three boys gathered their gear and set off across the island toward the rendezvous point.

Soon, Jeff and Barnes came into view near the hidden E3 bunker entrance. After a quick discussion, they collected the necessary supplies - flashlights, rope, tools, cameras - and headed as a group down the steps into the dark, vine-shrouded entrance.

The heavy steel door creaked open to reveal a dark passage sloping into the earth. Determined to uncover the bunker's secrets, the five explorers switched on their flashlights and ventured cautiously into the darkness. The cool, musty air carried a tinge of mystery as they descended deeper underground.

Up ahead, the passage opened into a wider space. Sweeping their flashlight beams around, they found themselves in a large central chamber with several hallways branching off into different sections of the bunker. They decided to split up to cover more ground, each taking a separate section to investigate.

Richie headed down the corridor leading to the personnel offices, hoping to find records that might identify who worked there. Pug made for the engineering section, eager to examine the machinery and equipment used for the shadow experiments. Wally went to check out the barracks and living spaces, imagining the soldiers who once resided here.

As the friends dispersed, a sense of anticipation hung thick in the air. What secrets would they uncover in this forgotten relic of wartime ingenuity? They could hardly wait to find out.

PUG AND BARNES SHUFFLED down the dim hallway, flashlights in hand. At first glance, this corner of the bunker's main room appeared to be a dead end. But upon closer inspection, the concrete wall curved inward, obscuring a narrow passage beyond.

"Well, what have we here?" Barnes murmured. He swept his flashlight beam along the walls and ceiling, revealing peeling military-green paint and exposed pipes. The passage sloped gradually downward into the earth.

Pug stepped over chunks of crumbled concrete and dangling wires. "Looks like this leads somewhere secret. Should we check it out?"

Barnes nodded, a glint of adventure in his eye. "Might as well see where this rabbit hole goes."

As the passage leveled out, they found themselves in a small room lined with metal lockers and cabinets. Barnes pried one open, the rusty hinges screeching in protest. "Well, slap me silly," he chuckled. "Take a gander at these."

Inside sat neat stacks of file folders, their labels weathered but legible. Orders, inventories, personnel dossiers. Pug's pulse quickened. "This must be where they kept all the classified stuff. We hit the jackpot!"

They explored further, finding a workshop with decrepit machinery and testing equipment. One locker held a logbook with observations of weather, tides and passing ships. Down the hall, they discovered what looked like crew quarters and a galley.

"A whole hidden base within the bunker," Pug breathed. "Just wait 'til the others hear about this!" They pressed on, hungry for whatever secrets still lay buried.

PUG SHONE HIS FLASHLIGHT around the small, dusty room, the beam illuminating old machinery, cabinets, and workbenches. Behind him, Barnes let out an excited gasp.

"Well, look at that," Barnes said, moving towards the far wall. Pug followed the old man's gaze to a large, antique telescope on a metal stand. Next to it sat a bookcase filled with leatherbound journals.

Pug stepped closer, examining the intricate brass accents on the telescope. "What on earth were they looking at, way out here?" he wondered aloud.

Barnes flipped open one of the logbooks, scanning the neat handwritten notes inside. "From these observations, I'd say they were studying the night sky and weather patterns." He pointed to a series of coordinates and measurements. "See here, they were tracking stars, planets, cloud formations. Important information for naval navigation and operations."

Pug's brow furrowed. "But why way out on this tiny island? Wouldn't somewhere on the mainland make more sense?"

"Perhaps," mused Barnes. "But conditions here on the bay may have provided unique insights. Remote, minimal light pollution at night. And the interface of land, ocean and atmosphere could reveal interesting meteorological data."

He continued paging through the book, Pug looking over his shoulder. Diagrams of constellations, weather phenomenon, and maps of the night sky filled the yellowed pages. Pug's mind spun with the implications of the telescope's presence on this secluded island. What had Dr. Sinclair and his team been observing out here, so many years ago?

RICHIE AND WALLY CREPT down the narrow hallway, flashlights in hand, casting erratic beams across dusty shelves and equipment. The air was musty and still as they entered a large laboratory, seemingly frozen in time.

Along the walls stood silent centrifuges, microscopes, and rows of mysterious vials, all neatly labeled with codes like VAM-346 and VAM-1722. Wally's light lingered on one rack labeled VAM-3.5, filled with an amber substance. "This must be the long-term storage," he murmured.

At the back loomed a small office with the words "Long Term Storage" printed above it. The frosted glass door was slightly ajar, revealing glimpses of more vials packed into upright cabinets.

Richie felt a chill run down his spine. "What do you think they were storing here?" he asked Wally nervously. As they peered inside, Richie's light fell upon a dusty logbook sitting open on the desk. He picked it up and read the title aloud: "'Ancient Microorganisms Growth Records' Top Secret."

"Whoa," Wally breathed. He shone his light at the cabinets again. "Do you think those vials could have ancient stuff in them?"

Richie turned the page, squinting at the faded entries. "Looks like they were studying it, growing cultures..." He trailed off as footsteps echoed down the hall. The boys exchanged an anxious look, switched off their lights, and crouched behind a lab bench, logbook in hand. They held their breath, wondering if their exploration had just taken a dangerous turn.

Chapter 5
The Hidden Bunker

Richie gave Wally the logbook and continued searching through the lab, looking through microscopes at various slides already labeled and prepared. Nothing interesting - just dust, dirt, and tiny crystals, mostly light brown or tan in color.

As Wally flipped through the log, he came to a recipe for sugar cookies. The last step in making the dough read "VAM-345 - 2 grams" and then the final instruction: store it at room temperature for 7 days before baking. Oddly, at the bottom of the page was a small footnote that read 'vision aid'.

Wally began to search long-term storage for a vial labeled VAM-345, eventually finding pint-sized jars of it. He took one and dropped it into his backpack with the logbook.

THE FADING DAYLIGHT casts a golden hue over East Matagorda Bay as the boys methodically stow their equipment into the jon boat. The familiar rattle of the anchor signifies the start of their journey back to Chinquapin. They navigate the still waters with practiced ease, the hum of the engine blending with the soft lapping of waves against the hull.

Meanwhile, Jeff "Seawings" Mitchell and Harold "Old Man" Barnes rest comfortably on the wooden dock abutting the bayou, their seaplane bobbing gently in the water nearby. They exchange stories and watch the horizon swallow the sun, awaiting the boys' arrival. As the boat appears, cutting through the water's calm surface, Jeff stands to help secure the vessel, his skilled hands making quick work of the rope.

The cabin is soon filled with the comforting aroma of brewing coffee as Richie, with his methodical nature, sets a pot to percolate. Pug, ever the determined organizer, and Wally, with his hands-on approach, collaborate in the kitchen nook, skillfully assembling shrimp Po' Boy sandwiches—a well-deserved reward for a day spent outdoors.

Gathered around the cabin's makeshift dining table, the group indulges in their hearty sandwiches, the tang of remoulade tingling on their tongues. Steaming mugs of coffee warm their hands as they pore over the day's discoveries. Amidst the savory bites and sips, the boys explain their impending two-week absence, casting a shadow of temporary parting on the gathering.

Jeff leans back, his blue eyes contemplative, while Barnes strokes his thick white beard, both men understanding the transient nature of such adventures. Plans for their young friends' return are woven into the conversation, the men's voices rich with experience and encouragement.

During the boys' time away, Jeff and Barnes agree to keep the exploration alive, their own sense of adventure undimmed by the passage of time. They will comb the shores and delve into local lore, gathering more pieces of the marsh's puzzle. Each clue uncovered in the boys' absence will be a stepping stone for the continued journey when the band reunites under the vast Texas sky.

MORNING CAME QUICKLY, the soft glow of dawn filtering through the fishing cabin's windows as Pug, Wally, and Richie stirred awake after a late night poring over the mysteries they had uncovered on Bird Island. Despite their eagerness to return home after the long weekend away, a sense of melancholy hung in the air knowing their adventure was drawing to a close, at least for now.

After a lite breakfast of coffee, eggs, and toast, the boys got to work cleaning up the cabin and preparing for their journey back. Dishes clinked as they were washed and stowed away. Sleeping bags were neatly rolled and packed. Trash was collected and disposed of. Throughout it all, the friends chatted lightly about school, sports, and other mundane topics, trying to infuse a sense of normalcy into their morning routine.

Once the cabin was tidied up, Wally and Pug headed outside into the damp bayou air to deal with the boat. They maneuvered it into the boat shed using the built-in roller system, guiding it up the ramp until it allowed for the double doors to be closed and secured.

Meanwhile, Richie loaded up his pickup truck, organizing their luggage and the mysterious artifacts they had found on the island. He took care to conceal the chest holding Dr. Sinclair's journal and the other sensitive documents under blankets and gear. As he worked, Richie's mind wandered, still spinning with unanswered questions about the true purpose of the island bunker and the secrets it held. He wondered when they might return to unravel more of the mystery.

Before long, the preparations were complete. After one final sweep of the cabin, the boys locked up and climbed into Richie's truck. As the engine rumbled to life, pulling away from the cabin, Pug gave a wistful look back, already longing for their next grand adventure.

The drive home was filled with lively discussion, the three friends reminiscing over the highlights of their trip - the thrill of finding the wooden chest, the mystique of exploring the abandoned bunker, the satisfaction of acquiring the confidential military documents. Their excited chatter made the three hours pass quickly until they pulled into Rudy's Cafe for a hearty breakfast.

The smell of sizzling bacon, black coffee, and homemade biscuits washed over them as they entered the cozy diner. Famished after the long journey, they ordered a feast - fluffy pancakes dripping with syrup, crispy hashbrowns, spicy sausage links, and frothy chocolate milkshakes. The rich, nostalgic flavors transported them back to childhood as they satisfied their appetites. Even Pug, with his notoriously big stomach, sat back contentedly once the last bite had been devoured.

Before leaving, they ordered a slice of Rudy's famous apple pie to share, the cinnamon and flaky crust putting the perfect sweet finish on their meal. Full and satisfied, the trio climbed back into the truck for the final leg towards home, the pie's warmth still lingering as they pulled into Richie's driveway.

Richie's wife was there waiting excitedly on the front step, waving as they arrived. After bidding Wally and Pug goodbye, Richie grabbed his bags and headed inside, giving his wife a deep hug and kiss, happy to be home. As Pug backed the truck out, he and Wally watched the couple disappear into the house, Richie's wife already chattering brightly, eager to hear all about her husband's adventure.

Wally was the next stop. As they turned onto his street, he gave Pug a brotherly slap on the back, both acknowledging how much they had enjoyed their time together in Chinquapin. When the truck rolled to a stop, Wally hopped out, collecting his things.

"See ya tomorrow," he called with a grin. Pug waved in return, watching as Wally strode up to his front door. His mom's excited voice carried down the street as she embraced her son.

Pug smiled, shifting the truck into drive and heading for home just a few blocks away. He breathed in the familiar scents of his neighborhood, knowing this place would feel a little smaller after the freedom of the open water and the thrill of discovery. But as he pictured his dad's proud face greeting him, Pug's heart swelled with contentment.

They were home.

WITH A SPARKLE IN HIS eyes, Wally set about preparing for his first venture into baking. He meticulously transcribed the recipe from the ancient logbook onto a fresh sheet of notebook paper, careful to capture every detail.

Holding the recipe, minus the enigmatic ingredient VAM-345, he sought out his mother. Her brows furrowed at the simplicity of the recipe—it reminded her of her own mother's traditional sugar cookie recipe. Agreeing to help, she decided to double the batch, ensuring there would be plenty for whatever Wally had planned.

In the warm glow of their kitchen, Wally watched as his mother combined flour, sugar, butter, and vanilla extract. The familiar scent of cookie dough filled the room, evoking memories of holiday baking sessions. Once she finished mixing the dough, she scooped half into a large jar and handed it to Wally. "I don't know what you're up to with this," she said with a knowing smile, "but here you go."

Cradling the jar of dough, Wally made his way to the garden shed—an ideal place for his secretive endeavor during winter's chill when gardening activities lay dormant. The smell of damp earth and potting soil enveloped him as he entered. He placed the jar on a dusty table under a small window that allowed a thin shaft of winter light inside.

Pulling out his instructions and the mysterious jar of VAM-345 from his pocket, he measured two grams of the powdery substance. With an air of reverence reserved for ancient rites, he sprinkled it into the dough.

Following the steps detailed in Dr. Sinclair's logbook was akin to maintaining a sourdough starter. Each day he would add a little flour and water to feed the culture and then gently mix it. As days passed in anticipation, Wally couldn't help but feel like an alchemist stirring up a magic potion in his clandestine lab. Patience, he reminded himself, would be the key to unlocking this ancient secret.

IN THE SPAN OF A WEEK, Wally's concoction had transformed. The mysterious substance, VAM-345, had swelled and bloomed within its glass confines, reaching out in a frothy, doughy expansion that defied the jar's limits. Quick on his feet, Wally had divided the mixture into two jars, diligently feeding each with flour and water to maintain their vitality.

Saturday was the day. With his mother off at her garden club meeting for several hours, Wally seized the opportunity to bake his experimental cookies. A symphony of activity unfolded in the kitchen as he measured out cookie dough onto a baking sheet and preheated the oven. He left off the customary sugar sprinkle; he didn't want any external factors to interfere with his experiment.

The cookies emerged from the oven with a golden hue and an inviting aroma. He let them cool before stowing them away in an airtight jar to prevent any moisture from spoiling their integrity.

Then came the crucial moment of decision—should he taste test the cookies himself or use Lacey, his faithful dog, as the guinea pig? After a moment of contemplation, he decided on safety first. Lacey was offered a whole cookie, which she gobbled down in an instant. Wally watched her closely, but there were no immediate effects. Emboldened by this lack of reaction, he offered her another cookie.

When Lacey still showed no signs of discomfort or change after two cookies, Wally felt it was time to take the plunge himself. With a newfound courage, he bit into half a cookie. It tasted good—no odd flavors or smells betrayed its unusual ingredient.

He waited anxiously for any sign of change—an energy surge or heightened senses—but nothing happened. Frustrated and slightly disappointed, Wally finished off the rest of the cookie and continued his vigilance. After an hour of waiting with no effects, he retreated to his room, falling into a light sleep.

The sound of the back door closing jolted Wally awake. His mother was home. He joined her in the kitchen, discussing her garden club meeting and helping prepare lunch. His experiment seemed to have yielded no results, a far cry from the adventure he'd envisioned. Little did he know that his exploration of Bird Island's secrets had only just begun.

NIGHT FELL ON WALLY'S small Texas town, a thick quilt of darkness enveloping the world outside. But not for Wally. As he blinked, his surroundings shimmered, each object outlined with an otherworldly glow. It was as if the world had suddenly switched on, lit by an unseen source.

Every leaf on the trees, each blade of grass underfoot, all hummed with an ethereal light. No corner of his world was left untouched by the unusual luminescence. The ordinary transformed into the extraordinary. His dog Lacey, usually a black and white blur in the night, was now a radiant beacon of light.

It wasn't blinding or overpowering; it was just right. Like a comforting lamp in a dark room, it provided enough illumination to navigate but not enough to sting his eyes. The night wasn't banished but bathed in a soft, ambient glow.

Wally gazed around in wonderment, his heart pounding with excitement and confusion. The familiar outlines of his backyard had taken on a surreal quality. The once dark corners now revealed hidden details - the weathered texture of the garden shed, the intricate veins on leaves, even the small pebbles scattered across the pathway seemed to radiate their own unique light signature.

This wasn't ordinary light; it was as if he could see the very DNA of things - their essence glowing from within. Each object, every living thing had its own light signature - a unique aura that made it stand out against its surroundings.

It was magical and terrifying all at once - to see the world in such detail, to see what no one else could. As Wally stood there under the stars that now seemed dim in comparison to his illuminated world, he realized that his life had changed forever. He had seen the unseen; he had stepped into a world beyond darkness and light - a world where everything was alive with an inner glow. The night would never be the same for him again.

PERCHED ON THE PORCH steps, Wally's mind was a whirlwind of questions and doubts. His gaze fell upon the silent town, its every detail glowing in an ethereal light that was visible only to him. The world was not as he had known it to be; it had transformed into a realm of luminous outlines and radiant auras. But how long would this last? Would he wake up one day to find the world had returned to its mundane colors?

He found himself torn between curiosity and caution. His scientific mind yearned to explore this newfound vision further, to perhaps even enhance it. But there was a nagging fear at the back of his mind—a voice whispering warnings about side effects and unknown consequences. Was this an irreversible change? Or would it gradually fade away like a dream upon waking?

With each passing minute, his resolve hardened—no more tinkering with cookies until he knew what he was dealing with. He owed himself that much safety, didn't he? Or had he already stepped too far into the unknown, rendering such caution meaningless?

Just as these thoughts were beginning to consume him, Lacey came bounding up to him. Her furry form glowed in the night like a beacon, her tail wagging enthusiastically as she greeted him. As he watched her, Wally felt a sense of relief wash over him—she seemed perfectly fine despite sharing the cookie experiment with him.

He stayed out on the porch late into the night, mulling over these revelations. The serene sounds of the night played in harmony with his racing thoughts. Finally, exhaustion began to creep up on him. He retreated indoors and, after what felt like hours of tossing and turning, sleep claimed him. His dreams were filled with radiant visions of a world unseen by others—a world that was now his reality.

EVEN AS CAPTIVATING as the color spectacle had been, Wally relished the return to normalcy during daylight hours. He pondered why this was so. Did the sun's rays somehow negate the effect? Was it his eyes or his brain that permitted this peculiar night vision? It had been over twenty-four hours since he'd consumed the cookie laced with the mysterious VAM-345, and still, the strange effects lingered.

The phenomenon had grown from a source of intrigue to a constant distraction. It permeated his thoughts, weaving its way into every corner of his mind until it was all he could dwell on. His mother had given him a few quizzical looks throughout the day. He wondered if his eyes bore some physical change that she could detect. Could she see something different about him?

The day dragged on in a slow march towards twilight, and once again, the sun surrendered to the encroaching darkness. Apprehension gripped Wally at the prospect of confronting his transformed night world again. He questioned what practical purpose this newfound ability served. If his vision didn't revert to its normal state, he supposed he would have to find out.

But tonight, he was reluctant to gaze out into the world bathed in those ethereal hues. Fear and uncertainty gnawed at him as he contemplated the possible permanence of his condition. Yet, despite these feelings, an undercurrent of curiosity lingered. His eyes drifted towards the window as he weighed his options against the setting sun.

THE SUN EMBARKED ON its daily retreat, its light seeping away from the world and leaving the promise of encroaching darkness in its wake. Wally, perched on the porch of his house, found himself caught in a tumultuous storm of anticipation and dread. The burning question that had consumed his thoughts throughout the day was soon to be answered: would he return to normalcy or would the world around him continue to glow with an otherworldly light?

He contemplated the mystery ingredient, VAM-345, that had sparked this bizarre change in his perception. It led him to wonder about a possible VAM-346. Could there be such a thing? If so, what effects might it hold?

As dusk approached, he could not help but sit and wait. The familiar landscape began to shift as day succumbed to night. His heart pounded with uncertainty, matching the rhythm of time ticking closer to twilight.

Slowly, the first hints of neon began to lace through his vision as darkness settled in. It was starting again—the night's performance was beginning its surreal dance.

But as Wally watched, something shifted. The once vibrant leaves and grass seemed less luminous than before. Their glow was muted, as if a dimmer switch had been turned down on their radiant light show. This change sparked a glimmer of hope within him—perhaps his night vision was fading back to normal.

With that small seed of hope planted in his mind, Wally allowed himself to relax. The sixth day since consuming that fateful cookie came to an end. Relief replaced fear, transforming into a joy that filled his heart and eased his troubled mind.

Sleep beckoned him into its peaceful embrace, promising respite from his concerns. As he surrendered to its call, sleep came easily for the first time since his world had been cast in a neon glow.

WALLY WAS UP AT FIRST light, now that his fear of not being able to return to normal had passed, he began to focus on the logbook. Knowledge was the key to being amazed. If the world found out about these microorganisms, it would be endless mayhem at the bunker. The only way to keep a secret is to keep a secret, for now he would tell no one.

How was "Shadow Masking" tied to microorganisms if at all? In trying to understand "Shadow Masking" it led them to find the microorganisms. Are microorganisms everywhere, we just don't know to look for them? Why Bird Island? As Wally began to read the logbook, he started to learn that the discovery evolved around military origins.

The logbook revealed that the microorganisms were first discovered inadvertently during WWII. Military scientists were monitoring water quality around Bird Island for possible biological warfare applications. During this surveillance, they stumbled upon unique microbial lifeforms in the bay that exhibited unexplained bioluminescent properties.

Intrigued, they collected samples and brought them back to the bunker laboratory for further study. Experiments showed the microbes could be concentrated and cultivated into a substance that induced temporary night vision enhancement in test subjects. Seeing military potential, the project was classified top secret under the code name VAM-345.

The serendipitous discovery on Bird Island launched a covert research initiative to weaponize the extraordinary microbes. However, difficulties in controlling the effects led the program to be shut down. Yet the dormant microorganisms endured in obscurity, their existence and abilities recorded solely in the forgotten logbooks that Wally now held in his hands.

WALLY HAD SPENT THE last 3 days consumed with the log book, it seemed that for now Microorganism ID: BRV-076 was his key to understanding what the boys had stumbled upon. They would soon resume their adventure in the exploration of the bunker. Wally knew he had to make the most of it without giving away his secrets about the research that occurred here.

He studied the logbook, poring over every detail about the mysterious microorganism BRV-076. Though its effects extraordinary, allowing photographic memory retention, the logbook frustratingly lacked specifics on the microbe's origins. Wally wondered what BRV stood for - was it an acronym? A code name? He had to crack this mystery.

Wally's mind churned as he memorized all he could about BRV-076. Diagrams of its chemical structure, incubation notes, test results - he absorbed it all, trusting his new abilities to retain this precious data. Once they returned to Bird Island, every iota could prove useful.

Yet Wally faced a dilemma - how much to reveal to Pug and Richie? The microbe's secrets were his alone for now. Still, its existence hinted at greater forces at play on the island. Wally had to tread carefully, providing only tidbits to spur the search while keeping his full knowledge guarded.

For now, Wally studied on, determined to uncover BRV-076's secrets before their next adventure. If answers lingered on Bird Island, within the crumbling bunker or beyond, Wally would find them. The microbe was the key - of this he felt certain. And soon, they would return to that place of mystery and discovery, where the shadows of the past still lingered.

Chapter 6
Shadows of War

With Pug at the wheel, Richie riding shotgun, and Wally holding down the jump set in the back of the extended cab pickup truck, they turned down the long shell road coming off of the main highway. The early morning sun filtered through the canopy of oak trees lining the road, casting flickering shadows across the truck's hood. Anticipation mounted as the fishing cabin came into view, the boys eager to reunite with Jeff and Barnes after their two-week absence and discover what revelations had emerged in their quest to uncover Bird Island's secrets.

As Pug steered the last bend, the dock jutted into sight, Barnes' familiar figure standing at its edge surrounded by drifting mist off the bayou. Pulling up alongside the shed, the truck's rumble ceased and doors swung open, the three friends vaulting over its sides with youthful energy.

"Greetings, glad to have you back," Barnes announced, breaking into a wide smile beneath his bushy white beard. His weathered hands gripped a steaming mug emitting the rich aroma of fresh coffee.

"We'll put on a pot of coffee, then please update us on what has happened since we left," Richie replied, matching Barnes' enthusiasm. The prospect of unraveling new clues in the island mystery had consumed their thoughts on the long drive back.

After quick handshakes and pats on the back, the group headed inside, Wally firing up the stove while Pug rinsed out the French press. Soon, the four were seated around the worn table, mugs in hand, as Barnes and Jeff relayed their latest findings. The friends soaked in every detail, minds racing to connect the new pieces in the complex puzzle spread before them.

WALLY LEANED AGAINST the railing of the cabin's dock, half-listening as Barnes enthusiastically recounted the logbooks and records he and Jeff had uncovered during their latest exploration of Bird Island. Details about radar calibration experiments and the mysterious SCR-520 filled the morning air, but Wally's mind kept wandering back to the two men from the island - Jack and Harry.

He hadn't told the others everything about his encounter with them. Only that he'd stolen a map and there'd been some kind of altercation back at their camp. But Wally knew there was more to it than that. What were they really up to out there on that remote shoreline? Did they somehow already know about the secrets hidden beneath the island's surface? The thought made Wally's skin prickle with unease. Information that valuable could tempt even the most principled of men to resort to violence in order to possess it.

Catching the tail end of the conversation, he heard Pug enthusiastically ponder the valuables such a discovery might reveal. Treasure, though, was the least of his concerns—his friends' safety and well-being were what truly mattered to him. His mind churned with possibilities, each darker than the last. If Jack and Harry caught wind of what they were uncovering on Bird Island, there was no limit to what they might do. The thought of Pug, Richie, Barnes, or Jeff coming to harm was too much for Wally to bear.

As the others laughed and planned over steaming mugs of coffee, Wally stared out at the marshlands surrounding the cabin. The secrets of Bird Island were deeper and more dangerous than any of them could have guessed. He had to find a way to keep his friends safe, no matter what it took. The sun glinted off the water as Wally's jaw set in determination. This time, he would be ready for whatever was coming.

AS THE MORNING SUN glinted off the calm waters of the bayou, Pug busied himself launching the jon boat while his friends Richie and Wally tidied up inside the fishing cabin. The three were eager to continue their exploration of Bird Island's mysterious bunker, hoping to uncover more of its hidden secrets.

Pug backed the boat down the ramp, the rollers rumbling under its aluminum hull. Reaching the water's edge, he hopped in and fired up the outboard motor. It sputtered to life as Pug steered toward the dock where the crab traps bobbed in the morning tide.

He cut the engine and began loading supplies for the day's journey – flashlights, rope, tools, and provisions. His mind wandered as he worked, pondering what revelations awaited them in the abandoned bunker's shadows. He thought of the strange vials and equipment they had found in the laboratory during their last visit. And the cryptic references in Dr. Sinclair's journal to experiments involving ancient microorganisms with supernatural properties. What were they researching here decades ago?

The screen door of the cabin creaked open and Richie and Wally emerged, having tidied the kitchen and loaded the last of their gear. Richie carried a bulky duffel bag which he passed to Pug before climbing down into the boat.

"Got the walkies, med kit, and some extra flashlights in there," Richie said, settling into his seat.

Wally clambered in next, seeming lost in thought. He had been acting distant and distracted all morning. As the boat puttered down the bayou, Pug glanced at his friend.

"You alright there, Wally? You've been quiet all morning."

Wally looked up as if shaken from some internal debate. "Huh? Oh yeah, I'm fine. Just thinking about that bunker and what we might find today."

Pug nodded, sensing there was more on Wally's mind but not wanting to pry. He knew Wally would open up when he was ready. For now, they had an island to explore.

The bayou soon opened up into the vast expanse of East Matagorda Bay. Pug increased the throttle, the boat bouncing through the choppy waves. Pelicans and terns circled overhead as they raced across the open water toward the rendezvous point.

In the distance, the low shape of Bird Island emerged from the mist. Pug scanned the shoreline until he spotted the familiar silhouette of Jeff's seaplane, its floats bobbing near the island's southern tip. He steered toward it, cutting the engine as they coasted the last few yards to shore.

Jeff stood on the beach next to Harold, waving as the boys beached their boat. After quick greetings, they hauled the gear up past the dunes and began trekking toward the hidden entrance to the bunker. Pug took the lead, following the subtle landmarks toward the concealed hatch.

Reaching a particular gnarled live oak, he paused and began sweeping aside sand and debris from the base of a small rise. The rusty cover of the bunker hatch soon emerged. Pug tugged at the handle, the heavy door creaking open to reveal the dark passage below. A cool, stale draft wafted up from the depths.

One by one, they descended the metal rungs embedded in the concrete shaft, their flashlights cutting through the gloom. At the bottom, they regrouped in the main tunnel, then split into pairs to investigate different areas of the expansive bunker.

Pug and Jeff headed toward the administrative wing they had discovered previously. Richie and Harold took the passage to the communications center and barracks. And Wally opted to explore the laboratory section, insisting he could manage it alone.

As Pug and Jeff poked through offices and storage rooms, a nagging curiosity about Wally's odd behavior remained in Pug's mind. He hoped they would uncover something soon to shed light on the bunker's purpose and secrets. Some piece of evidence that might explain Wally's distraction.

Little did Pug know, but Wally had his own covert mission today. As he crept through the derelict laboratory, he focused on locating the refrigerated storage unit that held the mysterious vials labeled CLF-532 and BRV-076. The microorganisms he had read about in Dr. Sinclair's journal which possessed incredible properties – one granting increased strength and endurance, the other a perfect photographic memory.

Wally was torn about taking them without telling his friends. But he worried that Richie's caution would prevail, stopping them from utilizing the microbes' powers to unravel the island's many mysteries. No, securing the vials was up to him alone.

Reaching the cold storage room, Wally surveyed the racks of labeled samples. There – CLF-532, just where he had last saw it. He pocketed the vial and located BRV-076 as well. This microbe was unknown to the others and could prove invaluable.

Footsteps echoed from the hall. Working swiftly, Wally re-hid the vacated spots on the shelves by shifting other vials. He slipped out just as Richie and Harold appeared around the corner. Wally nodded casually and said he was just finishing up. The vials felt like burning coals in his pocket.

"Find anything interesting?" asked Harold.

"Not really, just some empty offices and labs. This place has been cleaned out. We should probably start heading topside soon."

The others agreed. They were eager to meet up with Pug and Jeff to discuss their findings so far. Wally followed Richie and Harold toward the exit tunnel, contemplating the powers now in his possession. So much about this bunker still remained a mystery. But perhaps these microbes were the key to unraveling its secrets once and for all.

THE DARKNESS OF THE bunker had swallowed Wally whole, and yet, to his astonishment, he found he could see. Not with the clarity of daylight, but with an uncanny ability to discern shapes and movements in the obsidian black. The shadows seemed less dense, less impenetrable. His eyes drank in the faintest traces of light, teasing them into outlines that became a map of his surroundings. His night vision had transformed into a nocturnal compass.

This bunker was a world away from the dimly lit streets of the city where his vision had first been altered. The contrast was stark—city night versus bunker night—and it was in this deep darkness that Wally realized the extent of his sight's transformation. His vision had not just been enhanced; it had been reshaped.

Within this underground maze, Wally found an old office tucked away in a secluded corner. He slid into a worn chair behind a desk, now serving as his makeshift laboratory. As he laid out vials of mysterious powder—samples of CLF-532 and BRV-076—he began calculating doses based on the batch size of his homemade cookies.

Moisture and time were key catalysts for activating these microorganisms, according to the logbook he'd been studying. Some reacted quickly; others were like dormant spores needing days to awaken. Each had its own rhythm, its own tempo of transformation.

Selecting two candy bars from his backpack, he began his experiment. With meticulous precision, he dusted each bar with a different powder—CLF-532 on one for increased strength and

BRV-076 on the other for enhanced memory—then moistened them lightly with water before tucking them back into his backpack.

His plan was simple: one bite from each bar every day until they were gone or until something happened. Whatever came first. And so, in this secluded office deep within a World War II bunker, Wally began a personal journey of transformation, fueled by the mysterious powers of long-forgotten microorganisms.

WALLY REALIZED HE NEEDED to divert the others' attention away from the powder lab and its potentially dangerous contents. "I better find something else for us to focus on," he thought. There was already great interest in the SCR-520 radar system mentioned in the "Shadow Masking" documents. Drawing the group to explore that angle further would provide the perfect distraction while Wally decided his next steps regarding the lab.

Soon Wally came across Pug and Barnes rummaging through some old file cabinets in what appeared to be an administration section of the bunker. "Hey fellas, need an extra hand over there?" Wally offered.

"Sure, we'd love some help going through these old records," Pug replied, as Barnes nodded in agreement.

As the three of them sifted through the paperwork, Wally suggested, "You know, we should start marking the hallways with their codes like we saw on that map. It would really help us keep track of where we are in this maze."

Pug and Barnes thought it was a great idea. Wally grabbed a piece of chalk he had in his bag and handed a piece to Richie too. "Richie and I can start labeling the halls. We'll do it in big, bold letters right on the floor so it's easy to spot."

The two friends then set off down the dark corridors, chalk in hand, searching for hallways to identify. The first one they came across was dimly lit by a flickering light bulb. Large pipes and bundles of wires lined the walls and ceiling. The air was heavy with moisture and the smell of mildew.

"This matches the description of Hallway 300 from the notes," Richie said, consulting the crumpled pages in his hand. He and Wally knelt down, chalk scraping and squeaking against the rough concrete floor as they wrote "HW-300" in block letters large enough to spot from a distance.

They continued their search, traversing metal staircases and ducking under low-hanging ventilation shafts. After covering several hundred yards of claustrophobic passages, they arrived at an intersection where the hallway split in three directions.

"This must be where HW-400 and HW-500 meet up," Wally deduced, tracing his finger along their penciled-in map. The boys wrote the corresponding codes where each passageway began, hoping their breadcrumb trail would help navigation.

The duo pressed forward, finding and labeling several more hallways and junctions throughout the bunker's subterranean maze. Each time their chalk letters echoed off the cold concrete walls, it gave them a small sense of making order out of chaos.

Eventually, they reached a dead end with a heavy locked door. A faded stencil on the wall identified it as Hallway 010. After marking the code, they paused to catch their breath in the musty corridor.

"I think we've tagged most of the main routes now," Richie said. "This chalk trail will definitely keep us from getting lost down here."

Wally nodded in agreement, hoping their hallway hunting had provided an adequate diversion from the mysterious powder lab. As they turned to retrace their steps back, the chalk letters stood out like a guiding beacon, casting an eerie glow in the beams of their flashlights. The markings would now lead their crew on a deliberate path of discovery through the bunker—one that Wally could discreetly steer them along.

SHIELDING THEIR EYES from the sudden onslaught of sunlight, Richie and Wally exited the Southeast Bunker Entrance E3. A moment passed as they adjusted, their surroundings transforming from an inky void into a canvas of vivid greenery and vibrant blues. The bunker entrance, a hidden concrete mouth obscured by nature's shroud, had been their gateway into a forgotten world.

"Alright," Wally declared, turning his gaze to the dense foliage that swathed the island. He clutched a crumpled piece of paper bearing the entrance codes. "The Main Bunker Entrance should be about 70 yards north from here."

They began their trek, moving away from the concealed E3 entrance and into the labyrinth of trees and vines that veiled Bird Island. With every step, they brushed past broad leaves, ducked under low branches, and maneuvered around gnarled roots snaking across their path. Their eyes scanned the terrain for any hint of the bunker's primary access point.

Their search took them uphill through a thicket of cordgrass, their boots sinking slightly into the earth with each step. The path twisted and turned, but Wally and Richie persevered, drawn forward by a shared sense of adventure.

Suddenly, Richie halted, his gaze fixed on something ahead. "There," he pointed to a faint outline almost hidden within the undergrowth—a modest concrete portal no more than four feet high. Overgrown with vines and cordgrass, it blended seamlessly with its surroundings.

As they approached, the imposing steel door came into view—oxidized and weathered yet undeniably solid—its stern presence hinted at the historical significance hidden behind it.

Wally glanced at Richie, a triumphant grin spreading across his face. "Found it," he announced, satisfaction ringing in his voice as he looked at the Main Bunker Entrance—the primary access point leading to the Main Corridor of the Bird Island Bunker. Their first destination was discovered, but many more awaited. The island was still ripe with secrets to uncover.

BEFORE THE TOWERING steel door that served as the bunker's main gateway, a beam from his flashlight danced across its aged, rust-speckled surface. Age had not diminished its formidable presence; it stood as a steadfast guardian to deep-seated secrets, projecting an air of unyielding strength and mystery, resistant to trivial revelation.

"Let's see if we can enter the bunker," Wally said, gripping the cold metal handle tightly. "If not, we'll go back to 'E3', ok?"

Richie nodded, watching as Wally grunted with effort, trying to turn the stubborn handle. After several failed attempts, he leaned his shoulder into the door, throwing his full weight against it. The hinges barely budged. Stepping back, Wally studied the entrance pensively.

"I think it's rusted shut," he said. "This is the main way in and out. If we can't get it open, we'll have to try the southeast entrance again."

Richie ran a hand along the door's edge, his fingers tracing the intricate pattern of oxidation. "Too bad. I was hoping we could explore the interior more today. But you're right - we should head back to 'E3' and regroup with the others."

Wally clicked off his flashlight and returned it to his pack. With a last longing glance at the impenetrable bunker door, he turned and began navigating back through the scrubby undergrowth, Richie following closely behind. Their boots crunched over dried under growth as they retraced their steps to the southeastern entrance.

RICHIE AND WALLY RETURNED to the overgrown southeastern entrance of the bunker labeled E3. After some effort forcing open the rusted steel door embossed with a faded E3, they slipped inside, flicking on their flashlights to illuminate the pitch blackness.

The cool, musty air of the abandoned bunker enveloped them as they oriented themselves, consulting a makeshift map they had sketched. According to their notes, the main entrance to the bunker lay approximately 70 yards north of their current position.

With a large spool of baker's twine in hand, Wally took the lead, unwinding the string as they went to mark their path like a breadcrumb trail. He counted his steps aloud as they moved cautiously through the gloom, Richie close behind examining documents recovered on a previous trip.

Their flashlights danced irregularly over the rough concrete walls and debris-strewn floor, casting distorted shadows that played tricks on their eyes. After 52 paces, the passage split, and they paused to tie off the twine before choosing the left fork.

The left passage ended abruptly 20 yards later at a collapsed section, blocked by broken concrete and twisted rebar. Backtracking, they followed the right fork as it zig-zagged erratically. The occasional faded stencil or rusted pipe bracket on the walls provided cryptic clues to rooms and systems long forgotten.

At the next junction, a weathered sign reading "Central Hub" with an arrow pointed their way forward. Hopeful, Richie and Wally pressed on. The passage seemed to curve left, and the temperature dropped noticeably. Soon the staccato echoes of their footfalls revealed a larger space opening ahead.

As the passage ended, it opened into an expansive central chamber, just as depicted on the map. Scanning the space, their lights revealed a high, arched ceiling and metal rafters. But the promised exit was not readily apparent. They moved cautiously into the room, footsteps reverberating, as they searched for any sign of the main entrance to the outside world.

RICHIE AND WALLY MOVED methodically along the north wall of the massive central chamber, sweeping their flashlights back and forth across the rough concrete surface. The dim beams illuminated years of dust, cobwebs, and decay, but no sign of a doorway leading out.

"This doesn't make sense," Wally muttered. "The main entrance has to connect to the central hub according to the map."

Richie paused, leaning in to inspect an area of wall that looked slightly less weathered. "Hey, check this out," he said. Wally joined him, and they could just make out the faint outline of a wider crack in the concrete. It was barely visible underneath thick cobwebs and a layer of grime.

"I think this might be it!" Wally said excitedly. He began clearing away the webs with a stick, revealing the vertical seam of a large sliding door. They searched the walls on either side, finding heavy-duty handles recessed into the concrete.

"Here goes nothing," Richie said, grasping one handle. Wally took the other, and on the count of three, they pulled with all their

might. The massive door screeched in protest, but began to slide
open as decades of rust shed from its tracks. An intense musty odor
wafted out from the widening gap.

Beyond the doorway was a long descending passage, at the end of
which daylight was just barely visible. "We found it!" Wally shouted
triumphantly. They had discovered the main entrance to the bunker,
though it had been intentionally concealed. What other secrets
might it reveal? With rekindled excitement, the pair ventured
forward, using the twine to mark their path back while proceeding
towards the light.

WALLY AND RICHIE STEPPED out into the daylight, squinting
as their eyes adjusted after the dimness of the underground bunker.
They found themselves in a small clearing surrounded by thick brush
and tangled vines. The massive steel door they had emerged from was
nearly invisible, completely overgrown with vegetation.

"How could such a large entrance be so hard to find from the
outside?" Wally wondered aloud. "We walked all over this island and
didn't find it, yet we found the 'E3' entrance."

Richie nodded in agreement. "Let's check it out," he said.

The two boys examined the door and surrounding area closely.
The door itself was set deep into the entrance, only the very top
visible above ground level. The rest was buried beneath layers of dirt
and tangled roots. Camouflage netting stretched overhead, nearly
indistinguishable from the canopy of trees and vines.

"No wonder we couldn't spot this thing from the air or by
walking around," Wally remarked. "It's totally obscured by the island
itself."

Richie ran his hand along the deep grooves where the massive
door slid along its track, now jammed open by dirt and debris. "I

wonder if they kept it hidden even back then, during the war. Hard to imagine how they maneuvered vehicles or equipment in and out."

Wally pointed to some faded lettering etched into the steel frame of the door. "Look - HW-100. That matches one of the codes from the map we found in the chest!"

The two continued searching the area, looking for any other clues or markings. The clearing showed signs of long abandonment, with any paths or structures long since swallowed up by the encroaching forest. Wally snapped some photos with his phone while Richie jotted down notes and sketches in a small notebook.

After nearly an hour of careful investigation, they decided there was little else to uncover there. The entrance itself seemed to be the only remaining artifact of note. They gathered up their things and prepared to re-enter the bunker, hoping to find more clues inside about its mysterious past.

SUNLIGHT SPLASHED AGAINST the seaplane as Jeff and Barnes waved their goodbyes. The engine sputtered to life, and the craft danced across the waves before lifting into the sky. They watched it shrink into a speck, heading west along the island until it was swallowed by the horizon.

Richie broke the silence, his voice steady but carrying an undercurrent of urgency. "Fellows," he began, "I think we need to find all of the entrances and somehow mark them so as to tell if anyone has accessed the bunker."

Pug and Wally nodded in agreement. It was a prudent idea; an unknown entrance could mean an unexpected surprise. Besides, knowing all possible escape routes seemed only logical.

Pug scratched his chin thoughtfully. "Some time back, I saw somewhere a reference to the 'Service Entrance'. Let's find it, okay?"

Wally's eyes sparkled with anticipation. "Let's go," he responded.

The trio set off towards their new objective, their footsteps muffled by the undergrowth carpeting Bird Island. The jungle around them buzzed with life, a symphony of insects singing under the vast Texas sky.

Their journey led them westward along a barely discernible path that meandered through dense foliage and towering trees. Their keen eyes picked up signs of previous activity - footprints in the mud, snapped twigs, patches of trampled grass - all indications of a trail frequently used.

The 'Service Entrance' was not what they had expected. Nestled between two large live oaks was a steel door set flush with the ground - not imposing like the main entrance, but practical and discreet. The door was rusted from years of exposure to salt air and coastal weather, its original color lost under layers of corrosion. A weathered sign hung precariously above it reading 'Service Entrance', letters barely visible beneath decades-old paint peeling away from the wood.

Beside the entrance was a moss-covered stone slab. Etched onto it were faded letters spelling out 'SE-1', matching one of the codes from their map. The slab, they realized, was not just a marker but a discreet lid covering a small tunnel that led into the bunker, likely for maintenance or quick access.

They exchanged triumphant smiles. This was another piece of the puzzle, another key to unlocking the secrets held within Bird Island's bunker. Their mission was clear - mark this entrance, note its details, and move on to find more. Their adventure was far from over.

AS THE SUN BEGAN ITS descent towards the horizon, casting an orange glow across the sky, Pug, Wally, and Richie knew their time exploring the island that day was coming to an end. Though they felt they had only scratched the surface of the mysteries that lay buried beneath the dense foliage and aging structures of Bird Island, the light was fading fast, and soon it would be too dark to navigate the island safely.

Reluctantly, they gathered up their equipment and supplies, packing away notebooks, cameras, sample jars, and various tools into their backpacks. As the shadows grew longer, they made their way through the underbrush and back to the hidden cove where their jon boat was tied up, bobbing gently in the lapping waves.

Wally coiled the ropes neatly as Pug and Richie loaded their gear into the boat, distributing the weight evenly so they would ride steady on the open water. Once everything and everyone was situated, Pug pulled the ripcord on the outboard motor, and it sputtered to life as he steered them away from the island.

The sun hung low over the horizon now, casting a fiery glow across the glassy surface of East Matagorda Bay. A steady breeze came up from behind them, propelling them smoothly across the bay's rippled surface. Pelicans and seagulls circled overhead as the three friends cruised steadily towards home, keeping a watchful eye out for other boats or obstacles.

Before long, the scattered lights of Chinquapin came into view ahead of them, twinkling like fireflies along the wooded shoreline. Pug expertly guided the jon boat up the winding bayou until their fishing cabin emerged from the dusky trees. He throttled down and coasted smoothly into the dock, the hull gently kissing the weathered boards as they arrived home after their day's adventures.

"Whew, made it back just in time!" Richie exclaimed as he hopped onto the dock and tied them off. The sun had just dipped below the horizon, the western sky ablaze with fiery hues of orange, pink and purple.

"That was some smooth sailing across the bay," Wally said, clapping Pug on the back as they finished unloading. "Despite that big load we're carrying, this old girl handled it like a dream."

Pug grinned, giving the hull an affectionate pat. "She may not be the fanciest boat around, but she's gotten us out of a scrape or two. Ol' reliable here has never let us down."

The three of them carried their gear up to the cabin, excitedly recounting the day's highlights and discoveries. Though they were worn out from the long day's adventures, they were eager to further analyze some of the artifacts and samples they had uncovered in the island's mysterious bunker.

As Pug stowed away their equipment, Wally headed down the dock to grab the crab traps they had set out earlier that morning. He pulled up several nice sized blue crabs that were feistily snapping their pincers, excited for the crab feast they would enjoy later that evening.

Meanwhile, Richie started preparing dinner. He mixed up some cornmeal batter for skillet cornbread and put a pot of grits on to simmer. Once the cast iron skillet was sizzling with oil, he tossed in some fresh Gulf shrimp to fry up, their sweet succulent aroma filling the cabin.

Before long, they were sitting down to enjoy their southern spread of shrimp, grits, and cornbread. The day's adventures had left them ravenous, and they eagerly shoveled mouthfuls of the delicious food to replenish their energy. As they ate, they continued discussing the mysteries of Bird Island, speculating about what revelations tomorrow's exploration might bring.

When their plates were clear and their bellies full, they tidied up the kitchen then headed to the back room to shower and clean up before bed. The hot water felt soothing after a long day tromping through the island's rough terrain.

Soon they had all washed away the day's sweat and grime. A sense of contented exhaustion permeated the cabin as they settled into their cots. Despite their curiosity about what secrets may still lie hidden on Bird Island, the comfort of their cabin and the gentle lapping of waves outside soon lulled them into a deep and restful sleep. The new day would bring fresh opportunities to unravel more of the mysterious history of Bird Island and search deeper into the bunkers that lay beneath its surface.

Chapter 7
Unraveling the Mystery

Adhering to a rule of early to bed and early to rise, the boys found themselves up well before the sun, perched on the dock with steaming cups of coffee, eagerly outlining the day's agenda under the dim pre-dawn sky.

Richie, getting their attention, says "Fellows, let's keep looking for the hidden entrances. Wally, what's next on your list?"

Wally replies, "HC2, the hidden coastal access would be next. Sounds as good as any to me."

All agree.

Pug, while fixing po'boy shrimp and crab sandwiches for the day's lunch, replies "Sounds great to me. It will be interesting to find all of these entrances that we never knew about."

Richie pipes up, "Guys, sorry but it will be leftover shrimp and grits for breakfast. There was plenty left from last night, so let's eat it, okay?"

They all agree.

After breakfast, with coffee in hand, Wally walks out on the pier where the supplies are stowed, finds his backpack, retrieves the doctored candy bars, and takes a small bite off each before slipping them back into his backpack. It had been almost 18 hours since he had doped the bars.

Wally makes a note in his Mybook log.

Soon the boys have finished their morning preparations for the day and are on their way across the bay, the early morning sun glittering on the water around them. They chat lightly as they go, though Wally stays quiet, lost in thought. His mind keeps returning to the candy bars in his pack, wondering when their effects might hit. He feels a mix of trepidation and excitement.

They beach their boat in a secluded cove near where they believe the hidden coastal entrance HC2 to be located. After securing the boat, they shoulder their packs and hike inland, keeping their eyes peeled for any signs of a bunker entrance.

The coastal foliage is dense here, making progress slow. After about half an hour of searching, Pug spots what looks like a cleared path leading away from the shoreline. "Hey guys, over here!" he calls out.

The others converge on his location. Sure enough, an overgrown trail winds vaguely inland. "Nice find, Pug," Richie says appreciatively.

They follow the winding path slowly, watching for any clues. Wally notices drag marks in the dirt as if something heavy had been pulled along the trail periodically. "Look here," he points out to the others.

After several more minutes, the trail ends abruptly at a sheer rock face. The boys spread out, examining the stone wall. "There's gotta be something here..." Pug mutters.

Richie runs his hand along the rock, peering closely. "I think I see seams here, where the rock looks newer."

The boys brush debris from the rock face, gradually revealing a steel door camouflaged to look like the surrounding stone. "Jackpot!" Pug crows triumphantly. The others grin, pleased with their discovery.

Wally steps forward to inspect the door closer, and suddenly stumbles, his head swimming. He puts his hand against the rock to steady himself. As the lightheadedness passes, he feels his senses sharpening. Details of his surroundings he never noticed seem to jump out at him. The candy bars are kicking in, he realizes.

"You okay, Wally?" Richie asks with concern.

"Yeah, I'm good," Wally replies. "Just got a little lightheaded for a second. Probably need to eat something."

As the others discuss how to open the concealed bunker door, Wally hangs back, assessing the changes he feels. His vision seems hyper-focused, and he can hear Pug and Richie's conversation with perfect clarity from 20 feet away. He notices things about the forest that normally would have escaped his attention - the vibration of insect wings, the gentle swaying of leaves in the breeze. He feels his apprehension fading, replaced by fascination at this new perceptual world.

"Ready to head in?" Richie calls to Wally, snapping him from his thoughts. He joins them at the door, eager to test his enhanced senses further underground. Pug wrenches the handle and the heavy door swings open with a grinding screech, revealing a dark passage sloping down into the earth. One by one, flashlights in hand, the boys descend into the bunker, the door booming shut behind them.

PUG LED THE WAY, FLASHLIGHT in hand, as the three friends ventured forth into the dark corridors of the abandoned bunker. The cool, musty air clung to them as they moved cautiously through the shadows.

Their footsteps echoed off the concrete walls lined with peeling paint and rust stains. Following the winding hallway labeled "HW-010," they traced a path from the Hidden Coastal Access towards the bunker's core.

As the passage narrowed, remnants from the past emerged. Faded signs hung at intersections, directing personnel to various sectors—the Infirmary, Supply Depot, Machine Shop. At one turn, an old military jacket lay crumpled on the floor, still bearing its insignia.

"Man, this place is like a time capsule," Pug whispered. The others nodded, awed by the snapshot of history surrounding them.

Connecting through smaller utility tunnels, littered with debris, pipes, and cobwebs, the group eventually reached the wider expanse of the Main Corridor. Their flashlights danced over the central hub, hinting at its former purpose as the heart of operations.

Consulting Pug's hand-drawn map, they identified the route towards the Southeastern Entrance, following the signs for "HW-800." Their sense of direction wavered in the maze-like bunker, but they pushed on with growing excitement.

Passing a branch labeled "Command Center," Wally paused, peering down the dim passageway. "Let's check that out on the way back," Richie suggested, focused on reaching their destination.

After several more turns, Pug raised his hand, signaling the others to stop. Ahead, the weak beam of his flashlight revealed a weathered door, the paint faded but the bold stenciled letters "E3" still legible.

"We made it!" Pug exclaimed. Swinging open the creaky steel door, the three friends gazed with a mix of triumph and anticipation at the large chamber just beyond, eager to explore its secrets.

WALLY, PUG, AND RICHIE continued their exploration of the abandoned bunker, flashlight beams dancing ahead of them down the gloomy concrete corridors. They were following the signs towards the 'Central Command' section, hoping to uncover more clues about the bunker's mysterious past.

As they walked, their flashlights glinted off the metal door frames lining the passageway. Most of the doors were closed, but some stood ajar, allowing glimpses into the rooms beyond. They spotted what looked like a barracks, with rows of rusted metal bed frames and footlockers. In another room, the remains of a kitchen - shelves still lined with dusty tin cans and utensils.

"Man, this place is like a time capsule," Pug murmured. "It's weird to think people actually lived down here once."

Wally paused, shining his light on a faded poster hung crookedly on the wall. It depicted a serious-looking bald eagle above the words "Loose Lips Sink Ships."

"Yeah," Wally agreed. "It must have been intense, spending months sealed underground, cut off from the outside world." He imagined what it would have been like, confined below the earth in service of some mysterious mission.

They continued on, passing offices with metal desks and black rotary phones, documents strewn across the floors long ago abandoned. The deeper they went, the more cluttered and chaotic the bunker became. The ordered barracks gave way to rooms piled high with equipment, maps, and paperwork.

"We must be getting close," Richie said, consulting the crude map they had drawn.

Up ahead, they saw a large steel double door, the words "Central Command" stenciled across it in faded white paint. Excitement surged through them. What secrets lay beyond? Pug and Richie took hold of the door's large rusted wheel, grunting with effort as they turned it. The wheel groaned in protest, but the heavy door swung open.

Beyond was a cavernous room, filled with panels of switches, dials, and screens. At the far end stood an enormous metal console - the command center. The boys moved cautiously into the space, shining their lights in awe over the sophisticated equipment. This was the nerve center that had controlled the entire bunker.

Wally's light lingered on a swivel chair in front of the command console. He imagined an officer sitting there, holding the lives of the men below him in his hands. What had they been charged with, down here in the island's belly? What had they been hiding from the world above?

"Let's see if we can get some power going," Pug said, running his hands along the console. "Maybe some of these systems still work."

The three of them began examining the panels, looking for anything to bring the long-dormant technology back to life. Anticipation coursed through them. If they could restore power, who knew what secrets they might uncover within the bunker's depths?

RICHIE AND WALLY WANDERED through the dark, musty corridors of the abandoned bunker, their flashlights cutting through the gloom. They had split off from Pug to search for the bunker's power station, hoping to restore electricity and unlock its secrets.

The command center had yielded little, its consoles and equipment long dormant. But with power, there was a chance more could be discovered.

"Wally, let's find the power station, maybe we can somehow get the power on," Richie suggested, playing his flashlight over peeling signs and rusted pipes along the walls.

Wally nodded, equally curious what the bunker might reveal with lights on. "Good idea. Let's have a look around."

They searched through storage closets and barracks, finding useful supplies like tools and blankets but no sign of electrical access. After nearly an hour, Richie paused, shining his light on a faded directory sign.

"Wally, you got any idea what workshop would handle the power for this place?"

Wally studied the sign, brow furrowed. "Maybe Utilities? I don't know, let's find out."

Consulting the directory, they located a passage labeled 'Utilities Workshop B' and followed it deeper into the bunker's maze. The air grew cooler and damper, their footsteps echoing down the neglected corridor.

At last they arrived at a heavy steel door marked 'Utilities Power Control.' Exchanging an excited glance, Wally and Richie strained to slide the stubborn door open on its rusted track, revealing a dark room filled with transformers, breaker boxes, and thick cables.

"Jackpot," Richie grinned, playing his flashlight over the antiquated equipment. "Let's see about getting some lights on in this place."

Wally nodded, equally eager to restore power and discover what other secrets the bunker might reveal. With care and luck, its past might soon be illuminated before them.

WALLY STUDIED THE FADED directory he had found earlier, running his finger down the list of rooms until he came to 'WS-404 - Utilities Workshop'. He looked around the dimly lit workshop, taking in the panels of switches, gauges, and wiring. This had to be the place.

"Richie, I think we're in the right spot," Wally said. "This looks like it could be the power control room for the whole bunker."

Richie nodded, shining his flashlight over the equipment. "Yeah, this has got to be it. Look at all these panels and cables." He walked over to a large electrical cabinet and inspected the switches and labels. "Main Power Distribution - Sector 3," he read out loud.

The two friends began tracing the web of cables and conduits that snaked across the walls and ceiling, trying to understand how the bunker's electrical system was laid out. Wally located what looked like a master power switch, but it didn't budge when he tried to flip it.

"I think we need to check the fuel situation first," Wally said. "No use trying to turn on the power if the generator's bone dry."

Richie agreed and they began searching the room for any clues that might reveal the fuel status. As they dug through logbooks and inspected gauges, they started piecing together a rough idea of how the decades-old generator and distribution system worked. Their excitement grew as they anticipated bringing the bunker's equipment back to life and unlocking its secrets.

RICHIE WALKED ALONG the far wall of the workshop, scanning the faded signs and notices. He paused as one label caught his eye - "Generator Room."

"Hey, over here," Richie called out. "It's the generator room."

Wally made his way over to join Richie. Together, they entered through the heavy steel door into the generator room. Inside were two large diesel generators, standing side-by-side. One was the main generator, the other an identical backup. Behind them loomed a giant 1000-gallon fuel tank.

Wally rapped his knuckles against the large tank. The resulting hollow echo told them all they needed to know - if any fuel remained, it couldn't be more than a tiny amount.

The generators each had a hefty mechanical weight attached by gears, designed to be cranked by hand to start the engines without battery power. Wally grasped the crank handle on the main generator and began straining to turn it. The gears creaked and groaned as the weight lifted and dropped every 10 revolutions of the crank.

After several minutes of cranking, Wally was out of breath. "It's no use," he panted. "Without fuel, we'll never get these old dinosaurs running."

Richie scanned the room, looking for anything they may have missed. Along the back wall, he noticed a small locker. Inside were two 5-gallon jerry cans, a funnel, and a hand pump.

"Hey, check this out," said Richie. "We can use these to get some fuel from our boat's tank to start the generator. It's not much, but it could be enough."

Re-energized, the two friends gathered up the equipment and hurried back to their boat. After siphoning fuel into the jerry cans, they returned and poured it into the main generator's tank. Wally cranked the starter again, and this time the engine sputtered to life. The lights flickered on in the workshop as the bunker hummed with electricity once more.

PUG WORKED DILIGENTLY in the bunker's central control room, focused on restoring power to the ancient equipment. He traced cables and cleaned corroded connections, piecing together the complex electrical system.

Meanwhile, Wally and Richie explored the generator room, finally getting the old diesel units running again. But they knew the generators couldn't run for long on gasoline without proper lubrication. They shut the units down, deciding to bring diesel fuel when needed for temporary power.

With daylight fading, Wally and Richie returned to find Pug still engrossed in the control room. "Time to pack it up, Pug," Wally said. "We gotta head back before it gets dark."

Pug nodded, reluctant to leave the equipment he was so close to reviving. But he knew Wally was right—they needed to gather their tools and supplies and get back to camp at Chinquapin before night fell.

The three boys did a final sweep of the areas they had explored, making sure they left no trace of their presence. Soon they were motoring steadily across East Matagorda Bay in their jon boat, the bunker growing smaller behind them.

AS THE EVENING SKY bled into shades of pink and purple, Wally was on the pier, tying down their trusty jon boat with experienced hands. The last echoes of the day's adventure still rang in his ears as he completed the task and hefted his backpack onto a shoulder.

Meanwhile, Richie, armed with a well-worn skillet and a determined expression, had claimed the cabin's rustic kitchen. His nimble fingers worked to peel potatoes, the soft scraping sound joining the symphony of evening noises. He planned to serve a Southern feast of fried potatoes, hush puppies, and redfish. His tongue darted out in concentration as he chopped the peeled potatoes into even pieces, a quiet hum of satisfaction leaving his lips.

Out by the bayou, Pug was on crab duty. His sturdy hands moved with a practiced rhythm, hauling up the crab traps with grunts of effort. The crabs squirmed within their wire prisons, clicking their claws in futile resistance. He hummed an old tune as he worked, adding to the cacophony of sounds that made up their rustic home away from home.

Back on land, Wally unzipped his backpack and pulled out two candy bars - the ones he'd laced with microorganisms earlier. A sense of trepidation coursed through him as he took small bites from each.

The sweetness hit his tongue first followed by a rush of sensations - strange yet not unpleasant.

He replaced the half-eaten candy bars into his backpack and zipped it shut. His fingers fumbled slightly as he pulled out Wally's Log Mybook and jotted down his actions. The pen scratched against the paper in short bursts as he documented everything.

The moment passed, leaving him alone with his thoughts again. He slung his backpack over a shoulder and began the short trek back to camp. His steps were steady now; the earlier wave of dizziness had receded as quickly as it had come, leaving behind a heightened awareness that made his senses tingle.

He could hear the faint sizzle of potatoes frying in the cabin, smell the salty tang of the crabs Pug was handling, and see the vibrant colors of the sunset more vividly. The strange sensation he'd experienced earlier was gone, replaced by an almost superhuman acuity.

He reached the cabin just as Richie was flipping the hush puppies in the skillet. With a final glance at the setting sun, Wally stepped inside to join his friends. The night was young, and there were secrets yet to uncover.

WALLY ENTERED THE CABIN and went to the kitchen to get a glass of iced tea. As he took a seat at the table, he noticed several old research logbooks placed next to Richie's chair.

"Hey Richie, what are you reading about there?" Wally asked.

Richie looked up from the potatoes he was peeling. "Oh, I haven't had a chance to really look at them yet. The logs are right there on the table though, feel free to check them out."

Wally picked up one of the logbooks and flipped it open to a random page. On the inside cover, he saw a short synopsis:

Search and Rescue Aid: In a humanitarian twist, the SCR-520 radar could assist search and rescue teams in challenging terrain, such as dense forests or marshy landscapes around Bird Island. It could help locate lost individuals by picking up movements in areas where conventional visual searches are hindered.

Wally realized the radar could also be useful for patroling sensitive areas. He started to read through the detailed research contained in the logbook.

As he read, it dawned on him that he was effortlessly understanding everything on the pages before him. How was this possible? He flipped through several more pages. He grasped the concepts perfectly. Suddenly it hit him - the candy bars. The microbe BRV-076 was working.

Wally leaned back in his chair, amazed at his newfound comprehension. This changed everything. The secrets of Bird Island were now open to him.

RICHIE DIPPED A BUTTERY biscuit into the pot of spicy crawfish étouffée, savoring the flavor as he listened to Pug and Wally discuss the day's discoveries. The three friends were gathered around a weathered picnic table outside their fishing cabin, plates piled high with Richie's homemade Southern cooking. As the sun set over East Matagorda Bay, casting a golden glow, their conversation turned to the implications of the secret bunker they had uncovered on Bird Island.

Wally in particular seemed troubled, staring pensively into his iced tea as Pug rattled off ideas for getting the bunker's old equipment working again. "How could the military, knowing all this back then, just walk away?" Wally interjected. "How on earth could you keep something like this quiet forever? Whole generations have come and gone since World War II. It might as well be forever ago."

Pug paused his enthusiastic scheming and exchanged a look with Richie. "You got a point there," Pug said. "This stuff is so crazy top secret, I don't even think 'top secret' covers it."

Wally nodded, looking back out at the bayou. "Exactly. We've gotta really protect this information and be careful about who else knows about it." His brow furrowed as he thought of the men they had encountered on the island weeks earlier. "Harry and Jack can't find out any of this. They must not."

Richie could sense Wally's protective instinct surfacing. He reached over and gave his friend a reassuring pat on the back. "Don't worry, we'll keep it all between us for now," he said gently. "No one else will get their hands on what we found."

Wally gave a small smile, the worry in his eyes easing at his friend's reassurance. Pug raised his glass in a toast. "To the keepers of the secrets of Bird Island!" The three clinked their glasses together, the tinkling sound echoing across the quiet bayou. As the sunlight faded into dusk, they dug back into their meal, the mysteries of the past lingering in their minds.

ALONE ON THE DOCK WITH his thoughts in turmoil, he watched the sun slip beneath the horizon. Revealing what he knew to Richie and Pug weighed heavily on him—could he take that risk? And what of Jeff and Barnes? The entire ordeal had spiraled into perilous complexity since they'd unearthed secrets on Bird Island, perhaps some that were meant to remain hidden.

The effects of BRV-076 were undeniable now. His memory was sharper than it had ever been, recalling the smallest details with perfect clarity. And if that microbe worked so well, what about CLF-532? He had to find out.

Wally stood and walked deliberately towards Pug's pickup truck parked nearby. With hardly any effort, he grasped the front bumper with both hands and lifted. The front tires rose effortlessly off the ground as he held the truck's weight aloft. He stood in stunned silence. The microbe had made him as strong as ten men.

My God, he thought. I can't believe this is real.

Unsure what to make of his newfound gifts, Wally released the truck and it bounced back onto the dirt. He walked pensively out to the end of the dock, sat down on a plastic chair, and gazed out at the bayou as the sun dipped below the horizon. What was he going to do now?

WALLY LAY AWAKE LONG after Richie and Pug had drifted off to sleep, contemplating the plan that had been forming in his mind. He knew that if he was going to explore the bunker's secrets alone, he would need an advantage. Glancing at the glowing hands of his watch, he decided it was time.

Slowly and silently, he slipped out of his cot and felt around in the darkness for his backpack. Unzipping it, he retrieved one of the altered sugar cookies he had made using the mysterious VAM-345 compound. Wally took a bite, the sweetness spreading across his tongue as he chewed. He could feel the cookie taking effect, his vision sharpening until he could make out every detail of the cabin's interior, clear as day. His night vision had returned.

He hastily dressed in dark clothes and laced up his boots. Wally knew he only had a small window of time before the cookie's effects wore off. As he tiptoed past his slumbering friends toward the door, Pug snorted in his sleep, making Wally freeze. But Pug merely rolled over, and Wally breathed a sigh of relief as he slipped outside into the night.

The full moon illuminated the glassy surface of the bayou as Wally silently loaded his backpack and supplies into the Jon boat. Ever so carefully, he loosened the moorings and pushed off, paddling with focused determination until the cabin lights faded from view. Satisfied he was far enough, Wally pulled the starter cord and the outboard motor rumbled to life. Soon he was speeding across the bay toward the deeper secrets that awaited him on Bird Island.

The moon was dipping low on the horizon as Wally beached his boat on the island's shore. Slinging his backpack over his shoulder, he hurried inland through the underbrush until he arrived at the hidden southeastern bunker entrance, labeled E3. Swinging the heavy steel door open, he descended into the darkness, his night vision guiding the way.

WITH EASE, WALLY NAVIGATED the pitch-black corridors of the bunker, his vision unimpaired by the inky darkness that would overwhelm any normal human. The effects of the mysterious VAM-345 microorganism had imbued him with extraordinary night vision capabilities, allowing him to see every detail as if it were bathed in sunlight.

Making his way methodically through the abandoned facility, Wally searched for the microorganism research lab, relying on his enhanced eidetic memory to recall the maze-like layout of the bunker. His recollections were perfect - another gift granted by the experimental BRV-076 compound he had secretly consumed.

At last, Wally located the sealed door leading to the lab area. His prodigious strength, amplified massively by the CLF-532 microbe, allowed him to force the stubborn door open with ease. Inside, he found a treasure trove of log books, research papers, and files - a comprehensive record of the shadowy experiments once conducted here.

Meticulously gathering every document related to the microorganisms, Wally filled a large military footlocker with the precious research materials. Despite the locker's considerable weight when loaded, he lifted it effortlessly thanks to his superhuman strength.

With care, Wally transported the full locker through the bunker to the southeastern entrance marked "E3." His mind, expanded by BRV-076, guided him unerringly along the optimal route.

Emerging into the moonlit night, he carried the locker containing the microorganism research down to his jon boat. Wally knew these documents held the key to unraveling the mysteries of Bird Island, secrets he intended to protect and master. With the locker safely stowed, he piloted the boat away from the island under cover of darkness, his extraordinary gifts ensuring success in this covert mission.

WALLY RETURNED TO THE fishing cabin long before sunrise, while Pug and Richie were still fast asleep. He secured the jon boat to the dock with expert knots and then, with his newfound strength from the microorganisms, easily lifted the heavy chest containing all the research materials on microorganisms.

Carrying it carefully, Wally brought the chest into the boat shed. Inside, he found a shovel and dug a hole about three foot deep at the top of the ramp. Gently lowering the chest into the hole, he covered it back up with dirt and smoothed over the surface. Wally hoped this would keep the chest's valuable contents concealed and protected.

After securing the double doors of the shed, Wally quietly slipped back into the cabin. Pug was snoring softly on the cot across from him, oblivious to his nighttime activities. Feeling the fatigue setting in from being awake all night, Wally collapsed onto his bunk. Within moments, he fell into a deep sleep, comforted by the knowledge that the secrets of the microorganisms were safely hidden away.

When morning came, Pug and Richie awoke before Wally. They started coffee and breakfast, chatting about plans for the day's adventure. Wally stirred, yawning and stretching as if he had been sleeping all night. Joining his friends at the table, Wally felt a sense of satisfaction about his covert operation. For now, the mysteries of Bird Island were theirs alone to uncover, one step at a time.

Chapter 8
The Experiment Unveiled

The morning sun filtered through the windows of the cozy fishing cabin, casting shafts of light across the worn wooden table where Pug, Wally, and Richie sat with steaming mugs of coffee. An air of contemplation settled over the group as they considered their next steps in unraveling the mysteries of the abandoned bunker on Bird Island.

Wally had grown quiet, staring pensively into his coffee. His covert nighttime operation to secure the bunker's research documents weighed heavily on his mind. Though the materials were safely stowed away for now in the boat shed, Wally grappled with whether to reveal the full extent of his enhanced abilities to his friends.

Richie studied Wally with a look of concern. "You alright there, Wally? You seem extra distracted this morning."

"Hmm?" Wally glanced up, shaking himself from his thoughts. "Oh yeah, sorry just got lost in my head a bit." He took a bracing sip of coffee. "So, what's the plan for tackling that bunker today?"

Pug's eyes glinted eagerly at the prospect of exploring the subterranean maze. "Well, if we can get that backup generator running, I think I can get power restored to the central command center. That could give us access to control systems, records, surveillance..."

As Pug enthusiastically speculated over the possibilities, Wally nodded along, interjecting occasional comments while keeping his newfound knowledge guarded close to his chest. For now, patience

and care were needed to safely navigate the mysteries of Bird Island.
Soon enough, he hoped to share his revelations when the time was
right.

"GUYS, HOW ABOUT PANCAKES today? I'm a little tired of
eggs and grits," Wally ask.

Richie replied, "Well if we got the mix, I'm game."

Pug spoke up eagerly, "Sounds good to me too!"

Richie rummaged through the pantry and found a box of
pancake mix. He cracked a couple eggs into a bowl and began
whisking up the batter.

Meanwhile, Wally grabbed a skillet and turned on the stove,
letting it heat up in preparation for the pancakes.

Pug poured glasses of milk for each of them and took the syrup
from the fridge, setting the table.

Soon the savory smell of sizzling batter wafted through the cozy
cabin. Richie fried up a plate of bacon to go along with the pancakes,
the popping and crackling joining the symphony of smells.

Before long, stacks of fluffy pancakes and crispy bacon were piled
high on their plates. The three friends sat down at the table, ready to
dig into the hearty breakfast feast. With smiles on their faces, they
doused the pancakes in syrup and bit into the delicious morning
treat, fueling up for another day of adventure and discovery that lay
ahead. The good food and even better company put them in great
spirits.

THE EARLY MORNING SUN glinted off the calm waters of the
bayou as Pug, Richie, and Wally cleaned up after breakfast in the

fishing cabin's cozy kitchen. Plates clinked as they were washed and stowed away, while pots and pans sizzled as they were scrubbed of the remnants of pancakes, bacon, and grits.

As they worked, Wally's face was creased with thought. "Guys," he began tentatively as he dried the last plate, "I've been thinking a lot about those men we saw at the bunker - Jack, Harry, and Alexei. How did they even know about that place to begin with? And what was a Russian doing all the way out here?"

He paused, looking between Pug and Richie's attentive faces. "What if foreign governments already know about the bunker? What if they're interested in whatever secrets might still be hidden there?" His voice held a note of apprehension.

Richie nodded, considering Wally's concerns. Pug looked more skeptical. "It does seem fishy," Richie agreed after a moment. "We should be careful."

"I think we're getting ahead of ourselves," Pug countered, though not unkindly. "We don't really know anything about those guys. Could just be coincidence." He shrugged.

Wally didn't seem convinced, but he didn't argue further. "Well, you guys go on with your plan for today. I'm going to hang back on the island, take a closer look around for any signs those guys left behind. Tracks, campsites, anything unusual." He grabbed his backpack and headed for the door. "I want to see if there's any way for us to set up some kind of security system, maybe rig some kind of alarm in case anyone else shows up."

The three boys continued discussing possibilities as they loaded up their small motorboat. Though they didn't reach any definite conclusions, they agreed to proceed with caution. Wally seemed reassured to have shared his concerns as Pug steered the boat toward Bird Island's shore. He was determined to discover anything out of the ordinary that might reveal who else was interested in the island's secrets.

THE EARLY MORNING SUN glinted off the gentle waves as the
jon boat cut through the waters of East Matagorda Bay. Pug sat at the
motor, guiding them steadily toward the low shape of Bird Island on
the horizon. Wally was perched at the bow, binoculars in hand, while
Richie checked their equipment in the middle of the boat.

As they drew nearer to the island, Wally turned to Pug. "I think
we should circle the Island first, along the northern shoreline around
the tip on the west side and back to the southeast tip. Let's anchor
there and make sure no one else is already on the island."

Pug considered the suggestion and nodded. "Okay, but it'll take
an extra 30 minutes to make that run around."

"Better safe than sorry," Richie chimed in, looking up from
organizing their packs.

Pug adjusted their course, and the boat began a wide arc, giving
the island a wide berth as they motored up the east side. Wally
scanned the shoreline through his binoculars, looking for any signs
of life while Pug kept them far enough out to avoid detection. The
morning air was still and clear, making their passage smooth and
quiet.

They continued along the northern edge, seeing nothing but
empty beaches and grassy dunes. Rounding the western tip, they
began closing back in toward the southeast as the far side of the
island came into view. Wally saw only undisturbed marshland along
the shore.

Within thirty minutes, they had completed their cautious circuit
and were anchored off a secluded sandy cove near the southeastern
end. Their sweep confirmed the island was deserted this morning.
After a quick check of their equipment, the three friends set off
through the gentle surf onto the beach, ready to explore the island's

hidden secrets. As agreed upon, Wally stayed behind to scout the island.

PAUSING IN THE TREE line, Wally scanned for any signs of life before lowering his pack and retrieving three items - a slightly crumbling cookie wrapped in parchment paper, and two foil-wrapped rectangles that were, in truth, small candy bars. But these were no ordinary sweets. The cookie contained the microorganism VAM-345, which granted heightened night vision. The candy bars had been secretly laced with BRV-076 to amplify memory retention, and CLF-532 to increase physical endurance.

Wally unwrapped the ancient cookie, its rough texture evident even in the dim light. He took a bite, the flavors subtle and earthy. Then he unwrapped the candy bars, taking a small taste of each - just enough to ingest the microorganisms within. Their effectiveness remained uncertain, but if they worked as intended, they could give Wally the edge he needed.

After washing it all down with a sip of water, Wally re-secured his backpack. He moved steadily through the underbrush, homing in on the concealed bunker entrance. Soon, if all went according to plan, the effects of the microorganisms would begin to manifest. BRV-076 would grant him flawless recall. CLF-532 would push his endurance beyond normal human limitations. And VAM-345 would allow him to see in the pitch darkness that awaited within the abandoned bunker. For better or worse, Wally was about to enter a world beyond ordinary perception. His transformation had begun.

AS WALLY MOVED STEALTHILY through the brush, the effects of the microbe-laced cookies and candy bars took hold. His vision sharpened until he could make out the faintest impressions left by wildlife on the sandy paths—the paw prints of raccoons foraging at night, the slithering trails of snakes seeking sunshine. Energy and alertness surged within him, his muscles unfatiguing no matter the terrain. His mind cataloged each detail, etching it into memory with perfect clarity. Trails and landmarks that he had only glimpsed in passing were now fixed in his mind like photographs.

Empowered by these enhancements, Wally covered ground with astonishing speed, navigating by instinct through the island's interior. In no time at all, he had reached the western shoreline, not far from where he had spotted Jack's boat on that fateful day. Wally paused, listening for any sound of activity over the gentle lapping of waves. Satisfied he was alone, he slipped into a copse of trees and settled in to observe, ready to utilize his new gifts to unravel the island's secrets once and for all.

WALLY MOVED THROUGH the brush, retracing his steps along the winding trail back towards the campsite. As he glanced down, he was struck by how vividly his own footprints stood out, practically glowing with color against the muted landscape. It was as if someone had outlined each impression in the dirt with neon paint that only he could see.

He paused, considering the implications of this newfound ability granted by the microbe-laced treats. If he could see prints this fresh so clearly, how far back might that enhanced vision extend? Could he make out tracks from days or even weeks ago that would be invisible to a normal eye?

He decided to test this idea. Wally changing direction, crept towards the location where the tents had been set up, moving slowly and watchfully to avoid leaving any new disturbances. Once there, he scanned the trampled earth, seeking any signs of the previous inhabitants.

At first, he saw nothing unusual. But as he focused, subtle details began to emerge. Faded outlines of shoe treads, partially filled in and blurred by time, yet still faintly glowing to his augmented sight. He spotted one print, then another - soon realizing he could distinguish prints ranging from a few hours to several days old by their dimming luminosity.

It was fascinating, almost like reading a timeline etched into the soil. The most recent impressions shone brightly, while older tracks took on muted tones of blue and green. Wally stared in awe, comprehending the power this granted him. With some practice, he might be able to track anyone who had passed this way, however long ago. Lost in thought, he lingered at the site, studying the chronicle of faded footsteps only he could see.

WALLY MOVED WITH RENEWED purpose, invigorated by his heightened senses after consuming the microbe-laced treats. He decided to take advantage of his newfound tracking ability and circled the entire island, meticulously scanning for human footprints.

The midday sun beat down as Wally combed through the sandy shores and winding inland trails. He discovered faded tracks here and there, but none fresh enough to raise concern. As he walked, an intricate map of the island formed in Wally's mind. He realized he could now close his eyes and visualize details of the landscape - from the salt-weathered bunker doors to the tiny crabs scuttling across the beach.

By early afternoon, Wally had completed his circuit of the small island. The sweep revealed nothing alarming, just the ordinary signs of wildlife and the occasional fisherman passing through. With his mental map complete, Wally turned his thoughts to finding his friends Pug and Richie. The day was getting on and he knew they would be wondering about him.

Wally hurried back along the inland trail, retracing his own fresh footprints in the sandy soil. He felt energized by the microbes continuing to enhance his senses, but also relieved to have found no trace of the mysterious men from their last trip. For now, Bird Island's secrets remained undisturbed. As he neared the cove where they had docked, Wally could make out Richie and Pug's voices drifting through the trees. He called out to them, eager to share the revelations from his solitary trek around Bird Island.

WALLY MOVED THROUGH the dense underbrush of Bird Island with preternatural speed and perception, energized by the microbe-laced treats he had secretly consumed. Every detail of the environment was etched into his mind with perfect clarity thanks to the memory-enhancing effects of BRV-076. His vision pierced the island's shadows, granting him extraordinary night sight due to the influence of VAM-345. Most incredibly, Wally felt no fatigue or strain as he dashed over rough terrain with marathoner-like endurance gifted by CLF-532. These radical abilities had fueled his solo scouting mission across the remote island.

Satisfied that no threats lurked after thoroughly combing the area, Wally raced to the southeastern tip of Bird Island where his friends' boat was anchored in a secluded cove. There he found Pug and Richie, who greeted him eagerly, unaware of the transformations he had undergone. "No signs of anyone else on the island," Wally reported, concealing his enhanced explorations.

Eager to continue their subterranean adventure, the trio entered the familiar southeastern bunker entrance marked 'E3.' The heavy steel door groaned open to grant them access to the depths. Guided by their flashlights and driven by curiosity, they navigated the musty tunnels with growing excitement. Their destination was the bunker's Command Center, located not far from the Central Hub according to Richie's drawn map.

Wally led the way with tireless energy, mentally reviewing the route from his flawless memory. The microbe-induced gifts had made him the perfect guide through the dark maze of corridors. Yet only he understood the full extent of the changes within himself, kept secret even from his closest friends. Wally wondered, as they plunged deeper underground, how much longer he could conceal the bunker's true mysteries.

WALLY NAVIGATED THE dark corridors of the bunker with ease, his vision sharpened by the microbe-laced treats he had secretly consumed. Though his friends Pug and Richie struggled to see in the pitch blackness, Wally moved with confidence, mentally mapping their route.

Soon they arrived at a heavy steel door labeled "Command Center." Wally's acute hearing picked up the humming of dormant electronics beyond.

"Hang tight guys, I'll go start the generator," Wally said. "Just wait here."

"Gladly," Pug replied. "Just speak up if you need help."

Wally retraced their steps, arriving in moments at the utility workshop. His enhanced strength allowed him to easily crank start the old generator. Soon power surged through the bunker's veins, lighting up the abandoned control room.

Wally rushed back to his friends. "All set!"

Together they entered the command center, eyes wide with wonder. Dusty consoles and screens lined the room. A large tactical map dominated one wall, stuck in time decades ago.

"This must be how they coordinated missions on the island," Richie murmured.

"And tracked ships in the bay," added Pug, pointing to a radar screen.

Wally nodded, but his focus strayed to a file cabinet in the corner. While his friends explored the technology, Wally discreetly rifled through personnel records, his photographic memory absorbing every detail for later study.

"Jackpot!" cried Pug. "This logbook has daily operations reports. We can piece together what they were up to here."

Wally joined Pug and Richie at the central console, acting enthused. But inwardly, he pondered the secrets still hidden in his own mind, unsure if he should ever reveal the full extent of his transformations.

WALLY STOOD SILENTLY in the shadows of the command center, his senses heightened from the microbe-laced treats he had secretly consumed. The diesel generator hummed steadily, casting light across the dated controls and equipment that filled the room. Pug and Richie moved about with notebooks in hand, marveling at the relics of technology that surrounded them.

"This console must have been the nerve center," Pug remarked as he inspected a large panel covered in toggle switches, buttons, and analog gauges. He traced his fingers over the labels, reading out commands like "Deploy Radar" and "Initiate Patrol Pattern Delta."

Meanwhile, Richie was poring through a thick binder titled "RADAR Aided Military Patrol Operations Manual." As he turned the pages, studying the diagrams and procedures, understanding began to take root.

"Guys, I think this was a base for developing radar techniques to coordinate submarine hunting patrols," Richie said. "There's mention here of something called 'Abnormal Weather Event' experiments - I think they were testing systems in extreme conditions."

Wally stayed quiet but mentally filed away every detail thanks to the microbe's effects, while discreetly pocketing a few personnel dossiers to examine later.

"This console must have been where they simulated patrols and weather events," Pug added. "I'll bet this whole bunker was bustling with radar operators, patrol commanders, meteorologists - all to gain an edge in naval warfare."

As the boys pieced together details, the true nature of the forgotten base became clearer. Their excitement grew at uncovering this hidden fragment of military history. Wally kept his own discoveries to himself, unsure how much to reveal to his trusted friends.

WALLY MOVED THROUGH the bunker with heightened senses, the effects of the microbe-laced treats still coursing through him. As the day wore on, a realization dawned on him - the best way to protect the bunker's secrets was not to overtly shield them at all.

Such efforts would only stoke others' determination to uncover what lay hidden within these walls.

No, he would take a different tack. Let them find secrets, but only the ones he allowed.

He hatched a plan. He would locate all sensitive documents, research records, and logbooks and quietly stow them away in a concealed location only he knew about. For everything else, he would rearrange files and add misleading labels like "Top Secret" to throw off suspicion. The bunker's most critical revelations would be obscured, visible only to him.

The challenge was accomplishing this without his friends Pug and Richie around. He needed an opportunity to be alone in the bunker undisturbed. As the trio explored the abandoned rooms and corridors, Wally stayed alert for any distraction that could give him the opening he needed. The slightest lapse in the others' attention, and he would make his move, spiriting away the bunker's true history to his secret cache. Only then could he guide his friends toward more benign discoveries, protecting them from harsh truths they weren't yet ready to bear.

Wally moved through the shadows, biding his time, determined to keep the bunker's secrets even as he fed its explorers measured morsels of revelation. His enhanced abilities gave him the means to filter what his companions uncovered. All he needed now was the chance to enact his ingenious plan.

WALLY MOVED SWIFTLY and silently through the dark corridors of the abandoned bunker, his senses heightened by the microbe-laced treats he had consumed earlier. While his friends Pug and Richie were busy exploring the vintage command center, Wally was on a covert mission of his own.

He scouted out a remote corner of the bunker, far from where the others were investigating. This hidden nook would be the perfect spot for what Wally had already started thinking of as "WallyLab" - a secret lab for him to conduct private experiments and research, taking full advantage of the unique abilities the mysterious microbes had given him.

In the darkness, Wally's exceptional night vision allowed him to examine the space in detail. It was secluded and unlikely to be stumbled upon by happenstance. The thick concrete walls would provide sound dampening, and the bunker's maze of corridors would make it easy to come and go from WallyLab without drawing attention.

He imagined how he would outfit the lab - places to store samples and documents, space for a worktable. With his newfound strength, he could easily move any required equipment and furniture in here. A hidden exit could even be built, allowing a quick escape route if needed.

Satisfied with the spot after thoroughly scoping it out, Wally hurried back through the bunker's passageways. His impeccable memory guided him unerringly back to the command center where Pug and Richie were still engrossed in researching the dated equipment and records. Wally rejoined them, pretending to share in their fascination with the command center while keeping his side project to himself. Only Wally knew that soon, he would have a secret lab in the depths of the bunker for accessing the mysteries the microbes had unlocked within him.

WALLY MOVED SWIFTLY through the dim corridors of the hidden bunker, his enhanced senses guiding him effortlessly even in near-darkness. The last few days had passed quickly as he and his friends continued studying the abandoned complex, but Wally had other plans brewing.

In a remote corner, Wally had set up his secret laboratory, which he jokingly referred to as "WallyLab." It was here that he had moved most of the remaining microorganism samples found scattered around the bunker. Rows of vials and jars filled with exotic powders and liquids lined the makeshift shelves he had built along the walls. Logbooks and research notes were stacked neatly on an old desk in the corner. This was Wally's private sanctuary, where he could experiment and learn without interruption.

Wally was relieved to have the valuable samples protected in his lab. For now, he had decided it was safer not to attempt growing any cultures from the ancient microbes. Having active, multiplying spores around would be far too risky with his friends Pug and Richie still exploring the bunker daily. Better to keep the microorganisms inert for the time being.

Besides, Wally mused, separating the samples from any active research was wise. Keeping papers, cultures, and powders all in one place was dangerous. If his lab was ever discovered, the damage would be limited by the physical distance between elements.

Glancing at his watch, Wally realized it was already mid-afternoon. This was to be their last day at the fishing cabin before returning home. He gathered a few final items into his backpack and did a final check of his hidden lab before turning to leave. Wally took one long look at the secret space that had allowed him to learn so much in such a short time. Soon he would be back to continue unraveling the mysteries of the microorganisms and their extraordinary effects. For now, he re-sealed the lab and slipped away to rejoin his friends for the journey home, the vials and powders hidden safely within the bunker walls until his return.

Chapter 9
The Quest for Answers

Wally walked up the gravel driveway, the crunch of stones under his shoes the only sound breaking the stillness of the late afternoon. He could feel the effects of the microbe-laced treats he had consumed over the past four days finally beginning to fade, his senses dulling, his strength waning. Soon he would be no different than anyone else.

He turned to wave as Pug's pickup truck disappeared around the corner, already missing his friend's animated energy. Their conversation about college and returning to Chinquapin still rang in his ears. Pug believed it would be at least a month before he could get enough time off for another adventure. Too long in Wally's estimation. He yearned to uncover more of the bunker's secrets, to test his abilities to their limits. But he knew Pug was right. Responsibilities called them back to the real world for now.

He sighed and walked up the steps to the front door of his house. "Hey Mom, I'm home!" he called out, his voice echoing in the empty rooms. There was no reply. Wally wondered where his parents were as he made his way through the living room back to the kitchen. On the counter, he found a note from his mother saying she had gone with his father to a dental appointment in Pearland and would be back by dinner time.

Happy to have the house to himself for a bit, Wally changed and headed out the back door towards the shed at the rear of the property. Inside, he unlocked a metal cabinet bolted to the wall and removed two mason jars filled with a cloudy liquid. Holding them up to the light streaming in through the small window, he could see tiny motes swirling within the solution. His cultivated microorganisms, are still active.

Wally smiled, knowing that when the time came, he could easily whip up another batch of treats to reactivate his extraordinary abilities. For now, he replaced the jars in the cabinet, locked it securely, and headed back to the house to start preparing dinner for his parents' return. He felt content, despite the waning effects of the microbes, knowing that the secrets of Bird Island were not done revealing themselves. When the time was right, he would be ready to discover more.

AS THE SUN DIPPED BELOW the horizon, the last rays of daylight retreated from the quaint suburban neighborhood where Wally lived. Streetlights flickered on one by one, bathing the orderly rows of houses in a warm glow. Inside the cozy split-level home, Wally stood at the stove, wooden spoon in hand, tending to a bubbling pot of pasta sauce. The rich, tomatoey aroma filled the kitchen, making his stomach rumble in anticipation.

Wally glanced at the clock on the microwave as he gave the sauce a final stir before reducing the heat to low. Nearly 6 PM. His parents would be home soon. He moved the pot off the burner and lifted the lid on another pot filled with boiling water and pasta. The spaghetti noodles needed another minute or two. Wally grabbed potholders and opened the oven door to check on the garlic bread. Perfectly toasted. He removed the baking sheet and set it on the stovetop to cool.

Everything was coming together for the special dinner Wally had prepared. A homemade meal was a small way to show his parents how much he cherished them. How much he wished he could share everything that was going on with him lately.

Wally took a deep breath as he set the dining room table, centering the plates just so. He knew he couldn't keep his secret forever. The changes were too big to hide, and getting bigger by the day. His only hope was to break it to them slowly. Let them see how he had grown into himself before they learned the full truth, but this seemed to be impossible, too many days doing what at Chinquapin and missing class at the local college.

Headlights flashed across the front windows as his parents' sedan pulled into the driveway. Wally straightened his shirt and went to greet them at the door. As soon as they stepped inside, the delicious aroma drew them towards the kitchen.

"Welcome home! Go ahead and get comfortable. Dinner's just about ready," said Wally.

"Oh, honey, it smells wonderful!" his mom exclaimed, giving him a peck on the cheek before heading upstairs to change.

"You've been busy. What's the special occasion?" his dad asked, playfully ruffling Wally's hair.

"No occasion. Just wanted to do something nice since you've both been working so hard," Wally said with a shy smile.

His dad gave him an approving pat as they settled around the table.

AS THEY FINISHED EATING including a slice of mom's apple pie, Wally set down his fork and looked at his parents earnestly. "Mom, Dad, I have something very important to tell you."

His parents exchanged a glance, curiosity mingled with concern in their eyes. "What is it, son?" his dad asked.

Wally took a deep breath. "I know this will sound unbelievable, but I've come to possess some knowledge that could change the world. Knowledge that in the wrong hands, could cause terrible destruction, but in the right hands, could save mankind."

His parents stared, stunned into silence.

"Just let me explain everything first before you react," Wally continued. "I was hoping to break this to you slowly, but there's no easy way to say it. During my recent trip with Pug and Richie, we uncovered some...secrets. Secrets dating back to World War II experiments that happened right here in Texas, out on Bird Island."

Wally's mom opened her mouth, but Wally held up a hand. "Please, just listen. I promise I'll explain." She nodded hesitantly.

"Out on Bird Island, we found an abandoned military bunker. It was a research lab from the 1940s. Me and Richie and Pug, we found all kinds of weird equipment and files and specimens. Including..." Wally hesitated. "Including samples of certain microorganisms. Microbes with properties nobody could've imagined."

Wally's father furrowed his brow, but remained silent.

"I know it sounds crazy. But some of these microbes had effects on the human body. Enhancing strength, vision, memory, you name it. Almost like superpowers." Wally shook his head. "I didn't believe it either at first. Not until I experimented on myself."

His parents both stiffened, their eyes widening.

"I'm fine, I swear!" Wally said. "I was careful. I just tried a small amount, to test it. And..." He flexed his arm, feeling the muscles ripple beneath his shirt. "It worked. It really worked."

Wally's father found his voice. "Son, what on earth are you talking about? Microbes that give superpowers? That's absurd."

"I told you it would sound unbelievable. But I can prove it." Wally stood up from the table. "Mom, can you please put on a pot of coffee? I know it's getting late, but I think we're gonna need something to steady our nerves."

His mom looked uncertain, but rose and went to fill the coffee pot. His dad was still staring at Wally in disbelief.

Wally took a deep breath. "I didn't want to have to demonstrate this tonight. I wanted to ease you into it, over time. But I think you need to see with your own eyes."

His mom had gone pale. His father seemed unable to speak. The percolating coffee was the only sound.

"As hard to believe as it is, what I now know could change the world. It could create great wealth, or cause wars to break out. I know you must have a million questions. And I promise, I'll explain everything."

"I'm still your son, Mom. I'm still me. I just have...abilities, now. Abilities that I now know I have to dedicate my life to protecting." Wally's expression was grave. "The military, world governments—they would do anything to gain this knowledge. We would all be in great danger if anyone else knew what I know."

Wally's dad passed a shaking hand over his face. "Son, you have to turn over anything you took from that island. This is wildly dangerous—"

"No!" Wally said forcefully. Then, softer: "No. You don't understand, Dad. I'm the only one who can protect this secret now. But I can't do it alone. I need you both to trust me on this."

His mom and dad stared at him for a long, silent moment. The coffee finished brewing, the heady aroma filling the room.

Finally, Wally's dad nodded. "Alright, son. Keep talking. We'll try to understand."

Wally's shoulders slumped in relief. He sat back down at the table. "Thank you. I know it's a lot to take in. Here, Mom, let me help you with that coffee..."

As his mother brought over mugs and cream, Wally continued. "It all started when we first stepped foot on Bird Island. We found something strange there, something that set this whole crazy adventure in motion..."

WALLY SAT DOWN WITH his parents at the dining room table, taking a deep breath before continuing his incredible tale. Though uncertain how they would react, he knew it was crucial to reveal the full truth about the discoveries made on Bird Island.

"There's more I need to tell you about what we found in that bunker," Wally began. "I didn't mention it before, but during our last trip, I gathered up all of the most critical research documents, logbooks and samples of the microorganisms. I smuggled them off the island and have been keeping them hidden away ever since."

His parents exchanged a look of surprise and concern.

"I knew the information was too sensitive and powerful to leave behind," Wally explained. "So I selected the most revealing papers and specimens and concealed them in my backpack. I was worried about who else might come looking and what they might do if they found it."

"Where did you put all of this material?" his father asked cautiously.

"I have it secured in a locked chest, buried in the back corner of the boat shed," Wally revealed. "I also staged some fake documents in the bunker to throw anyone else off the track of what really went on there. I'm still not even sure myself exactly what happened, but I know it needs to stay hidden."

His mother nodded, though her eyebrows knitted together in concern. "That seems rather extreme, don't you think? To take all of that without telling your friends?"

"I know, but someone had to protect these secrets," Wally said. "There's no telling how dangerous this knowledge could be if it got into the wrong hands. I did what I thought was right."

His father sat back in his chair, arms crossed as he pondered this new information.

"Well, I can't say I fully understand what would drive you to do all that," he said. "But I appreciate you being upfront with us now. Just don't let this turn into an obsession."

Wally nodded. "Thanks. I know it might sound crazy but let me show you something that will help explain."

He went and fetched his mother's gardening magazine from the other room, sitting back down and rapidly scanning through the pages. "Okay, now pick any page you want and I'll recite it back to you word-for-word," he challenged.

Skeptically, she flipped through and pointed to a spot. Wally took a breath and then perfectly recited the entire page she had indicated, stunning his parents.

"How on earth did you do that?" his mother exclaimed.

"It's from one of the microorganisms I told you about - BRV-076," Wally revealed. "It gives me almost perfect recall ability. I can memorize anything after just a quick look."

His awestruck parents sat in silence, processing this demonstration.

"There's more," Wally continued. "Let me show you something else."

He led them out to the driveway, where his father's pickup truck was parked. Gripping the front bumper, Wally lifted the front tires a few inches off the ground as his parents watched in shock. After holding it briefly, he gently set it back down.

"I have enhanced strength now too, from the microbe CLF-532," he explained. "Pretty crazy, right?"

"I'll say!" his father responded, kneeling to examine his truck. "And that didn't even look hard for you. Just be careful, the last thing we need is you throwing out your back trying to be a show-off."

They headed back inside, where Wally picked at the remains of his dinner.

"I know this is a lot to take in," he said. "I'm still wrapping my head around it too. But the island holds incredible secrets that I feel compelled to protect. I hope you understand why I had to keep parts of this to myself until now. Are you okay with me telling you everything?"

His parents exchanged a thoughtful glance. "We appreciate your honesty, Wally," his mother said. "This is certainly alarming, but if you feel it's that important, we will try to understand and support you through this unusual situation. Just promise you'll be smart and stay safe with all...this."

Wally let out a relieved breath. "I will, and thanks for trusting me. There's still more I should fill you in on so we're all on the same page."

Settling in, Wally continued unveiling everything he had kept hidden about the mysteries of Bird Island, his parents listening with a mix of fascination and concern. Though an improbable tale, the proof he demonstrated compelled them to keep an open mind. They talked late into the night, laying the groundwork for an alliance built on truth and trust, as Wally shared his full experience of the extraordinary discoveries made during that fateful summer.

WALLY SAT WITH HIS parents at the dinner table, the remains of pasta and garlic bread scattered across their plates as he prepared to divulge the full extent of the changes brought on by the microorganisms. Though apprehensive, he knew it was crucial they understand the scope of his new abilities.

"There's one last thing I should mention about the effects of the microbes," Wally began. "I can see incredibly well in the dark now - even better than in daylight. And I can track almost anything, anywhere. Human, animal, snake - you name it. I can tell how old tracks are too."

Wally's father pursed his lips, processing this latest revelation. After a moment, he stood and began clearing the table. "Let's take our coffee outside. I need your help making some plans."

Wally nodded, relief flooding through him. He began helping clean up the remnants of dinner, heartened that his father seemed willing to hear him out further. A breeze drifted in through the open window as the two soon stepped out into the quiet of the night, mugs in hand. Settling into patio chairs, his father spoke. "Alright son, let's figure this out together."

WALLY SAT ACROSS FROM his father on their back patio as the fading light of dusk settled over their yard. He took a deep breath, gathering his thoughts before breaking the comfortable silence.

"Dad, I need to talk to you about something important," Wally began. His father nodded, his expression open.

Wally proceeded cautiously. "You know those abilities I told you about at dinner? The ones from the microorganisms?"

His dad nodded again. "I have to admit, it's pretty incredible stuff. And more than a little hard to believe."

Wally gave a small smile. "I know it sounds unbelievable. But it's all real, I promise." He paused. "The thing is, now that I have these abilities, I feel...responsible. Responsible for protecting the knowledge I found on Bird Island."

Wally's father leaned forward, intrigued. "Go on."

"Well, some of what I learned could be dangerous if it got into the wrong hands," Wally explained. "Things that could really hurt people, or alter them permanently. I don't feel right about that knowledge being out there unchecked."

His dad looked thoughtful. "That makes sense. But it's a big responsibility for someone your age."

"I know," Wally acknowledged. "But I'm the only one who really understands the full extent of what's there. I need to be the guardian of those secrets."

Wally's father smiled slightly. "Guardian of Bird Island secrets, eh? Well, it does suit your abilities." His expression grew more serious. "But guardianship is no small task. It will require wisdom and discretion to know what to reveal and what to conceal."

"I know," Wally said. "I've been thinking a lot about the best way to handle this. And I think the first step is making sure no one sees the island as any kind of treasure trove."

He leaned forward. "If people think there's gold or something valuable there, they'll tear the place apart looking for it. But if I can spread the word that it's just an old military base with mostly mundane records and junk, it won't attract much attention."

Wally's father nodded. "That's smart. Downplay anything that seems valuable."

"Right. I'll hide any research that seems risky or open to misuse. And obscure anything related to personal gain, so no one gets tempted by thoughts of wealth." Wally ticked the points off on his fingers. "I'll conceal anything catastrophic, anything that could be turned into a weapon. Basically remove all the incentives that would make that island a target."

"That all makes good sense," his dad agreed. "Though it's a lot for a 19-year-old to take on."

"I know," said Wally seriously. "But I brought this on myself by taking those microbes. And I have the abilities now to pull it off."

Wally's father looked at him appraisingly. "Just don't take on too much at once. And know that you can rely on your mother and me for support."

Wally smiled, relieved. "Thanks, Dad. That really means a lot. This won't be easy, but knowing you guys have my back helps a lot."

His father gripped his shoulder. "Of course. That's what family is for." He gestured at the darkening yard. "Now, you said your abilities let you see at night?"

Wally nodded, and his father grinned.

"Well let's see what else these old eyes can pick up then."

They rose from their chairs and descended from the patio into the night. Wally felt the familiar tingle behind his eyes as his vision shifted, bringing the world into sharper focus. He smiled to himself, leading his father into the darkness. He still had much to learn about his new purpose, but with his family's support, he felt ready to embrace his role as guardian of Bird Island's secrets. There were challenges ahead, but he would face them with wisdom, discretion, and care.

UNDER THE SUBTLE CONTROL of the microorganism, Wally dedicated his day to unraveling the threads of the World Wide Web. Ensconced within the hushed confines of the college library, he navigated a sea of information, his focus zeroed in on unearthing lucrative employment opportunities. His mind, usually teeming with thoughts of outdoor escapades and machinery, now hummed with figures and future possibilities.

The realm of information technology glimmered like a gold nugget in a prospector's pan. He sifted through various job descriptions and profiles, his eyes drawn to software contracting - an occupation that seemed to offer a balance of autonomy and financial gain.

Eager to sharpen his mental faculties, Wally consumed another microorganism-infused cookie. The subtle effects rippled through him like a wave, imbuing him with an almost uncanny memory retention. He felt as if he could remember every word he read, every diagram he saw. With this newfound intellectual prowess at his disposal, he plunged into learning about programming languages for cloud-based data storage.

As he swam through a sea of jargon and complex concepts, the threads began to weave together in his mind. Python, Java, SQL - each language became another tool in his mental toolbox. He immersed himself in this newfound knowledge until it became part of him.

Next came the hunt for opportunities. Wally dove back into the digital ocean, seeking a company in need of his newfound skills. A local company named Bake-RiteZ emerged from his search results. Their need? To migrate their manufacturing software to a cloud-based system.

With a newly polished repertoire of technical language and a boosted memory, Wally made his pitch to Bake-RiteZ's IT manager. His confident demeanor and seemingly innate understanding of their needs won them over; they offered him the contract.

On the way home, he detoured to a local computer center. The scent of fresh electronics filled the air as he purchased a Dell workstation running Microsoft Server, a high-end desktop computer, a sleek monitor, and a professional-grade printer.

Returning home, he transformed his bedroom into an office. His single bed found a new home in the sun-drenched back room while his desk took center stage, adorned with his new equipment.

The transformation was complete; Wally's bedroom was now the command center of his new business venture.

WALLY SAT AT HIS DESK in his makeshift home office, his mind buzzing with enhanced focus and retention thanks to the microorganisms he had consumed. Spread out before him were piles of documentation, specifications, and user notes from Bake-RiteZ, a local bakery looking to move its systems to the cloud.

Utilizing his exceptional abilities granted by the microbes, Wally swiftly parsed through the materials, grasping the bakery's data and functionality needs. His fingers flew across the keyboard as he began constructing a robust database architecture using Java and SQL. He normalized the data requirements for efficiency, occasionally referencing the docs to ensure alignment with Bake-Rite's goals.

In just a few short days, Wally had produced a working cloud-based system for the bakery. All of the core functionality was in place, with just the reporting features remaining. Wally diligently built out three basic reports for each database table, providing the analytics and summaries that the client had requested.

Finally ready, Wally packaged up the finished software and sent it off to Bake-RiteZ's IT department, along with instructions for setup and configuration. Now, he just needed to wait for them to test it out and provide feedback. Leaning back in his chair, Wally smiled with satisfaction. He knew this was just the beginning of his budding software contracting business, with many more opportunities to come. The microbes had unlocked exceptional skills within him, and Wally was determined to put them to good use.

WALLY SAT AT HIS DESK, reviewing the contract from Bake-RiteZ one more time before submitting his invoice. Thanks to the extraordinary cognitive abilities granted by the microorganisms, he had been able to develop their cloud-based system with ease in just a few short weeks. Now his fledgling software business was poised to take off.

The initial $12,000 payment had covered his expenses for new computer equipment and converting his bedroom into a professional home office. With the next $80,000 payment due upon delivery, along with minimum monthly support and training fees of $6,000 for two years, Wally would have plenty of capital to continue operations. He could keep his parents in the dark about the true origins of his sudden business success.

Wally submitted the invoice to Bake-RiteZ's accounting department, confident that the delivery of the functional cloud system met all their specifications. He included instructions for the monthly support payments, making sure to retain ownership of the source code until the final payment cleared.

Leaning back in his desk chair, Wally smiled with satisfaction. His software business would provide the perfect cover for his role as the guardian of Bird Island. The steady income would fund any equipment and travel needed to keep its secrets safe from outsiders who might exploit the power of the microorganisms. Wally's transformation into a protector empowered by extraordinary abilities was well underway.

Along with this new business adventure, Wally discovered as BRV-076 wore off, his new memory and knowledge were not lost, just the ability to understand and store new information returned to normal. This was in itself, a nice windfall.

WALLY WALKED DOWN THE gravel path leading to his mother's potting shed, a sense of purpose propelling his steps. He unlocked the wooden door and stepped inside, immediately greeted by the earthy aroma of soil and foliage. Making his way past terra cotta pots overflowing with flowers and herbs, Wally arrived at his secret workbench tucked away in the back corner.

On the bench sat three large mason jars, each filled with a bubbling tan liquid - his carefully cultivated sourdough starter that had been fermenting for weeks. Wally inspected each jar closely, noting their activity. It was time to begin the next phase of his experiment. But first, Wally would save a little out of each jar, adding it to another starter jar that would grow with time and continue to feed the process.

From his backpack, Wally produced a small vial labeled 'DNX-109' and held it up to the light. The lite tan powder inside seemed innocuous, but Wally knew its incredible power - the ability to accelerate healing. He carefully measured out a precise amount two grams and added it to the first jar of starter. After sealing the jar, he gently swirled the contents until the DNX-109 was fully incorporated.

Wally repeated the process with the vials labeled 'BRV-076' and 'CLF-532', enhancing the starter in the other two jars with the microorganisms' respective abilities to boost memory and endurance. Satisfied with his work, Wally neatly labeled each jar and placed them on a storage shelf to culture.

In a week's time, the sourdough would be ready for the next phase - baking into bread. By consuming the bread, Wally hoped to safely ingest the abilities of the microorganisms. A plausible cover for his covert experiments.

Wally next inspected his remaining supply of cookies enhanced with VAM-345, granting him temporary night vision. He still had over a dozen left, enough for now. Carefully repacking his backpack, Wally made his way out of the shed, locking it securely behind him.

After lunch, he set out to run some errands, stopping at the local home goods store. There, he purchased a top-of-the-line air fryer oven that could also be used for dehydration and baking. Wheeling the large box out to his truck, Wally felt a swell of excitement imagining the possibilities with this new tool.

Back at the shed, Wally unpacked the air fryer and found a spot for it near an outlet. He read the manual front to back, absorbing all the features and functions. Soon he would be able to bake his enhanced bread, cook up powders, and experiment further with the incredible microorganisms. But for today, his work was done.

Wally locked up the shed once more and headed up to the house for dinner, content with the progress made. In one week's time, he would return to check on the sourdough and move to the next step of his clandestine operation. With patience and care, he would unlock the potential of the powerful microbes from Bird Island. Their secrets would be revealed in time.

LATE IN THE AFTERNOON, the phone rang in Wally's house, cutting through the soft hum of his coding efforts. It was Richie, full of life and enthusiasm as always. He announced that he and Pug had decided on a bowling game, a return to the All-Pro-Lanes that held years of their shared memories. The plan was set for the following day at 3:45 PM.

Wally welcomed the break from his usual routine. He spent his early mornings deeply immersed in software development, tweaking and improving the program for Bake-Ritez. The feedback from IT was encouraging; they deemed his work beyond expectations with only minor hiccups. Time had slipped away unnoticed amidst his work, bringing him to the day of the bowling game.

He arrived at All-Pro-Lanes to find Richie and Pug already settled into a booth, sandwiches half-eaten and Cokes fizzing on the table. He joined them, ordering a coffee for himself as he slid into the booth. Richie, always ready for action, wasted no time before suggesting their next adventure.

"Guys," he began, an eager glint in his eyes, "when are we going back to Chinquapin? Maybe we could fit in some duck hunting?"

Pug considered this, a thoughtful look crossing his face before he replied. "I'm ready when you guys are. How about the last week of December? Classes will be out, and Richie will still be on vacation."

Their agreement echoed around the table, settling like a promise in the air. As an afterthought, they decided to check out Bird Island during their trip to see if any boats were around.

With plans made and excitement simmering under the surface, they turned their attention back to their game. Bowling balls rolled down the lanes with familiar thuds and clatters, filling up their afternoon until it was time to head home again. Their shared anticipation for the upcoming trip to Chinquapin and Bird Island cast a warm glow over their goodbyes, promising more shared adventures to come.

TIME SEEMED TO WARP around Wally, the rhythm of his software work blurring the days into a seamless flow. As he sat down to breakfast, his father was already off to work, and his mother soon departed for her grocery run. Alone, Wally saw his chance.

The shed welcomed him with familiar smells of dough and machinery. A work table stood ready for him, upon which he spread a layer of wax paper. From each jar, he scooped out a cup of dough, rolling it into a thin layer until he had enough to cut out a dozen squares.

With methodical precision, he greased a pan and arranged the first batch of squares onto it before transferring it into the waiting jaws of his air fryer. Forty-five minutes later, the squares emerged, transformed into cookies under the fryer's steady heat. He repeated this ritual with each batch until he had a dozen cookies each laced with 109, 076, and 532.

Cooling on the counter, the cookies received their final touch - a drop of food coloring to distinguish them: green for 109, blue for 076, red for 532. Wally then carefully vacuum-sealed them in groups of three, ensuring that each cookie could be individually extracted.

His cache complete, Wally started on a fresh batch of 345. This time, however, he added an innovative twist by incorporating the food coloring directly into the dough. A deviation from his original formula indeed - would it matter? Only time would tell. As the new batch began its week-long fermentation process, Wally felt a sense of accomplishment. He was not only a software entrepreneur but also a pioneer in harnessing microbial powers - two worlds that seemed worlds apart yet were intertwined in his life.

Chapter 10
The Ties That Bind

As the festive season of Christmas drew near, a blanket of anticipation and cheer wrapped itself around the town. However, for Wally, the yuletide merriment was a distant hum beneath the buzzing symphony of his thriving software business. Bake-RiteZ, with their incessant demands for new features, provided a relentless rhythm to his workdays. It was a tempo that would have overwhelmed an orchestra of six, but Wally managed to conduct this symphony solo, thanks to occasional doses of 076. The result? A steadily swelling bank account that was music to his ears.

While Wally immersed himself in the world of code and cloud, Pug held down the fort on the Bird Island front. His connection with Old Man Barnes had grown into a strong link, their conversations filling in the gaps of distance and time. Several times a week, their voices bridged the miles between them, ensuring Bird Island's activities didn't fade into oblivion.

Barnes and Seawings took it upon themselves to become vigilant guardians of the island from above. Their routine flyovers kept them tethered to Bird Island, their keen eyes scanning its contours for any unusual activities. This aerial vigilance provided Wally with a sense of relief - an invisible safety net allowing him to focus on building his business empire.

The countdown to their December Duck Hunt had begun, and Wally had every intention of entering this adventure with his business in shipshape. With every passing day, he navigated through the tumultuous seas of start-up life with unyielding determination.

The anticipation for what lay ahead fueled him, and he knew he would be ready when it was time to trade his keyboard for a shotgun.

AS DUCK SEASON APPROACHED, Wally became consumed with surveillance technology to protect Bird Island's secrets. He focused his research on cloud-connected cameras and sensors capable of detecting activity. Seeking enduring battery life, positive reviews, and reputable brands, his search was meticulous.

Ultimately, Wally chose ten units for installation across the island, especially near the bunker. Using his business identity, he kept the purchase removed from his personal records.

Eager to master the gear, Wally set up a unit in his driveway - his own test site. Through manuals and hands-on tinkering, he dissected every specification, seeking total familiarity.

As the detector blinked and pinged his phone, it echoed his resolve. When night fell, the sentinel stood guard, capturing each shadow that crossed its lens.

With this new addition to his arsenal, Wally was ready. Come sunrise, he would join Pug and Richie duck hunting at Chinquapin. But his true purpose was greater than sport - to safeguard Bird Island's mysteries hidden beneath its verdant cloak.

AS DAWN BEGAN TO PAINT the sky with shades of pink and gold, Pug was already on the move. The old pickup truck, a family heirloom, groaned under the weight of hunting gear and boxes filled with sophisticated detectors. He navigated the familiar route to Richie's house with an eager grin on his face.

Pulling up in front of Richie's house, Pug leaned out the window. "Morning, Richie! You ready? I'm raring to go," he called out.

Richie emerged from his front door, a wide smile on his face as he replied, "Ready as I'll ever be."

Minutes later, they were outside Wally's house, loading up his cargo – ten boxes of detectors that would soon serve a purpose beyond their imagination. The morning air was crisp as they set course for Chinquapin.

"If we hustle," Pug said, breaking the comfortable silence in the truck, "we can still catch breakfast at Rudy's."

As they drove through the gradually waking countryside, Pug filled them in on Jeff and Barnes' recent adventures. His voice blended with the hum of the engine and the soft murmur of the morning radio show.

Before long, they were pulling into Rudy's Cafe. The scent of sizzling bacon and freshly brewed coffee wafted out as they entered. No sooner had they placed their orders when Richie began to fidget in his seat.

"Guys, if we hustle," he said between glances at his watch, "we can be on the water in an hour or so."

Pug laughed at his friend's impatience and clapped him on the shoulder. "Slow down there, Richie," he advised. "This ain't gonna be our last hunting trip. Let's enjoy our breakfast and savor this coffee. The ducks aren't going anywhere."

PUG WAS BUSY UNLOCKING the boat shed to launch the jon boat as Wally and Richie finished unloading the truck. Richie gathered up a couple of dozen decoys while Wally placed their shotguns and 4 boxes of shells on the dock and then started filling up water jugs. With guns, shells, backpacks, surveillance equipment, snacks, box of crackers, the boys were ready to head out.

As the boys approached the mouth of Live Oak Bayou it was well after mid morning. There was a light gulf breeze in their face and the sky for the most part clear, a front had blown through the day before. It was chilly, in the mid 40s, cold for this part of Texas. "Guys, why don't we try hunting off of Bird Island, that way we get two birds with one stone, and I can get rid of this pile of electronics while you guys hunt." They were on their way, the bay was choppy but running full speed was still possible.

The three friends sped across the choppy waters of East Matagorda Bay, the strong winds whipping their faces. Pug expertly navigated the boat while Richie and Wally held on, bracing themselves against the cold spray. Soon the silhouette of Bird Island appeared through the morning mist.

They pulled up to a secluded shoreline, flanked on one side by tall cordgrass. While Richie and Wally unpacked the guns and decoys, Pug hid the boat with camouflaging branches. Despite the cold, they were energized, moving with precision to set up their hunting spot. Richie laid out the decoys in a small inlet as Wally prepared the shotguns and shells. Before long, they were set up and ready, concealed in the reeds, shotguns loaded, waiting for ducks to take their bait.

The stillness of the marsh sharply contrasted the blustery boat ride. Hunkered down in the cordgrass, the three friends waited with quiet anticipation, constantly scanning the skies and waters. The minutes crawled by without sight nor sound of ducks. The lack of action tried their patience, but their perseverance persisted.

Suddenly, Wally spotted a flock emerging from the mist. He alerted Pug and Richie with a subtle gesture. The birds circled above the decoys, considering the inlet. Richie hit the duck call, with a flap of their wings, they began their descent, committed to landing. The friends froze, shotguns ready. As the ducks drew near, almost within range, a deafening roar shattered the silence - a military jet screamed overhead, scaring off the flock. The boys were crestfallen, their hard work foiled. However, with hunting time left, their hopes remained high.

FOR WALLY, IT WAS TIME to work on securing the island. Stashing his gun close to the boat, he grabbed his backpack and the large bag of boxes containing the surveillance equipment he had prepared. Once out of sight from his friends Pug and Richie, Wally unzipped his backpack and broke out his specially laced cookies - one red, one orange, and one blue. He hoped he would not need the green one, reserved for more dire situations requiring healing due to injury. After consuming the cookies, Wally began to feel their effects taking hold as the unique microorganisms they contained entered his system. His eyesight started to shift and enhance while his movements became effortless and efficient.

Empowered by the cookies, Wally was ready to carry out his mission of finding all seven bunker entrances on the island in order to set up surveillance monitors at each one. With two detectors in hand, he set off into the brush, traversing the landscape with precision and ease granted by the microbes now flowing through his body. Methodically sweeping the area, Wally searched for any indication of the concealed bunker access points. He relied on his heightened senses, granted by the orange cookie, to spot clues invisible to the average eye.

Before long, Wally successfully located one of the bunker entrances, identifiable by the weathered concrete façade covered in vines and detritus. He quickly set up a surveillance camera, strategically positioning it to capture any activity at the entrance.

Wally continued his search, covering ground with supernatural speed and efficiency. Within minutes, four more entrances were found and outfitted with cameras.

With his enhanced capabilities, Wally was able to achieve in a short time what would have taken an ordinary person hours of grueling effort.

As he walked back, Wally contemplated where he would place the final three cameras. One would go where Harry had set up his camp, based on Wally's recollection. Another was destined for the east side of the island where he had spotted Jack anchoring their skiff during a past encounter. The last would be positioned at the overgrown end of an old runway that bisected the island. Satisfied with his plan, Wally pushed through the last bit of brush and emerged to find Pug and Richie waiting near the water's edge. To them, he appeared ordinary, unaware of the extraordinary transformation triggered by the cookies. Wally kept this secret to himself, knowing the microbes would enable him to safeguard the island and its hidden bunker. After briefly chatting with his friends, they continued their duck hunt, with Wally's abilities giving him a distinct advantage unbeknownst to his companions. He was determined to protect the island at all costs, even if it meant harnessing powers beyond human limitations.

WHILE THE WEATHER WAS perfect for a lazy picnic, it was far from ideal for duck hunting. The ducks flew high in the sky, specks of life too distant to beckon, diminishing their chances of a successful hunt.

Pug's voice cut through the quiet afternoon like a sharp knife. "Well guys, it looks like we're wasting our time today, maybe tomorrow," he said with an air of resignation.

Richie chimed in with his usual enthusiasm undeterred by their lackluster day, "Ok, how about the old bunker? Want to give it a look?"

An odd silence fell over them. It was as if Richie's suggestion had evaporated into thin air. There were no nods of agreement or eager smiles this time around. The thrill and mystery of the bunker that had once sparked their curiosity seemed to have lost its allure. Perhaps the charm of the unknown had worn thin, replaced by the comfort of familiar routines and simple pleasures. Wally's silence lingered the longest; his thoughts were elsewhere, caught in a private world of microorganisms and secrets yet to be uncovered.

UNDER THE COVERT INFLUENCE of microorganisms, Wally turned to his companions. His voice broke the silence of the bayou, "Ok, guys, want to trade your gun for a rod, maybe catch a red or two?" His eyes held a spark that suggested more than just a shift in activities.

An immediate chorus of agreement echoed through the quiet morning air. The allure of fishing held an irresistible charm for the trio. As they navigated the meandering curves of Live Oak Bayou, their camp came into view, an oasis of familiarity in the vast wilderness.

They docked their boat with practiced ease, unloading hunting gear that was still fresh with morning dew. The equipment shed on the dock opened its maw to swallow their paraphernalia. The doors closed behind them, sealing away shotguns and camouflage until their next adventure.

As the last piece found its place in the shed, Richie turned towards his friends. "How about we brew some coffee and make sandwiches before we cast our lines?" he suggested. His voice held an undercurrent of anticipation, already imagining the comforting warmth of a hot drink and the satisfying bite of a well-made sandwich.

WALLY SAT SILENTLY at the worn wooden table in the cozy fishing cabin, his mind clearly preoccupied as Richie busied himself with preparing a fresh pot of coffee. The rich, earthy aroma of the grinding beans soon filled the small kitchen, but Wally seemed oblivious, lost in thought.

Nearby, Pug hummed softly to himself as he assembled the ingredients for their favorite po'boy sandwiches—fresh slices of fried fish layered with shredded lettuce, tomatoes, and a zesty remoulade sauce, all tucked into a crusty French bread roll. But Wally's gaze remained fixed on some distant point beyond the cabin's window, his brow faintly furrowed.

After several moments, Wally finally spoke, his words measured and thoughtful. "Guys, you know my software business has really taken off recently, even though it requires a lot of my time. The thing is, I can work from pretty much anywhere as long as I've got an internet connection. So I've been thinking about maybe moving down here to the Chinquapin area permanently."

This announcement caused Pug to pause his sandwich preparations, a jar of pickles still clasped in his hand as he turned to look at Wally with surprise and curiosity. Even Richie glanced up from the gurgling coffee maker, one eyebrow raised.

"Really, dude? You'd leave the city and move all the way out here to the boonies?" Pug asked.

Wally nodded, a spark of excitement growing behind his eyes. "I heard fiber internet is coming soon to a lot of rural areas, at least partially subsidized by the government. If that's true, I could work perfectly fine from a place near the bayou. And if I did move down here, I think I'd also want to learn how to fly a plane."

Richie and Pug exchanged an intrigued look. The idea of their friend relocating to their beloved fishing retreat full-time, not to mention taking up aviation, was unexpected.

"What brought this on, Wally?" Richie inquired. "You've never mentioned wanting to move here before. Or fly, for that matter. That's pretty out of the blue."

"I know, I know," Wally sighed, leaning back in his chair. "It's just...with the success of my business, I feel like I've got more options opening up, you know? And I love it out here by the water. It's so peaceful. Like I can think clearly and just be myself."

He gazed wistfully out at the shimmering bayou beyond the window. Somewhere in the distance, a heron's lonely call echoed over the water.

"Plus," Wally continued, "I have to confess: ever since we started exploring Bird Island and found that old bunker, I feel kind of...called to understand it more. Like there are still secrets there I'm meant to uncover. I know that sounds crazy..."

"Not at all" Pug assured him sincerely. "This place gets under your skin. It becomes a part of you."

Richie nodded in agreement as he brought three steaming mugs of coffee over to the table. "I think it's a great idea, Wally. You've always loved it here."

Wally's face brightened at his friends' encouragement. "Thanks, guys. I really appreciate you being so supportive. If good internet really does come through, I think I'll start looking at property around here. And also," he added with a grin, "I'm going to give Jeff a call and get his take on learning to fly a plane out here. Oh, and find out if he's heard anything about the internet."

Pug chuckled and slid a freshly assembled po'boy across the table to Wally. "Leave it to you to want to start flying your own plane. But hey, we'll be your first passengers when you get your pilot's license!"

The three friends dug eagerly into the delicious sandwiches, the comfortable quiet broken only by their satisfied murmurs. Overhead, a ceiling fan spun lazily, circulating the savory scents of their meal.

As he ate, Wally felt a swell of contentment. Maybe it seemed impulsive to others, but something in him knew this was the right path. He belonged here, connected to the mysteries of this place—and with his two best friends at his side, he felt like anything was possible. Propelled by purpose, he would uncover whatever secrets still lingered beneath the island's surface. And when he wasn't exploring, he would build a good life here, one of peace and meaning.

Outside, the cry of a seagull echoed over the shimmering bayou, beckoning him on toward undiscovered horizons. With a confident smile, Wally took a sip of coffee and leaned back to enjoy the rest of his meal, his mind filled with visions of the future.

WALLY SET HIS COFFEE mug down on the wooden dock and leaned back in the patio chair, watching Pug haul up a crab trap at the end of the pier. The morning's duck hunt had proven fruitless, but their growing haul of blue crabs promised a hearty lunch. Behind him in the cabin, Richie's voice drifted through the open window as he put away the last of the dishes.

He pulled out his phone, quickly scrolling to Jeff's number. After two rings, the familiar gravelly voice answered.

"Jeff here. What's going on, Wally?"

He smiled, launching right into his questions. "Hey Jeff, it's Wally. Got a couple things I wanted to run by you. I've been thinking hard about moving down here permanently once I finish up college. My software business is taking off, and with Starlink improving rural internet, I could work remote easily."

He paused, gauging Jeff's reaction so far over the phone. "Plus, I'd be closer to continue investigating that bunker on Bird Island we found. And I was hoping maybe you could teach me to fly too. I could get my pilot's license, and buy a small plane even. What do you think?"

Jeff chuckled in his characteristic hearty laugh. "Slow down there, turbo. That's a whole mess of big life changes. But I like your style, kid. The area would suit you, and I'd be glad to show you the ropes of flying. Just promise me you'll take all your new freedom in stride. No need to rush into everything at once."

Wally nodded, reassured by Jeff's encouragement. They chatted a few more minutes about seaplanes and flight lessons as Pug walked up with three plump crabs to add to their growing collection in the trap. Wally said his goodbyes to Jeff, then joined Pug and Richie to prepare their fresh crab feast, his mind buzzing with dreams of the future.

UNDERNEATH THE CLEAR Texas sky, the wooden dock creaked in rhythm with the lapping waves of the bayou. Pug, Wally, and Richie huddled over a table, their hands busy sorting through their impressive crab haul. Each crab was subjected to a brief examination before a swift twist and pull claimed one of its pinchers. Released back into the water, the crabs skittered away, leaving behind a growing pile of claws on the weathered wood.

Pug wiped his brow, his gaze drifting over their bounty. His grin stretched wide as he let out a satisfied chuckle. "Man," he said, "we hit the mother lode today."

His gaze slid over to Wally, an idea sparking in his eyes. "Wally," he called out, "check if Jeff's game for a crab feast this afternoon."

Nodding, Wally fished out his phone from his pocket. The call connected quickly, Wally's invitation met with an enthusiastic acceptance from Jeff.

"Jeff will be here in an hour or so," Wally announced to Pug and Richie as he ended the call. Their successful crabbing expedition had just turned into an impromptu feast, promising laughter and stories shared over heaps of fresh crab claws.

JEFF IDLED HIS SEAPLANE up to the dock and stepped out into the late afternoon sun. "Greetings guys, thanks for the invite, pinchers are my absolute favorite," he announced cheerfully to Pug, Richie and Wally.

Wally's senses were heightened from the red, orange and blue microorganisms he had consumed earlier. The sound of the seaplane's engine seemed amplified and the glint of the sun off the water was almost blinding. He took a deep breath, steadying himself against the onslaught of sensations.

Jeff looked over at Wally with an easy smile. "While there is plenty of daylight left, if you are interested, let me show you my seaplane," he offered.

"Jeff, absolutely, thanks," Wally replied, eager for the distraction to take his mind off the effects of the microorganisms.

"'Sally' is my girl, we have been through a lot together," Jeff said affectionately, leading Wally over to the seaplane. "She's a Cessna 172M on straight floats. Take a look."

Wally examined the aircraft, admiring its bright white and blue paint job. Jeff pointed out various features and mechanics, clearly proud of his plane.

"If you have time I'll take you for a ride," Jeff added. "These old birds were built for adventure."

He readily agreed, excited by the prospect of seeing the area from the sky. He followed Jeff aboard, pushing down his apprehension about how the flight might affect his enhanced senses. As they taxied across the water and lifted off into the clouds, Wally took a deep breath and allowed his worries to slip away.

WALLY SAT IN THE PASSENGER seat of the seaplane, feeling the effects of the blue 076 cookie coursing through his system. His senses were heightened, his mind laser-focused. As Jeff piloted the Cessna over the shimmering waters of East Matagorda Bay, Wally watched his every move with intense concentration.

The plane banked gently to the left as Jeff adjusted the controls. Wally's eyes darted between Jeff's hands on the yoke and the instrument panel, noting the altitude, airspeed, and other readings. Through the windshield, the glassy surface of the bay neared.

"Watch how I transition from a descent to landing configuration," Jeff said. Wally nodded, his enhanced memory cataloging every detail.

Jeff slowed the plane and steadily lowered the flaps. The pitch changed, and the seaplane glided down towards the water. Wally glanced at the altimeter as it wound down, then back at Jeff, who was focused and calm.

At the right moment, Jeff leveled off, sending the plane skimming smoothly across the bay's surface. Spray misted the windshield as the pontoons made contact. With a gentle splash, they were down.

Wally had absorbed it all, every instrument reading, control input, and sensation thanks to the microbe cookie's effects. He knew that with practice, he could soon pilot the seaplane himself, mastering its complexities and freedoms.

JEFF WATCHED INTENTLY as Wally took control of the seaplane, impressed by the young man's natural piloting instincts. Though initially apprehensive about letting an amateur take over, Jeff couldn't help but grin as Wally smoothly lifted off and banked the plane in a wide arc over the shimmering bay.

He nodded in approval as Wally adeptly lined up for landing, adjusting the flaps and easing back on the throttle. The plane touched down with barely a bounce, skipping along the water's surface before coasting to a stop.

"Well I'll be damned," Jeff chuckled as he patted Wally on the shoulder. "For your first time up, that was some damn fine flying! You sure you haven't done this before?"

Wally shook his head, beaming with pride at having impressed the seasoned pilot. Jeff's years of experience told him the young man had a natural talent. As they taxied back towards the pier, Jeff envisioned a day when he'd pass the torch and let Wally take over piloting duties. The old seaplane would be in good hands.

"She handles like a dream, doesn't she?" Jeff said. "With some more practice, you'll be ready to solo in no time. And between you and me, I believe you've got the makings of a great aviator."

Wally took in the praise, glimpsing a future where he could protect the secrets of Bird Island from high above. Under Jeff's guidance, he was determined to master the skies.

Chapter 11

A Glimpse into History

Wally sat alone on the dock, a peaceful stillness settled over the water, but Wally's mind churned with unrest.

He longed to have someone to share this extraordinary secret with, someone he could trust to help protect the knowledge he had uncovered on Bird Island. Telling his parents had been necessary, but it still left Wally feeling isolated, the weight of secrecy heavy on his shoulders.

Ideally, Pug and Richie would be the perfect confidants. But confiding in them posed risks. What if Pug felt compelled to tell his parents? And what if Richie told his wife? Wally cared deeply for his friends, but he wasn't sure he could rely on them to keep this monumental secret.

The temptation to unburden himself and share everything with Pug and Richie tugged at Wally. Yet he knew that expanding the circle of knowledge increased the chances of exposure. For now, Wally determined, he must continue keeping his own counsel. The microbes, the bunker, his extraordinary abilities - all must remain hidden, shared only with his parents.

As the first stars blinked into view overhead, Wally sighed, wishing once again for a trustworthy companion in this lonesome quest. But some secrets, he realized, are best kept by remaining secrets. The stillness settled around him as he gazed over the glimmering water, resolved to stay silent and stand as the solitary guardian of Bird Island's mysteries.

AS HE SAT ON THE DOCK, his mind racing as he debated whether to share the incredible secret he had discovered on Bird Island. The knowledge of the powerful microorganisms and their unbelievable effects weighed heavily on him. He had already told his parents but feared revealing the truth to his closest friends, Pug and Richie.

Yet keeping this monumental secret to himself felt isolating, especially now as darkness fell over the bayou. Wally yearned to unburden himself, even just partially. A thought struck him - what about Jeff? The veteran pilot was an old-timer who lived nearby in Chinquapin. And he was close with Old Man Barnes, someone Wally trusted.

Wally considered the idea further. Jeff lived alone, seemingly unencumbered by family or friends. His military background suggested he could understand the implications of Wally's discovery. Perhaps he would be receptive, even helpful if Wally shared a portion of the truth with him.

Yes, Jeff might make a good confidant. But Wally knew he couldn't rush into this. First, he would casually ask Barnes about Jeff, to get a better sense of the man's character. He didn't need to explain the reasons behind his curiosity - not yet, anyway. If Barnes' opinion aligned with Wally's developing trust in Jeff, then Wally would reach out. He hoped Jeff might provide the guidance and companionship he sorely needed as the keeper of this astonishing secret.

For now, Wally would be patient. He rose from the dock and walked slowly back to the cabin, the lights glowing warmly to welcome him home. The decision could wait until morning. Tonight, he would simply rest and prepare for the conversations to come.

AS WALLY ENTERS THE cabin, Pug says, "Old man Barnes called, said he found out Jeff was here, said it was too late for him to visit, that he would come by for coffee come morning."

Wally thought it was like Barnes had read his mind.

By first light the next morning, Wally sat on the dock sipping coffee when Barnes came rolling up the driveway in his pickup truck.

Barnes spots Wally on the dock, comes over, and sits next to him.

Barnes says, "Good morning, how about some of that fine brew your drinking?"

Wally tells Barnes as he walks toward the cabin, "I'll get you a cup, be right back".

Handing Barnes a cup of coffee, Wally sits and says, "Mr. Barnes, is there any reason I should not be able to trust Jeff? You've known him a long time."

Barnes tells Wally that he has known Jeff for ages, so long now, not even sure how many years, and Jeff has never given him a reason to mistrust or question him, that Jeff has been a great friend, the best.

Barnes, cradling the warm mug in his hands, looked out at the tranquil waters of the bay. He let out a sigh, appreciating the quiet morning, before turning his attention back to Wally.

"Thank you for the coffee, Wally," Barnes said, his voice as rough as sandpaper yet imbued with a warmth that only years of camaraderie and wisdom could bring. "But I reckon I best be on my way. Didn't realize how late it was."

Wally nodded, understanding. Barnes was a man of routine, as predictable as the tides. He was always up with the dawn, ready to tackle whatever tasks awaited him. And though age had slowed him down somewhat, it hadn't dampened his spirit.

Barnes stood up from the dock, his movements careful and measured. His old bones creaked like a rusty hinge as he stretched out his legs. With a nod of acknowledgment towards Wally, he started walking towards his truck parked nearby.

Wally watched him go, admiring the resilience of the old man. Despite the trials life had thrown at him, Barnes had remained steadfast and resolute.

"Tell Richie and Pug I said hello," Barnes called over his shoulder without breaking stride. "I'll catch you all later today."

Wally lifted his coffee mug in a silent salute. "Will do, Mr. Barnes," he replied. "Take care."

With that, Barnes climbed into his truck and rumbled down the driveway, leaving behind a trail of dust that danced in the morning sunlight.

WALLY SAT ON THE DOCK, sipping his coffee as the morning sun peeked over the horizon. Though his friends were still asleep in the cabin behind him, his mind was already racing with the possibilities of the day ahead.

He thought back to his conversation with Barnes about Jeff. The old man's assurances had convinced Wally that the veteran pilot could be trusted with the secret of the microorganisms and their incredible effects. But how to broach such an unbelievable subject? Where to even begin explaining his covert operations and enhanced abilities without sounding crazy?

He took a deep breath, reminding himself that Jeff was a military man, conditioned to keep classified intelligence. Surely he would recognize the need for utmost discretion regarding the powerful compounds Wally had discovered.

His contemplations were interrupted by the screen door squeaking open. Richie shuffled out, yawning and stretching his arms overhead. "Morning," he mumbled sleepily. "You're up early."

"Hey Richie," Wally replied. "Couldn't sleep. Too much on my mind I guess."

Richie poured himself some coffee and joined Wally on the dock. For a while, neither spoke, both content to welcome the new day in pensive silence.

Eventually, Richie said, "So what's the plan for today? More exploring?"

Wally considered how to respond. He wasn't ready to reveal anything yet. "I think maybe we should take it easy today. Do some fishing, relax a bit. The bunker's not going anywhere."

Richie nodded. "Sounds good to me. We could all use a little R&R."

At that moment, the cabin door creaked open again and Pug stumbled out. "Please tell me there's more coffee," he said groggily.

Richie chuckled. "Fresh pot's still hot."

Pug trudged back inside, returning a minute later with a full mug. He took a long sip and sighed contentedly.

"So, what's on the agenda today boys?" Pug asked.

"I was just telling Wally a laidback fishing day sounds good," said Richie. "Take a breather from the exploring."

"Music to my ears," Pug said. "Now who's hungry? I can whip up a mean scrambled egg sandwich."

Wally smiled as he followed his friends inside, comforted by the familiar camaraderie of their trio. The bunker's secrets would keep - for today, time with true friends took priority.

WALLY, PUG, AND RICHIE had just finished their scrambled egg sandwiches that morning when one of the surveillance monitors that Wally had set up on Bird Island was triggered. The monitor that had been tripped was near the location where Wally had previously seen the three men - Jack, Harry, and Alexei - come ashore near their tent camp.

Hurriedly, Wally grabbed his phone and called Jeff. "Jeff, one of my surveillance monitors on the island has been triggered. Could you pick me up in your seaplane and then do a flyover of the area?"

Jeff replied, "Yes, I'll be there within 15 minutes. I may need to stop and gas up first."

Wally felt a surge of apprehension. Who could be on the island triggering his monitors? Were Jack, Harry and Alexei back? He needed to find out as soon as possible. Pug and Richie looked concerned as well, realizing the implications of the tripped monitor.

After ending the call with Jeff, Wally quickly gathered a few supplies into his backpack. He checked to make sure he had his binoculars, a flashlight, and a couple of the microbe-laced cookies and candy bars that gave him enhanced abilities. Their presence reassured him.

Soon Jeff arrived in his seaplane. Wally said a hasty goodbye to Pug and Richie and climbed aboard. As Jeff piloted the plane into the air, Wally scanned the water below, the takeoff was smooth and soon they were soaring at altitude toward Bird Island.

"Let's do a low pass over the southeast side of the island first," Wally suggested. As Jeff banked the plane, Wally peered intently out the window. He caught a glimpse of the island through the trees but saw no obvious activity.

"Okay, bring us back around to the west side where I set up the monitors," Wally said. As the plane circled and descended, he felt his apprehension rising. What would they find?

THE EARLY MORNING SUN glistened off the gentle waves of East Matagorda Bay as the seaplane carrying Wally and Jeff again made its approach to Bird Island. Despite the tranquility of the scene below, both were filled with a tense apprehension about what the surveillance alarm might signify.

As Jeff circled the island in a wide reconnaissance pattern, Wally scanned the terrain intently through binoculars, searching for any signs of intruders. The island's beaches and inland brush appeared undisturbed, with no obvious indications of human activity.

"I'm not spotting anything out of the ordinary so far," Wally reported, frustration creeping into his voice. "Let's make another low pass along the western shore."

Jeff banked the plane and dropped lower, providing a closer view of the island's rugged western coastline. Wally continued his meticulous surveillance, examining each cove and inlet for boats or equipment. Still nothing.

The men were nearing the conclusion of their patrol when Wally suddenly spotted some unusual markings in the sand near a grouping of rocks along the southern beach. "Wait, swing back around to 2 o'clock. I want to take another look at that area," he directed.

As Jeff looped the plane back towards the southwest tip of Bird Island, Wally felt his pulse quicken. Adjusting his binoculars, the mysterious markings came into sharp focus - footprints. Multiple sets of footprints dotted the beach, confirming his worst fears.

"It's just as I suspected. We've got company," Wally reported grimly. "Let's do one more pass and then set down in the lagoon. We need to get boots on the ground and figure out what's going on here."

Jeff nodded in acknowledgment, exhibiting the steady calm of an experienced pilot. After completing their aerial reconnaissance, he smoothly landed the seaplane in a sheltered inlet.

JEFF CUT THE ENGINE and let the seaplane drift silently toward the muddy shore of Bird Island. He dropped a small anchor into the soft bottom, anchoring them a prudent distance from land.

Wally took the lead as they disembarked, his senses heightened by the microbes he had consumed. Jeff followed close behind as Wally adeptly tracked through the tall cordgrass. To Wally's enhanced vision, human footprints glowed like neon signs against the dark mud and grass. He effortlessly spotted and followed the trail, picking up on the most subtle impressions invisible to normal eyes.

Wally's tracking skills, amplified by the microbes, allowed him to discern details - the number of trespassers, their relative sizes, and how recently they had passed. He could detect the faint lingering aura around the disturbed blades of grass, indicating the freshness of the trail. With Jeff relying on Wally's supernatural ability to uncover their uninvited guests, they pressed on following the trail, anticipating who or what lay ahead.

HE LED THE WAY INTO the dense foliage, relying on his heightened senses to track the trespassers on Bird Island. The footprints glowed faintly to his enhanced vision, allowing him to discern subtle impressions and determine the path taken inland. Jeff followed close behind, impressed by Wally's preternatural tracking skills.

They moved swiftly yet silently through the brush. Wally paused periodically, tilting his head as he listened for sounds of disturbance ahead of them. The island was quiet except for the usual wildlife sounds. After some time, Wally crouched and signaled Jeff to do the same. Up ahead, voices could be heard.

Peeking through the vegetation, they spotted two men in combat gear inspecting a concealed bunker entrance. "This is it alright, matches the coordinates," said one. The other nodded. "Let's get this door open and see if the intel is correct about what they were hiding here."

His eyes narrowed. He recognized these men from an earlier encounter. Harry and Jack - mercenaries who had accosted him on the island before. Wally clenched his fists. He would not let them access the bunker and its secrets. He turned to Jeff and whispered urgently. They needed a plan to stop Harry and Jack before it was too late.

WALLY, ENERGIZED BY the special microbes he had consumed, felt his senses heightened as he and Jeff arrived at Bird Island via seaplane. Anchoring at a safe distance, they proceeded inland, alert and ready to confront any trespassers.

As they reached the tree line, with barely a sound, Wally grasped a rock the size of a dodgeball and hurled it with uncanny strength into the trees just beyond the men. The rock smashed into a trunk with a loud crack, startling Jack and Harry. They turned towards the noise, listening intently for any further sounds. After a tense minute, the men slowly began walking in the direction of the impact, searching for the source.

Seizing the opportunity, Wally signaled to Jeff and they swiftly approached the nearby bunker entrance. Slipping inside, Wally pulled the heavy steel door closed behind them with ease, the blackness of the abandoned bunker enveloping the pair. "Find something to jam the door so it can't be opened," Wally whispered to Jeff urgently. Jeff scanned the darkness with his flashlight, locating a discarded steel rack leg that he passed to Wally. Jamming the pole through the door handle, they ensured it was securely wedged shut.

With his enhanced senses, Wally effortlessly navigated the pitch black bunker, leading them southeast towards Entrance E3 - his favored access point. Despite the darkness and threat of intruders, Wally felt energized and focused, ready to utilize his extraordinary abilities to protect the bunker's secrets.

WALLY AND JEFF EMERGED from the concealed bunker entrance labeled E3 into the bright coastal sunlight. Shading their eyes, they oriented themselves and began walking westward along the southern shoreline, their shoes sinking into the soft sand. The rhythmic shush of small waves lapping the beach accompanied their passage.

Up ahead, Jeff's seaplane rested just off shore, bobbing gently on the rippled surface. As they approached, Wally put a hand on Jeff's shoulder and said, "Wait here, I'll be back shortly." Before Jeff could respond, Wally had slipped away, deftly moving northwest and disappearing into the scrub brush and palms.

Meanwhile, at the bunker entrance, Jack and Harry strained and struggled to pry open the heavy steel door that Wally had secured shut. But despite their efforts, the door refused to budge. Frustrated, they slammed their shoulders against it over and over to no avail.

Having reached their skiff, Wally nimbly climbed aboard the boat and located the fuel line. With a quick slash of his knife, he opened up a tiny slit in the rubber hose. His task complete, he silently slipped back off and returned through the foliage to where Jeff was faithfully waiting.

"We shouldn't start the engine yet, the noise could draw them. We'll have to wait here until those men leave or find another way in,"

Wally explained. Jeff nodded, understanding the prudence of laying low until the trespassers had gone. And so they settled in to keep vigil, alert for any indication the intruders' persistence had paid off.

AGAIN WALLY ASKED JEFF to wait until he returned on shore by the seaplane. Jeff nodded, trusting his young friend's judgement.

Wally was off into the bush in an instant, moving with preternatural speed through the dense foliage. He honed in on the hidden bunker entrance, where he saw two men, Jack and Harry, struggling to pry open the steel door.

Crouched in the shadows, Wally watched as Jack and Harry pulled and pried on the steel door, again and again to no avail. After a few more futile minutes, they retreated towards their skiff.

"We need tools, we'll try again later," Wally heard one of them mutter in frustration.

They climbed onto their skiff and motored westward towards Bay City across the bay. Wally watched them intently until they were out of sight, his sharp vision tracking their departure.

Satisfied they were gone for now, Wally turned and raced back through the island's interior, his limbs pumping steadily, energized by the microbes flowing through his system. He reached the seaplane in mere minutes, where Jeff waited faithfully.

HE RETURNED TO JEFF, who was waiting patiently by the seaplane. "I tracked the two men, Jack and Harry, to one of the bunker entrances," Wally explained. "They were trying to get inside but couldn't open the heavy steel door. So they left, probably to go get some tools to try and break in."

Jeff nodded, taking in the information. "Good work, Wally. We'd better hurry then before they make their way back."

The two climbed aboard the seaplane. Jeff went through his pre-flight checklist with practiced ease before starting up the engine. The propeller began spinning, churning up the water behind them into a frothy wake. Once they were up to speed, Jeff pulled back gently on the yoke and the seaplane lifted effortlessly into the air.

Gaining altitude, they scanned the bay below for any sign of the intruders. The bright turquoise water glittered beautifully in the morning sun, but there was no boat in sight. "Let's do a sweep around the island's perimeter," Jeff suggested. "With any luck, we'll spot them before they can do any real damage."

Wally nodded in agreement. Perched up high in the seaplane together, they continued their airborne search, determined to protect the island's secrets.

"LET'S CIRCLE OUT A little further west towards Bay City," he suggested a glint of satisfaction in his eyes. "I put a cut in their fuel line, maybe it worked. Take a look."

Jeff's experienced eyes quickly spotted the boat they were looking for, sitting like a lone sentinel in the vast expanse of the bay. Its usual rhythm of movement was disrupted, and the boat was dead still - an unusual sight in these bustling waters.

The stranded vessel was marooned in no man's land - an area typically avoided by all but the most daring or desperate seafarers. Only an occasional Mexican shrimper, bold enough to risk capture for an illegal catch, would dare venture into this remote part of the bay.

"They could be there for hours, maybe a day or two," Jeff observed with a dry chuckle. His voice held no sympathy for their predicament; rather, there was a note of satisfaction at their ill fortune. It was as if the tide had turned, shifting from a chase to a waiting game they were now winning.

JEFF BANKED THE SEAPLANE and headed back towards Bird Island. As the small island came into view again, Wally spoke up from the passenger seat.

"Jeff, if you have time, let's sit down on the southeast tip of the island and go ashore for a while," he said. "I want to show you something."

Jeff nodded. "No problem, we've got some time to kill before meeting up with the others."

He gently brought the seaplane down on the calm waters on the southeastern side of Bird Island, coasting up to a small beach. After securing the aircraft, Jeff and Wally hopped out onto the beach and pulled the seaplane further up onto the sand.

Wally guided Jeff through the dense underbrush, following a path that was all but concealed by nature's embrace. Moments later, they emerged into a modest clearing. There, Wally crouched and motioned to Jeff to help him clear an assortment of fallen leaves and twining vines. As they did so, the hidden majesty of the Southeast Bunker Entrance "E3" began to reveal itself. The greenery receded to uncover the broad steps that descended defiantly into the earth, leading to the formidable, vine-draped threshold of the Southeast Bunker labeled "E3". This entrance, the portal protected by an impressive steel door, whispered of secrets lying in wait beneath their feet.

"This is entrance E3 to the bunker," Wally explained. "It's one of the more concealed ones and a good access point to the central areas."

Jeff let out a low whistle as he inspected the door and surrounding earthworks. "Incredible. Even when you know it's here, it's almost impossible to spot."

Wally nodded, a glint of pride in his eyes. "Exactly. Come on, let's head inside. There's a lot more to show you."

After ensuring the area was clear, Wally pulled open the heavy steel door. It let out a screech of protest as decades of disuse were overcome. Jeff followed Wally as he made his way down the steps into the darkness below. After descending about 10 feet, they reached the bottom and clicked on their flashlights. The powerful beams cut through the pitch-blackness, illuminating a hallway leading deeper into the bunker.

Wally glanced back at Jeff with an adventurous smile. "Let's go!"

The two continued on, ready to explore the secrets contained within the hidden depths of the bunker.

Chapter 12
The Final Revelation

Wally moved with purpose through the dark corridors of the abandoned bunker, his vision sharpened by the lingering effects of the microbe-laced treats. Though the winding tunnels appeared pitch-black to Jeff, Wally could discern every twist and turn with precision. His memories of exploring this bunker were crystal clear thanks to the boost from BRV-076, allowing him to effortlessly navigate to the central command hub.

As they entered the expansive command center, Wally and Jeff paused to take in the dated technology and instrumentation. Banks of analog gauges, switches, and dials covered the walls, while large circular radar scopes sat dormant in the center of the room. Wally walked slowly past each station, inspecting volt meters, ammeters, pressure indicators, and other controls. His extraordinarily keen senses picked up details that would be impossible for Jeff to notice in the dim light. Meanwhile, Jeff struggled to make out more than vague shapes and silhouettes in the darkness.

"This equipment was state-of-the-art in its time," Jeff remarked as he squinted at a dust-covered analog frequency display. "It's amazing to think what they were able to accomplish with such primitive technology compared to today."

Wally nodded in agreement, but his mind was already racing ahead, contemplating the valuable insights they could gain from this relic of the past. With his enhanced abilities, he knew he would be able to unlock secrets that were invisible to Jeff. Wally realized this command center held enormous potential, if only he could explore it alone, unencumbered by the need to conceal the full extent of his transformed abilities. For now, he maintained his focus on the task at hand, determined to glean whatever useful information he could without rousing Jeff's suspicions.

WALLY AND JEFF CLIMBED back into the seaplane, eager to depart Bird Island after ensuring the bunker remained secure. Jeff started the engine and it roared to life, the propeller cutting through the humid island air.

"Let's get out of here," Wally said. Though his abilities granted by the microorganisms were still active, he was ready to leave the island behind for now.

Jeff taxied the seaplane into position and increased the throttle. The aircraft steadily picked up speed across the water until it lifted off, wings outstretched, gaining altitude.

Looking out the window as they flew away, Wally watched Bird Island shrink into the distance. He knew its secrets still awaited below the surface, but was satisfied they remained protected for today.

Jeff leveled the seaplane off and set their course west, back towards the mainland. As Bay City appeared on the horizon, an idea struck him.

"Hey Wally, you want to buzz by those characters one more time?" Jeff asked with a wry smile. "Might be their last chance to appreciate air conditioning for awhile."

Wally chuckled, knowing exactly who Jeff meant - the men whose boat he had sabotaged, leaving them stranded.

"Sure, let's take a look," Wally agreed.

Jeff dipped the seaplane lower, heading for the coordinates where they had last spotted the lifeless boat. Scanning the waves, he soon pinpointed the vessel - and the two unfortunate souls still aboard.

As they made their low pass overhead, Wally felt a sense of satisfaction seeing the men's plight. Thanks to his tampering, they would be stuck for some time, unable to access the bunker or threaten the island's secrets.

"Bon voyage, fellas," Jeff muttered as they soared past. He pulled back on the yoke, guiding the seaplane up and onwards toward home.

JEFF GUIDED THE SEAPLANE smoothly along the coast as they neared Chinquapin. In the passenger seat, Wally gazed out at the marshy landscape passing below, his senses heightened from the microorganisms flowing through his system.

"Jeff, I know this is a rather odd request, but I would very much like to see your place, where you keep Sally. Would that be okay?" Wally asked, turning to the veteran pilot.

Jeff glanced over with a look of surprise, but it quickly turned to an easy smile. "That would be just fine, I'd love to show it to you," he replied amiably.

Wally nodded, a hint of excitement in his eyes. Soon the seaplane banked gently as Jeff lined up for his approach to the small coastal community. They touched down smoothly on the bayou near Jeff's property.

After securing the Cessna at the private dock, Jeff led the way up a crushed shell driveway to his modest wood-framed house overlooking the water. He gave Wally a brief tour of the place, culminating in a peek inside the metal hangar where the seaplane was housed when not in use. Wally took in every detail, imprinting the layout and surroundings into his enhanced memory. Their excursion ended on Jeff's back porch, where they sat gazing out at the shimmering bayou as the day drew to a close.

"JEFF," WALLY STARTS, his tone serious yet infused with a sense of camaraderie, "I've been giving a lot of thought to Bird Island and everything it stands for—its peace, its wildlife, and its untamed beauty."

Jeff nods, wiping his hands on a cloth. His demeanor suggests he's open to a deeper conversation. "It's a special place, Wally. Not many like it left around here."

Wally hesitates for a moment, but the trust they've built emboldens him. "Exactly. And that's what concerns me. You know, the island is more than just a playground for us. It's home to countless animals, plants... it's got its own rhythm, its own life."

Jeff agrees, his eyes reflecting an understanding, a shared sense of stewardship for the natural world.

Wally takes a deep breath and continues, "I want to protect it, Jeff. Not just from the usual threats, but from whatever might come our way. Development, pollution... you name it."

"You think something's coming?" Jeff asks, a crease of concern forming between his brows.

"Possibly. And I've been contemplating moving to Chinquapin for that very reason. To be closer, to watch over the island," Wally explains, his gaze steady on Jeff.

"That's a big step. But it sounds like you're set on this," Jeff observes, considering Wally's words.

"I am. But I can't do it alone. I could use someone with your skills—someone who knows the land, who can pilot a seaplane, and who gets why this is important." Wally pauses, allowing the weight of his request to settle.

Jeff's expression softens with the honesty of Wally's appeal. "Well, I've got to say, I admire your dedication. And I've grown pretty fond of this place myself."

Encouraged, Wally leans in slightly. "I could use your help, man. Not just with the plane or the island, but with creating a solid plan. To safeguard this place. To keep it as it should be."

There's a silence, filled only by the distant cry of birds and the gentle lapping of water against the shore. Finally, Jeff extends his hand, his decision clear in his eyes. "Alright, Wally. You've got my help. Let's protect Bird Island."

JEFF NOTES THE SUDDEN shift in the atmosphere; the air seems heavier, laden with Wally's unspoken thoughts. After a moment of contemplative silence, he prompts Wally with a nod, indicating he's ready to receive whatever it is that's weighing on him.

He glances around, ensuring the privacy of their conversation. He takes in the surroundings—the untouched expanse of Chinquapin, the serene bayou, the distant silhouette of Bird Island. He then locks eyes with Jeff, finding in them a quiet understanding that gives him strength.

"Wally, whatever it is, you can trust me," Jeff reassures him, sensing the hesitancy in his friend's posture.

Wally draws a deep breath, his resolve solidifying. "Jeff, I've seen things, discovered things on Bird Island that hardly anyone would believe. They're not just powerful; they could change everything we know about the natural world."

Jeff's eyebrows lift, his interest piqued by Wally's earnestness. "What kind of things?"

Wally's voice drops to a near whisper, the words tumbling out with a mix of awe and trepidation. "Microorganisms, Jeff. Hidden in a World War II bunker. They're not like anything documented before."

The revelation seems to hang suspended above the lapping waters. Jeff digests the information, his face a mosaic of curiosity and disbelief.

"Microorganisms?" Jeff repeats. He leans in closer.

Wally nods vigorously. "Yeah, and they grant abilities, Jeff—enhanced vision, superhuman strength, extraordinary memory... I've experimented on myself." Wally hesitates, then adds, "And it worked."

A beat of stunned silence follows, and then Jeff's laughter breaks through, lightening the moment. "Wally, you're pulling my leg, right?"

But Wally's expression remains serious, unwavering. "No, Jeff. I'm dead serious. But you have to promise to keep this between us. It's a matter of protecting not only the island but potentially everyone."

Jeff's laughter fades, replaced by the realization that Wally is entirely sincere. "You're not joking. Are you?" he whispers, now observing Wally with a newfound respect and hint of concern.

"With these... abilities... and the island's secrets, I have an upper hand in protecting it. I've been feeling isolated carrying this weight alone. I want you in this with me, Jeff. We need a foolproof plan, and I need someone I can rely on."

Jeff sits back, the magnitude of the secret he's been entrusted with setting in. It's not every day one encounters a revelation that feels straight out of science fiction. After a moment to collect his thoughts, Jeff gives Wally a firm nod. "Alright. I'm with you. Let's make sure Bird Island stays safe—with or without super microbes."

Wally lets out a sigh of relief, a smile breaking through his serious demeanor. "Thank you, Jeff. With you onboard, I really believe we can do this. But remember, secrecy is paramount."

"To protecting Bird Island," Jeff raises his hand, and Wally clasps it in agreement.

"To keeping its secrets," Wally affirms, a sense of camaraderie and shared purpose fortifying the bond between the two men.

Jeff could hardly believe his eyes as Wally grasped the front bumper of his Chevy 1500 pickup and lifted the front end clear off the ground with seemingly little effort. The early morning sun glinted off the chrome cattle guard as the tires hovered a good foot above the gravel driveway.

"Wally, that's... that's incredible!" Jeff stammered, shaking his head in disbelief. Just yesterday, the two of them had struggled to load a broken outboard motor into the back of that same truck. Now here was scrawny little Wally holding up the entire front end like it was made of styrofoam.

Wally let the tires settle back to earth with a crunch of gravel and turned to Jeff with a knowing smile. "Told you those microbes were something else," he said with a hint of pride.

Jeff walked around the truck, inspecting it as if to make sure Wally hadn't rigged something up to make this all an elaborate trick. But the truck seemed perfectly normal.

"I don't know how, but they've given you some kind of super strength," Jeff conceded, giving Wally an incredulous look. "Makes me wonder what else they're capable of."

Wally's smile broadened. "Oh, that's just the beginning. My vision and stamina are enhanced too. But I figured a strength demonstration would be the most convincing."

Jeff let out a low whistle, leaning back against the hood of the truck. "Well consider me convinced. That bunker of yours is hiding some serious secrets." He looked at Wally with newfound awe and curiosity. "Makes me wonder what else is in store on that island of yours..."

Wally nodded, his expression growing more solemn. "I know, and that's exactly why we need to make sure it stays protected. This kind of knowledge in the wrong hands..." He left the implication hanging in the air.

"Don't worry Wally, your secret's safe with me," Jeff assured him, placing a hand on his shoulder. "And we'll make sure Bird Island stays just the way it is - a sanctuary."

The two exchanged a look of understanding. Come what may, they were in this together now. Jeff cast a glance back at his truck, still struggling to wrap his mind around what he'd just witnessed. With abilities like that, he realized, Wally really could become a guardian of sorts over the island and its secrets. And Jeff aimed to help in any way he could.

WALLY STOOD WITH JEFF outside the seaplane hangar as the last rays of daylight faded over the bayou. He was still feeling the effects of the microbe-laced treats coursing through his system, heightening his senses. Turning to Jeff, he said, "Let's do one other thing to ensure your belief in case you decide it was some kind of trick. Go inside the hangar, walk some sort of pattern with the door closed so I can't see. Then I'll come in and walk the same path."

Jeff looked at him skeptically but nodded. "Alright, let's give it a try." He stepped inside the hangar, pulling the large sliding door shut behind him.

Wally waited outside, listening intently. He heard Jeff's footsteps tracing an irregular path across the concrete floor, occasionally stopping, turning, and doubling back. After a minute, the footsteps receded and Jeff called out, "Okay, come on in!"

He slid the hangar door open and stepped inside the dark interior. Immediately he perceived the glowing footprints on the floor, weaving in meandering switchbacks. He followed the shining trail precisely, matching each turn and pause until he reached the end where Jeff stood watching in astonishment.

"Well, I'll be darned," Jeff murmured, shaking his head. "I didn't think there was any way you could do that without seeing me walk it first. Guess you really weren't kidding about those abilities of yours." He gave Wally an appraising look. "Alright, you've convinced me. Now let's talk about how we can work together to keep that island protected."

Wally smiled, relieved that Jeff finally believed him. With the seasoned pilot on his side, he felt more confident that the secrets of Bird Island would remain safe from harm.

WALLY LOOKED AT JEFF with a serious expression, knowing that the time had come to fully reveal the truth behind his extraordinary abilities. After their experience at the hangar, there could be no more doubts or skepticism from his trusted friend and mentor.

"Jeff, now you know how I learned to fly your seaplane so quickly," Wally began. "It wasn't just raw talent or beginner's luck. The enhanced skills - all of it - comes from the microorganisms I discovered on Bird Island."

He went on to explain how he had first tested the powerful compounds on himself, gaining incredible benefits ranging from perfect recall to night vision to uncanny strength. He described the potent cookies and candy bars he had crafted to harness the microbes' effects, clarifying how they had allowed him to master the seaplane controls with ease during Jeff's lessons.

Jeff listened intently, stroking his beard as he processed Wally's incredible account. Everything he had witnessed started to make sense - the inexplicable tracking abilities, the swift mastery of complex tasks, the uncanny grasp of details. It was all due to the remarkable microorganisms Wally had uncovered and managed to utilize through his ingenious delivery methods.

"I know it sounds unbelievable," Wally continued. "But the microbes are very real, and their effects even more so. I wanted you to know the full truth, now that I can trust you completely. With your help, I believe we can protect Bird Island's secrets and prevent these organisms from falling into the wrong hands."

Wally extended his hand. Jeff grasped it firmly, his weathered face breaking into an admiring smile.

"Well, I'll be," Jeff said. "Never thought I'd see something like this in my lifetime. You can count on me to assist you however I can. Those secrets are safe with us."

The pact was sealed. Wally's disclosure had unlocked their path forward. Together, they would safeguard the extraordinary knowledge contained on Bird Island, confronting whatever challenges arose.

"THERE'S ONE LAST BIT of information I need to tell you," Wally said, turning to look Jeff in the eyes. "Pug and Richie know nothing about this. Only my parents know, and even they know very little."

Jeff nodded slowly, understanding the gravity of what Wally had shared with him so far. "I appreciate you trusting me with all of this," he replied. "Your secret's safe with me."

Wally smiled, relieved to have finally opened up to someone about the incredible discovery he had made on Bird Island.

A comfortable silence settled between them as they gazed out at the bayou. After a few moments, Wally's expression shifted to one of curiosity.

"Hey Jeff, what do you think about an ICON A5?" he asked. "I've been looking into maybe getting a sport plane that could land on water. Might be useful for quick trips out to Bird Island to keep an eye on things. The A5 seems like a good option but I wanted to get your take since you know planes so well."

Jeff rubbed his chin thoughtfully. "The A5's a fine little machine. Maneuvers well on both land and water," he said. "With your new talents, I'm sure you could handle her no problem. And you're right, it'd be perfect for your needs. Quick and nimble enough to zip out to the island whenever you needed."

Jeff went on to describe some of the A5's capabilities and features, clearly knowledgeable about the aircraft. The ICON A5 is a versatile two-seat light sport aircraft designed for adventure and utility. Its amphibious capabilities, with retractable landing gear for water landings and a lightweight airframe, make it ideal for exploration and leisure flights. The A5 is powered by a Rotax 912 engine, reaching a max speed of 110 miles per hour, and offers a range of 490 miles. Safety is paramount, featuring a spin-resistant frame, a predictable flying profile, low stall speed, and an emergency parachute system. With a cockpit boasting 46 inches of width and panoramic views, this aircraft combines functionality with an unforgettable flying experience. Wally listened intently, picturing himself piloting the sleek white and blue plane over the bayou. The prospect of taking to the skies in his own plane, keeping watch over Bird Island, filled him with excitement.

JEFF DROPPED WALLY off at the cabin just after dark. The fading light of dusk cast long shadows across the weathered wooden boards of the pier as Wally stepped out of Jeff's pickup truck.

"Thanks again for letting me in on the secrets of Bird Island," Jeff said appreciatively as Wally grabbed his backpack from the truck bed. "It's given me a renewed sense of purpose. Knowing that place needs to be protected...well, it makes me feel like I have something meaningful to contribute."

Wally nodded, understanding completely. "I'm glad I can trust you with this, Jeff. We'll talk soon."

With a wave, Jeff put the truck in gear and headed off down the shell driveway as Wally turned towards the cabin. Inside, he could see Richie and Pug sitting at the table finishing up their dinner. The aroma of fried fish and hushpuppies still lingered in the air.

"Hey Wally, we saved you a plate!" Richie called out as Wally stepped inside. He grabbed the heaping plate of food from the counter and joined his friends at the table. As he dug into the crispy fish, Wally recounted the day's events for Richie and Pug.

"So those two guys, Jack and Harry, showed back up on the island today," Wally explained through mouthfuls of food. "Jeff and I flew over and spotted them trying to get into one of the bunkers. We didn't want them finding anything important, so we snuck in ahead of them and secured the entrance."

Pug and Richie listened intently, their eyes widening at the tale of intruders and adventure. Wally went on to describe how they had stranded Jack and Harry's boat before making their escape. It had been a close call, but the island's secrets remained safe for now thanks to quick thinking and a bit of luck. Wally just hoped their luck would hold out. There was too much at stake.

WALLY AWOKE AT THE crack of dawn, the pale light filtering in through the window of the fishing cabin. Today marked the end of their adventurous winter break, with Pug needing to return for college classes and Richie heading home to his wife and job at the plant.

A sense of melancholy washed over Wally as he realized this magical time was drawing to a close. But he was also excited to embark on the next phase of his plan. With his friends departing, he would need his own transportation. Wally flipped open his laptop and began browsing for vehicles, thinking an SUV would suit his needs well.

His research then turned to real estate listings in the Chinquapin area, focusing on properties near Jeff's house. Wally dreamed of having a permanent foothold near the serene shores of East Matagorda Bay. Most of all, he was set on acquiring an ICON A5 amphibious sports plane. Its compact size, lightweight, and ability to take off and land on both land and water made it the perfect aircraft for quick trips to Bird Island. Wally could practically feel himself sitting in the cockpit, masterfully piloting the nimble plane over the bay.

The sound of voices outside pulled Wally from his daydream. It was time to load up with Pug and Richie before they set off on the long drive home and the beginning of a new solo chapter for Wally. He took a deep breath, ready to put the next phase of his plan into action. Bird Island was calling, and he would answer.

WALLY WAVED GOODBYE to Pug as the pickup truck pulled away, leaving him standing alone in the driveway with his duffel bag. His mother emerged from the front door and walked over to greet him, a warm smile on her face.

"Welcome home, honey. How was the trip?" she asked.

He set his bag down and gave his mom a big hug. "It was great, Mom. The fishing was awesome as always."

"I'm so glad to hear that. It looks like you got a little sun," she said, noticing his tanned face. "Oh, by the way, your office phone has been ringing a lot the last couple of days. I think it was that bakery client of yours."

Wally nodded, the information sinking in. Bake-RiteZ must be calling about more cloud migration work. This new project would keep him busy over the next two weeks.

He gave his mom a quick kiss on the cheek. "Thanks for letting me know. I better give them a call back right away."

Wally grabbed his bag and headed upstairs to his home office. He set his bag down and sank into his desk chair, then picked up the office phone and dialed Bake-RiteZ. As expected, they wanted to get another production plant's systems moved over to the cloud. Wally jotted down notes about the new plant's specialized equipment and proprietary processes that would need cloud integration. The project timeline was tight, but doable if he dedicated his time fully over the next two weeks.

After hanging up, Wally leaned back in his chair, contemplating the project. He knew he had the skills to handle it, but wished he had someone to collaborate with who understood complex factory systems. He closed his eyes, trying to remember the name of that retired systems analyst he met at the barbershop a few weeks back. The guy had 30 years of experience handling exactly these kinds of integrations. If only Wally could recall his name, he might be able to bring him on as a consultant.

Wally racked his brain, conjuring up the memory of sitting in the worn leather barber chair, chatting with the white-haired gentleman in the next chair over. He could picture the man's weathered face and faded tattoos on his forearms hinting at a Navy past. After a few moments, it came to him - Frank, that was the guy's name. Frank McMillan.

With this spark of recall, Wally reopened his eyes and turned to his computer. He did a quick search for Frank McMillan in the area and, thankfully, found contact info for a Frank McMillan, Navy veteran and retired systems analyst. Wally smiled and picked up his phone again, dialing the number. The gruff but warm voice that answered told Wally he had the right Frank.

After a brief chat, Frank enthusiastically agreed to come on board as a consultant and help Wally with the new Bake-RiteZ project. Wally felt a wave of relief wash over him. With Frank's experience, he was confident they could handle the aggressive timeline. This collaboration would also give Wally a chance to learn from the veteran analyst.

After hanging up with Frank, Wally glanced at the time. It wasn't too late to make one more call he had been meaning to make. He picked up a business card sitting on his desk for Aero Lift Aviation, the local dealer for ICON aircraft. Though Wally knew the A5 sport plane would be a major purchase, he couldn't get the sleek aircraft off his mind since Jeff let him pilot his seaplane.

Wally took a breath and dialed Aero Lift's number. A cheerful sales rep answered promptly. Wally explained his interest in purchasing an A5, with the intention of using it to visit family properties along the Gulf coast. The rep covered all the specs - the cruising speed, fuel efficiency, safety features, and of course, the price. The figure was substantial, but within Wally's growing budget, especially with the new Bake-RiteZ contract. After discussing financing options, Wally promised to follow up once he was ready to move forward.

After ending the call, Wally stood up and stretched. He gazed out the window at the darkening sky, contemplating the future. The A5 would enable convenient trips to Bird Island whenever needed.

And with Frank's assistance, Wally could take Bake-RiteZ's project in stride while continuing to prepare for his next adventure. He smiled to himself, feeling that familiar mix of contentment about his capabilities and anticipation for the mysteries still to uncover.

Wally headed downstairs to join his parents for dinner, his mind swimming with thoughts about cloud servers, sport planes, and secluded islands. But for now, he would enjoy the comfort of home.

WALLY AWOKE TO BRIGHT sunlight streaming through his bedroom window. Groggily, he glanced at the clock and realized he had slept in much later than usual. "The effects of CLF-532 must have worn off overnight," he mumbled to himself, recalling the microorganism he had consumed to enhance his endurance.

After getting dressed, Wally headed to his home office, ready to start on a new cloud migration project for his client Bake-RiteZ. He was looking forward to diving into the technical details of moving their systems over to the cloud. Before that, he had a brief check-in scheduled with his new consultant, Frank McMillan, to discuss the scope of the project. Frank's decades of IT experience would provide valuable guidance.

Wally also planned to go SUV shopping later - his old sedan was feeling cramped with his outdoor adventures lately. But first things first, he picked up his phone to give Jeff a callback. Jeff had done an aerial reconnaissance flight over Bird Island earlier that morning to check for any suspicious activity.

"Hey Jeff, what's the report from Bird Island?" Wally asked when his friend picked up.

"All's quiet on the western front," Jeff replied lightheartedly. He went on to describe circling back over East Matagorda Bay on his return. Squinting down at the waves, he had spotted a familiar boat still adrift - it belonged to the nefarious Jack and Harry. Thanks to Wally's sabotage, the men remained stranded, their boat subject to the winds and currents. Jeff figured they were still a day or more from reaching shore.

Wally smiled upon hearing the update. "Excellent news. Thanks for keeping an eye out, Jeff." They said their goodbyes and hung up. With the reassurance that Bird Island remained secure for now, Wally turned his focus to the tasks at hand - a busy day lay ahead.

Chapter 13
Legacy of the Island

A subtle hum echoed in Wally's home office as he peered into his computer screen, the soft glow casting an ethereal light onto his focused face. His fingers danced across the keyboard, setting up an automatic monthly payment to Jeff Mitchell for surveillance services over Bird Island. The figure - $1500. It was a substantial amount, but Wally deemed it a worthy investment to protect the island's secrets.

The soft ring of his phone broke the quiet concentration of the room. A representative from the Hyundai dealership on the other end of the line had good news. A used Santa Fe, only a year old and within his price range, was ready for him. A smile curled on Wally's lips as he agreed to finalize the deal later that day.

As the sun dipped lower in the sky, painting the horizon with hues of pink and orange, thoughts of Jack and Harry gnawed at Wally's mind. He picked up his phone once again and dialed Jeff's number. His voice carried an edge of urgency as he relayed his concerns.

"They'll probably hit land by nightfall," he explained, "It might be best to tip off the Coast Guard about them."

The silence on the other end of the line was detectable before Jeff responded with a gruff agreement. The pair knew well enough that if Jack and Harry were picked up by authorities, they'd have some explaining to do about their presence near Bird Island.

With their plan set in motion, Wally leaned back in his chair, a small sigh escaping his lips as he looked out into the evening sky, bracing himself for whatever tomorrow would bring.

JEFF WAS UP EARLY THAT morning, working diligently on routine maintenance tasks for his beloved Cessna seaplane. As he tinkered away, the sounds of a local Bay City radio station filled his hangar. Jeff half-listened to the benign chatter of the morning show hosts while focusing intently on his work.

That focus was broken when an intriguing news report came over the airwaves - a story about a recent Coast Guard rescue of two men who had been stranded for days in the remote tidal flats of East Matagorda Bay. The newscaster identified the rescued men as Jack Sparrow and Harry Locke, both recently released from federal prison after convictions for smuggling stolen military artifacts.

Jeff's ears perked up at the mention of those familiar names. He quickly cleaned his hands on a rag and reached for his cell phone. After a few rings, his call was answered by Wally, who Jeff had been working with to protect the secrets of the mysterious bunker on nearby Bird Island.

Jeff relayed the news report to Wally, who instantly made the connection - Jack and Harry were the trespassers they had thwarted from breaking into the bunker just days earlier. A wave of relief washed over Wally as he realized the threat had been neutralized, at least for now. The two men were in Coast Guard custody, stranded at sea by his own covert actions. The secrets of Bird Island were safe once again, thanks to quick thinking and a little help from the tidal flats of East Matagorda Bay.

WALLY WAS UP EARLY, focused on the implementation of Bake-RiteZ's requirements needed to bring another one of their plants online. By early afternoon, he had picked up his Santa Fe from the dealer and was on his way back home when one of the monitors tripped. What bad timing this was with his mind solely on Bake-RiteZ. Wally gave Jeff a call and brought him up to date.

After a short discussion, a plan began to form. Jeff would pick up Wally at the local small-town airport. Together they would fly back to Jeff's home and gas up the seaplane. As Wally and Jeff traveled, they continued to work on a plan.

He knew he needed to act quickly to investigate the monitor alarm on Bird Island, but he was determined to balance his software business responsibilities as well. With Jeff's help, he hoped to handle both situations efficiently. Though tired from a long day, Wally's mind raced with contingency plans as Jeff flew them towards his seaplane hangar under the fading evening light. There was no time to waste if they wanted to reach Bird Island before whoever tripped the alarm could find what they were looking for.

WALLY SPENT THE NIGHT in Jeff's hangar, the two of them staying up late to prepare a surprise for the smugglers Jack and Harry. Jeff, being an old military veteran, had quite an unexpected stash of supplies hidden away in the hangar.

Wally dug into his backpack and took out three of his special cookies - one red, one orange, and one blue. He ate them quickly, feeling the microorganisms within immediately start to take effect, enhancing his senses and abilities.

Under the cover of night, Wally and Jeff worked tirelessly, utilizing the supplies Jeff had gathered over the years. Wally's consumption of the cookies allowed him to see clearly even in the dark hangar, his strength and stamina heightened thanks to the microorganisms now coursing through his system.

It was very late by the time the two finished their preparations, both exhausted yet satisfied with their efforts. They unrolled sleeping bags beside the seaplane and settled in to get some rest before the coming day, when they would enact the surprise they had worked so hard to prepare for their unwelcome guest. Wally's mind raced with anticipation as he eventually drifted off, wondering what the smugglers' reactions would be.

JEFF BANKED THE CESSNA over the sparkling waters of East Matagorda Bay, the drone of the engine a steady companion as he and Wally scanned the landscape below for signs of trouble.

Bird Island loomed ahead, its marshy expanse interspersed with hidden dangers and forgotten relics of war—and now, clandestine visitors unwelcome in its tranquil solitude.

Wally squinted through binoculars, the island's details coming into sharp focus thanks to his enhanced vision granted by the microorganisms. He spotted faint disturbances in the foliage, footprints along the muddy shoreline, glints of light that betrayed manmade objects nestled amongst the natural landscape.

"We've got company," Wally said. "Looks like at least two, maybe more, landed on the southwest side, then headed inland."

Jeff nodded, easing back on the throttle and dipping the Cessna lower, spiraling gently over the coordinates Wally indicated. He couldn't make out the subtle signs his companion had described, but years of experience told him Wally was right.

As the plane banked, sunlight flashed off something metal by the tree line. "There," Jeff said, "solar panels. They've set up camp, and looks like more than just an overnight stay."

Wally's expression hardened, knowing the implications. Outsiders settling in could threaten everything he had worked to protect here. But whoever they were, they had no idea what they were walking into, or who they now faced. The microorganisms coursing through Wally's body made him more than a match for any trespassers.

"Take us down along the west shore," Wally instructed. "We'll access the bunker through the concealed sea entrance and find out what these uninvited guests are really after."

Jeff smiled slightly. "You got it, cap'n. Hang on."

The seaplane dipped lower still, skimming along the coastline. Wally's hands tightened on the binoculars as the Cessna banked gracefully over Bird Island, which guarded its secrets as it always had - but now relied on him for its defense.

WALLY MOVED ALONG THE southeast shore of Bird Island, his senses heightened from the microbes coursing through his system. Beside him, Jeff matched his brisk pace, relying on Wally's enhanced abilities to guide them.

Though the morning sun shone brightly, casting the beach in radiance, Wally's vision pierced the glare, discerning details otherwise hidden. Each grain of sand and blade of grass appeared illuminated to his augmented eyes.

He led them to a nondescript spot along the tree line, an area Jeff would have overlooked if not for his companion's firm sense of direction. Here, Wally cleared away a tangle of branches, revealing a weathered steel door.

"E3," Wally said, pointing to faded lettering on the steel door. "Southeast Entrance. It's our best chance of getting in unnoticed."

Jeff nodded, deferring to Wally's judgment. Though initially skeptical of the young man's claims of enhancement, Jeff now witnessed clear evidence of Wally's extraordinary gifts.

As Wally pulled open the rusted door with ease, the hinges emitted a faint squeal. He paused, listening intently for any signs of activity from within. Hearing nothing, he waved Jeff forward and they descended into the cool darkness of the abandoned bunker.

Wally wondered if the trespassers had already gained access to these hidden depths. But the undisturbed cobwebs and dust seemed to indicate the passage had remained unused. Still, he knew appearances could be deceiving. He focused his senses, probing the shadows for clues as they moved silently onward.

Chapter 14

A New Dawn

Wally and Jeff cautiously made their way through the dark, musty corridors of the abandoned bunker on Bird Island. Though the passageways appeared untouched by human activity in decades, Wally's heightened senses remained on high alert. The special microorganisms he had consumed granted him extraordinary sensory capabilities - he could perceive minute details even in the pitch blackness that surrounded them. Jeff followed closely behind, relying on the narrow beam of his flashlight to navigate through the gloom.

As they ventured deeper into the maze-like bunker, Wally detected a faint hint of smoke and ash in the air. He held up his hand to stop Jeff, signaling for absolute silence. Focusing intently, Wally picked up the unmistakable crackling of a dying fire somewhere ahead of them. He gestured to Jeff that there were likely intruders in the bunker. Jeff nodded in understanding and patted the holstered pistol at his hip, prepared to confront whoever had trespassed onto the island.

Moving as stealthily as shadows, they continued toward the source of the fire. Soon, the corridor opened up into a large chamber with a high, domed ceiling. In the center stood the remains of a campfire, tendrils of smoke still drifting up from the embers. Around it were signs of a temporary settlement - sleeping bags, packs of gear, and a portable electric lamp. But there was no one in sight.

Wally's acute hearing picked up the echoing sound of footsteps hurrying away down an adjoining tunnel. He pointed toward the noise, indicating the intruders were fleeing deeper into the bunker. A determined look passed between Wally and Jeff.

WALLY AND JEFF MOVED swiftly and silently through the abandoned bunker, their flashlights casting ominous shadows along the concrete walls. Wally led the way, his senses heightened from the microbes coursing through his system. He could detect the faintest sounds echoing down the corridors - the intruders were still here, and not far ahead.

"This way," Wally whispered, gesturing towards a small storage room. Jeff followed wordlessly, his arms loaded down with supplies scavenged from their makeshift campsite. Sleeping bags, flashlights, cooking gear - anything they could grab in their haste to disappear.

He selected a corner of the room that was partially obstructed by old filing cabinets and gestured for Jeff to stash the gear there. They worked quickly but carefully, concealing the items beneath some moth-eaten wool blankets that had been left behind decades ago. Satisfied that the supplies were adequately hidden, Wally did a final sweep of the room with his flashlight, relying on his enhanced vision to ensure they had left no trace.

"Let's move," he said. Jeff nodded, sweat beading on his forehead. He was out of his element down here, but he trusted Wally's judgment completely.

They moved back out into the corridor, their footsteps light and careful. Wally tracked the intruders by sound, leading Jeff through the maze of tunnels with certainty. He was determined to intercept whoever had invaded their sanctuary - and ensure the bunker's secrets remained safe.

WALLY AND JEFF MOVED stealthily through the dark corridors of the abandoned bunker, relying on Wally's enhanced senses to track the intruders they had heard moments before. Wally's microbiome-augmented abilities allowed him to see even in the pitch blackness and pick up sounds imperceptible to normal hearing. He gestured for Jeff to follow as he tracked the intruders' footsteps and hushed voices.

They wound through a maze of tunnels, passing remnants of the bunker's past life - old maps, rusted tools, and piles of paperwork. Wally paused at a junction, cocking his head as he listened intently, then pointed left down a passageway. As they crept forward, a dim light became visible ahead.

Approaching cautiously, they discovered the source - a camping lantern resting on top of a crate in what appeared to be the intruders' makeshift shop. Tools and backpacks were scattered around, evidence of an extended stay. But the occupants were nowhere to be seen.

Wally inspected the camp, his enhanced senses picking up clues. "They left in a hurry, probably less than 5 minutes ago," he whispered to Jeff. "We might still catch them if we move fast."

With haste fueled by determination, they continued their pursuit, Wally tracking the intruders' path through the bunker. The footsteps led to a heavy steel door marked "Restricted Area." Exchanging a nod, Wally and Jeff pushed through into the unknown space beyond, ready to confront whoever had invaded this secret island bunker.

ROUNDING A CORNER, they came upon a second makeshift camp, recently abandoned by its occupants. Warm ashes in the fire pit and half-eaten rations scattered about indicated a hasty departure. Wally's acute senses determined that whoever had been here had fled just moments before their arrival.

Pressing forward, they followed the trail towards a restricted area of the bunker. Wally paused, a vague memory surfacing in his mind. This section, marked as off-limits, was a dead end - only one way in and out.

An idea formed in Wally's head. Turning back, they passed through the heavy steel door that secured the restricted sector. Wally then took a sturdy metal pipe and wedged it through the door handle, preventing the door from swinging open.

He had effectively trapped anyone inside, cutting off their only escape route. Satisfied, Wally stepped back, hoping his improvised lock would enable them to finally confront whoever had infiltrated the hidden bunker.

FOR THE MOMENT, IT appears Wally and Jeff are in control. Wally remembers AXI-218, the microorganism that enhances auditory perception. With this, he would be able to eavesdrop on the intruders' conversation from a distance. Wally leads Jeff to the bunker entrance closest to where the seaplane is anchored and tells him to wait outside, hidden, until he returns.

Wally then hurries to his hidden lab to locate samples of AXI-218 in hopes of gaining extraordinary hearing abilities. He searches through his meticulously organized storage and finds a vial of AXI-218, quickly pocketing it before rushing back to where Jeff is concealed near the seaplane.

Wally meets Jeff and they quietly board the seaplane, casting off swiftly from the island shore. Now airborne, they are on their way back to Jeff's hangar on the mainland.

While en route, Jeff and Wally discuss the unknown men they trapped inside the bunker. Jeff speculates they could be antiquities thieves or foreign agents seeking classified information. Wally considers the possibility they are connected to Jack and Harry, who previously trespassed on the island. Despite the uncertainty, both are relieved that the interlopers are contained for now, unable to access the bunker's secrets. They agree to keep monitoring the island closely.

He does not disclose to Jeff that he took a sample of AXI-218. He intends to consume it to gain exceptional hearing that may prove useful but wants to keep the full extent of his enhanced abilities private for now. Their conversation continues casually as the seaplane cruises over the glimmering bay, returning them home with a sense of accomplishment about thwarting the latest threat to the island's hidden mysteries.

JEFF GUIDED THE SEAPLANE expertly onto the water near his hangar as the sun dipped below the horizon, casting a warm orange glow across the bayou. Wally peered out the window eagerly, taking in the familiar sight of Jeff's property. It had become like a second home to him over the past few months, a place where he could talk openly about the secrets of Bird Island without fear of being overheard.

As soon as the plane was secured at the dock, Wally grabbed his backpack and hopped out, his mind already racing ahead to the next steps in their ongoing mission. Inside the hangar, he made a beeline for the small kitchen area, where he had stored a supply of his microbe-infused candy bars for just such an occasion. Rummaging through the bag, he found one of the small, brown bars labeled "218" and pulled it out.

Wally worked quickly, not wanting Jeff to see what he was up to. He rinsed the candy bar briefly under the faucet, just enough to dampen the surface ever so slightly. Then, from a small glass vial, he tapped out a tiny sprinkle of powder-dried and crushed AXI-218 microorganisms. It clung easily to the dampened chocolate. He re-wrapped the candy bar in its foil and tucked it back into the side pocket of his backpack. There, it would have several hours for the microbes to infuse into the chocolate before he needed its effects.

By morning, the AXI-218 should be fully activated, and give him the exceptional hearing abilities that he was counting on. Ever since they had discovered signs of intruders in the bunker on Bird Island, Wally had been wracking his brain trying to figure out their motives. With his enhanced senses, he hoped to eavesdrop on the trespassers and uncover their true purpose. Were they looking for wartime relics to sell? Seeking lost records or technology? Or were they agents of some foreign government, trying to exploit the bunker's secrets? The possibilities troubled Wally deeply.

"Ready to head into town for some dinner?" Jeff called from the doorway, breaking Wally's train of thought. He zipped up his backpack and turned to Jeff with a smile.

"You bet," he replied. "I'm starving after all that excitement."

The two friends locked up the hangar and climbed into Jeff's old pickup truck. As they bounced along the dirt road into town, Jeff chatted lightheartedly about his plans to repaint the seaplane. But Wally's mind was still back in the hangar, running through all the possible scenarios that could be facing them on Bird Island. He knew that with the AXI-218 assisting him, he would be able to uncover the truth...but would he and Jeff like what they found? The secrets of Bird Island had already proven more complex than he could have ever imagined.

As Jeff pulled the truck into the parking lot of their favorite local burger joint, Wally pushed his worries aside for the moment. He would tackle things one step at a time, starting with dinner. Then, tomorrow, they would return to Bird Island and he would put his augmented hearing to the test.

The next morning, Wally awoke to sunlight streaming through the windows of the guest room in Jeff's house. He blinked his eyes groggily, then smiled as he remembered the candy bar tucked away in his backpack. Reaching over, he carefully unwrapped it and took a small bite. The chocolate had taken on a slightly gritty texture from the AXI-218 powder, but otherwise tasted normal. Wally ate the rest in a few quick bites, washing it down with some water.

Within minutes, he could feel the effects beginning. At first, sounds seemed slightly muffled, as if he was underwater. But then, his hearing sharpened more and more, until even the faintest noises became audible. The chirping of a lone bird across the field was as clear as if it was perched on the windowsill. He could hear the soft lapping of water against the dock posts outside. Every creak and groan of the old house was amplified. It was like a curtain being lifted, allowing him to hear the world in incredible detail.

Wally dressed quickly and went to meet Jeff, eager to test his augmented abilities further. As they fired up the seaplane and began the flight to Bird Island, Wally focused intently on each sound of the engine and mechanisms, comparing them to his memory. It was like hearing them for the first time. By the time they touched down in the secluded lagoon on Bird Island, his hearing was so attuned that he could pinpoint the location of animals moving through the brush from a hundred yards away.

They secured the seaplane and headed inland, towards the concealed entrance to the bunker they had entered the day before. Approaching as stealthily as possible, Wally's hypersensitive ears picked up the murmur of voices from deep within. Two distinct voices, though he could not make out words yet. But the intruders were definitely still here.

WALLY STOOD PERFECTLY still, head tilted slightly as he focused his enhanced hearing on the muffled voices coming from behind the heavy steel door. The AXI-218 microorganism he had secretly consumed was working its auditory magic, allowing him to pick up the conversation inside the restricted room with crystal clarity.

"I'm telling you, we're trapped," came an exasperated male voice. "No way out but that damn door, and it won't budge."

"Keep trying, you idiot," snapped another man. "There's got to be a way to get it open."

He recognized the second voice - it was Jack, one of the men who had trespassed on Bird Island before. He tensed, signaling Jeff to remain quiet as he continued eavesdropping.

"I already checked the hinges, there's no removing those pins," said the first man wearily. "And we can't get enough leverage to lift the bar they've wedged in there. Face it Harry, we're stuck here until someone lets us out."

Harry and Jack. Wally clenched his fists. The two men who had repeatedly tried to access the island's secrets were now trapped inside the bunker.

"This is ridiculous," fumed Jack. "How the hell did this even happen? The door was wide open when we came in."

"Someone must have followed us and locked us in," said Harry. "They're probably long gone by now. We're just gonna have to sit tight until they come back."

Wally nodded to Jeff, confirming the identities of their captives. Jeff's expression hardened.

"I don't get it, there's no food or water in here," complained Harry. "What are they playing at, leaving us stuck in this empty room?"

"Maybe they intended to just keep us contained, prevent us accessing the rest of the bunker," suggested Jack. "Doesn't matter now, we're not going anywhere until they return."

The two men descended into frustrated silence. Wally waited, expecting them to speak again. Finally Jack piped up.

"You really think someone followed us in and trapped us?" He sounded unconvinced. "I didn't notice any signs of another boat arriving. And I swear that door was open when we came through."

Harry sighed loudly. "Well how else would we get locked in here Jack? You think the door swung closed and barred itself? No, someone else is on this island and they made sure we couldn't wander around."

"Alright, say you're right," said Jack slowly. "Why haven't they come back then? Just gonna leave us in here to starve? Because if so, we need to find another way out, and fast."

Wally looked at Jeff and shook his head. Let them continue thinking someone else was behind this. They didn't need to know he had abilities that allowed him to secure the door and trap them inside.

"I'm telling you, there's no way out!" yelled Harry in frustration. "No windows, no air vents, nothing but solid concrete walls. We're not breaking out of this room without some serious firepower."

"Keep looking, there's got to be something!" shouted Jack. "A hidden hatch, a loose panel, anything. I don't plan on dying in this godforsaken bunker."

Wally heard the sounds of them searching every inch of the small room, pounding on the walls and floor in desperation. But Harry was right - the chamber had been designed to keep its contents securely locked down. Without help, the door wasn't opening.

He glanced at Jeff and pointed upwards, signaling that they should return to the surface. Jeff nodded and they silently retraced their steps back through the dim corridors until they reached the entrance.

After securely closing the bunker door behind them, Wally finally spoke. "It's Jack and Harry. Somehow they got onto the island again."

Jeff's expression was grim. "Reckless fools. Don't they realize this place isn't meant for sightseeing?"

"At least they're contained for now," said Wally. "But we need to decide what to do next. We can't just leave them in there."

Jeff crossed his arms. "Can't say I'm inclined to let them out anytime soon. The longer they're stuck in there, the less harm they can do to this island."

They would have to keep monitoring the situation. But for now, the secrets of Bird Island remained secure.

WALLY WORKED METHODICALLY under the bunker's dim lights, assembling the components for a tracking device that would allow him to monitor Jack and Harry's movements even after they left Bird Island. Though currently trapped, Wally knew it was only a matter of time before the men's resourcefulness and determination resulted in their escape.

He had consumed a cookie laced with the microorganism BRV-076 earlier, granting him flawless recall and manual dexterity. Each twist of the screwdriver and placement of the tiny parts was executed with precision as he constructed the inconspicuous tracker. Wally envisioned concealing it within the lining of a bag or seam of their clothing when the opportunity arose.

His enhanced capabilities from the microbe allowed him to work quickly and efficiently. Within an hour, the tracker was complete and ready for deployment. Wally turned it on briefly, observing the pulsing marker on his cell phone app that indicated its active status. Satisfied with his work, he switched it off and tucked it into a pocket.

When the time came to confront Jack and Harry, Wally would rely on his augmented senses to surreptitiously plant the device. They would never realize they were being tracked as they finally departed the island. He would appear to merely inspect their gear when in reality, he was ensuring the ability to monitor their movements remotely once they were beyond Bird Island. For now, the tracker remained safely concealed until Wally could execute the next phase of his plan.

WALLY AND JEFF LEFT Jack and Harry confined in the bunker, exiting into the bright daylight. As they walked along the sandy shoreline back to Jeff's seaplane, Wally explained his rationale for leaving the men trapped.

"I think we should leave them in there for a few days, let them sweat it out a bit. It'll soften them up for when we finally make contact and find out what they're really after here," Wally said, skipping a stone across the water.

Jeff pondered this, stroking his silver beard pensively. "Not a bad idea. The isolation and lack of provisions will surely have an effect on them mentally. Might make them more willing to cooperate when the time comes."

WALLY AND JEFF BOARD the seaplane, preparing for the flight back to the mainland. As Jeff goes through his pre-flight checklist, Wally tells him, "I need to get back home to continue working. I just started a big new project for a client and I want to keep the momentum going."

Jeff checks the fuel gauges and sees he has plenty to make the round trip flight. "No problem, we'll have you back in no time," Jeff replies as he finishes his checks and starts the engine.

The seaplane lifts off smoothly from the water and Jeff pilots it across East Matagorda Bay towards home. Wally sits quietly, lost in thought as he watches the coastal waters pass beneath them.

After a short and uneventful flight, Jeff sets the seaplane down gracefully at their local airport. As Wally gathers his things to disembark, he pulls out his wallet. "Here's $500 for expenses," he says, handing the cash to Jeff. "Have a safe trip back. I'll be at the Chinquapin camp the day after tomorrow."

Jeff pockets the money with a nod. "You got it. Take care of that big project now. I'll see you back at the camp soon." Wally gives a small wave as he heads off, eager to get back to work. Jeff does a final check of the seaplane before also departing, anticipating their next rendezvous at the fishing cabin, as the propeller spins down and the engine ticks while cooling in the midday sun.

Chapter 15
Beneath the Surface

Wally was still under the influence of the microbe-enhanced cookies he had consumed earlier. He sat in his home office, rapidly wading through the software requirements for his latest Bake-RiteZ project. His fingers flew across the keyboard at an astonishing pace as the microbes granted him increased focus and cognitive abilities.

Working late into the night, Wally made amazing headway on the new project, plowing through complex features and optimizations. The microbes allowed his mind to analyze problems from multiple angles simultaneously, devising elegant solutions. Where an ordinary programmer might struggle for days, Wally breezed through in mere hours.

By the time dawn's light began to creep into the office, Wally had accomplished nearly a week's worth of work. At this rate, he would likely finish the entire Bake-RiteZ project before needing to return to Chinquapin in a couple days. The microbes had proven their worth once again, enabling Wally to leverage his software skills to an extraordinary degree. He leaned back in his chair, contemplating the code he had just brought into existence, made possible by the remarkable secret of Bird Island.

WALLY WOKE UP FEELING refreshed after a restful night's sleep. The previous day, he had consumed a microbe-laced candy that granted him extraordinary hearing abilities. But as he went about his morning routine, Wally noticed the effects had already worn off - his hearing was back to normal.

In some ways, he felt relieved. While the hyper-acute hearing had been fascinating, it was also incredibly distracting at times. Wally was accustomed to the comings and goings of ordinary life, not a constant deluge of sounds from every direction.

It wasn't long after breakfast when Wally's phone rang. It was the aviation dealer calling with exciting news - the ICON A5 sport plane Wally had ordered had arrived and was ready for its first flight. The dealer had already completed all the necessary servicing and prep work.

He could barely contain his enthusiasm upon hearing the news. If all went well on his initial solo flight, he planned to fly the sleek new aircraft out to Pug's family fishing cabin near Chinquapin. Thanks to the boost in skills from a recent microbe, Wally had earned his pilot's license just days earlier at a nearby airport.

Donning his bomber jacket, Wally headed out the door, eager to take his prized plane for its maiden voyage. The microbes had opened up new worlds for him, both on the ground and now in the skies. But he remained measured in their application, using their power judiciously as he charted the course ahead. For now, the freedom of flight beckoned.

WALLY ARRIVED AT THE small local airport, eager to take his first flight in the ICON A5 sport plane he had recently purchased. He met with the dealer who handed him the keys and did a final walkaround of the sleek white aircraft.

He climbed into the A5's cockpit, taking in the state-of-the-art glass cockpit and carbon fiber interior. Though compact, the cockpit was optimized for comfort and visibility. Wally went through his pre-flight checklist methodically, familiarizing himself with the plane's advanced avionics. Satisfied everything was in order, he started the engine and felt the thrum of the turbocharged powerplant.

After receiving clearance from the tower, Wally taxied the A5 to the runway. With a surge of excitement, he pushed the throttle forward for takeoff. The A5 accelerated rapidly down the runway and lifted smoothly into the air. Once airborne, Wally marveled at the responsive controls and stability of the aircraft. He banked gently left and right, getting a feel for the plane.

As the A5 climbed, Wally took in views of the countryside stretching to the horizon. He flew east, following the coastline over beaches and wetlands. The A5 handled beautifully, almost like an extension of his own body. Wally executed standard maneuvers with precision, continuously impressed by the aircraft's capabilities.

After an exhilarating hour of flight, Wally returned to the airport for landing. He lined up on final approach, reducing power and descending smoothly. The A5 touched down softly on the runway. Taxiing back to the hangar, Wally wore an ear-to-ear grin, thrilled by the phenomenal flight characteristics of his new airplane. This was just the first of many adventures to come exploring the boundless skies with the ICON A5.

AFTER RETURNING HOME to pickup supplies for his return to Bird Island, Wally slid into the cockpit of his gleaming new ICON A5, running through the preflight checklist with practiced ease. Though only a novice pilot, he felt completely at home behind the controls of the sleek sport plane. The enhancements granted by the microbes flowing through his system gave him an almost preternatural sense of the aircraft and how it would respond to his touch.

After receiving clearance from the tower, Wally taxied the plane to the runway and smoothly applied power. The A5 accelerated rapidly down the tarmac and lifted gracefully into the evening sky. Wally banked the plane gently, relishing the nimble responsiveness of the controls. As the ground dropped away, he felt a swell of exhilaration. This was freedom, adventure, the gateway to protecting all he held dear.

He flew low over the glimmering coastal waters, weaving effortlessly between scattered clouds. The A5 cut through the air with sports-car agility, living up to its reputation for speed and maneuverability. Wally reveled in the plane's performance, already planning future flights to Bird Island and beyond.

As the sun dipped low over the horizon, Wally descended towards Jeff's waterfront home. He lined up for his approach, slowed to just above stall speed, and flared expertly for a picture-perfect landing on the glassy surface of the bay. Taxiing to the private dock, Wally breathed deep, savoring the salt air. Another successful flight under his belt, and a restful night ahead before his flight back to Bird Island in the morning.

WALLY AND JEFF MADE their way to Jeff's favorite burger joint that evening, with Wally still experiencing the effects of the special microorganisms he had consumed earlier. Though the two tried to keep the conversation light, enjoying their juicy burgers and fries, their minds kept drifting back to the dire situation unfolding on Bird Island.

Jack and Harry, the men that Wally and Jeff had trapped in the old bunker, had now been without food and water for almost 3 days. Wally knew the men must be growing desperate, which could make them dangerous and unpredictable. He and Jeff would need to handle the situation carefully when they returned to the island in the morning.

As they finished up their meal, Wally and Jeff began discussing their plan for the next day. They would take Jeff's seaplane out to Bird Island at first light, bringing some supplies like food and water. Though wary of the criminals, their humanity made them unwilling to simply leave Jack and Harry to die in the bunker. It would be a delicate operation, but they hoped they could provide some relief without compromising the bunker's secrets.

He could tell Jeff was troubled by the moral dilemma they faced. But he also knew how important it was to safeguard the powerful discoveries hidden on the island.

WALLY MOVED WITH DELIBERATE focus as the first light of dawn crept over the horizon. Despite the early hour, he was energized and determined, the various microorganisms coursing through his system granting him heightened abilities. In the privacy of his room, he had consumed a precise combination of the bio-augmented cookies and candy bars, each calibrated to a specific dose. Their effects were beginning to take hold.

His vision sharpened, allowing him to discern minute details in the low light. His hearing attuned itself to the subtlest of sounds. His muscles felt primed for any challenge, and his mind was clear and focused. Satisfied with his preparations, Wally donned his backpack and headed out to meet Jeff.

The seasoned pilot had the seaplane loaded and ready for takeoff by the time Wally arrived. Jeff gave him a knowing look but said nothing about Wally's transformed state. The two men had a mission

- to reach the stranded and surely desperate Jack and Harry on Bird Island.

Jeff expertly piloted the light aircraft over the bay as the sun rose, its rays glinting off the calm waters. Wally peered out the window intently, his enhanced vision picking out the island long before Jeff. As they approached, Wally's sharp ears could make out the cries of gulls and lap of waves breaking on the shore.

They landed smoothly in a secluded lagoon and secured the seaplane. Slinging packs loaded with food, water, and medical supplies over their shoulders, Jeff and Wally headed inland toward bunker entrance E3. Wally led the way, his tracking skills allowing him to avoid obstacles and find the clearest path.

At the hidden door, Wally spun the lock with ease, the numbers crystal clear in his mind. With a heave, he hauled the rusted door open, a task that would normally require both men. Peering into the darkness, he knew it was time to face whatever state they would find Jack and Harry in after three days trapped inside. His abilities would help ensure everyone made it out safely.

WALLY MOVED SWIFTLY through the dark corridors of the abandoned bunker, his senses heightened from the microbes he had consumed. Though Jeff struggled to see in the pitch blackness, Wally navigated with ease, guided by his extraordinary hearing.

Faint noises echoed through the passageways - the scurrying of rats' claws against the concrete floor, the slow drip of water seeping through cracks in the ceiling. But as they drew closer to the restricted area, Wally detected other sounds - the low murmur of human voices, the shuffling of feet, the clinking of metal tools against the stubborn door.

He raised his hand, signaling for Jeff to stop. He tilted his head, focusing his enhanced hearing on the trapped men just ahead.

"...gotta get this blasted door open," a gruff voice muttered.

"We tried everything, it won't budge," came the defeated reply.

Wally could detect their ragged breathing and the rumbling of empty stomachs. He sensed their desperation after being confined for days with no way out.

Turning to Jeff, he whispered, "They're still trying to escape, but they're weak. This is our chance to get the upper hand."

Jeff nodded, deferring to Wally's superior senses. They pressed on, prepared to confront the men who had trespassed on the island and threatened its secrets. Wally was ready - with his abilities amplified, he would ensure that the mysteries of this place remained safely hidden.

WALLY STOOD BEFORE the heavy steel door, the effects of the special microbes coursing through his body. His senses were heightened - he could hear the muffled cries of the men trapped behind the door, begging for release. Jeff stood back, hand on his holstered pistol, prepared for whatever may emerge.

"Stand back," Wally cautioned, gripping the rusted pipe wedged across the door handles. With his enhanced strength, he yanked the pipe free and tossed it aside. The door creaked open an inch before jamming again. Wally grabbed the edge and heaved, muscles bulging, forcing the swollen door to scrape open.

Two disheveled men tumbled out onto the floor, coughing and wheezing in the musty air. They were gaunt, with ragged clothes and dirt-smeared faces. One of them - Harry - peered up in confusion, then anger flashed across his face. He leapt at Wally with a guttural cry. Jeff reacted quickly, pistol aimed, stopping him in his tracks.

"Easy now," Jeff warned. Harry froze, then backed away slowly. The other man - Jack - simply sat slumped against the wall, depleted.

Wally was prepared to defend himself, but relaxed when Harry retreated. There was no more fight left in these men. Jeff kept his gun raised as Wally approached with water and food rations. The men gratefully accepted them, their desperation outweighing any remnants of pride.

It was clear they posed no threat in their current state. Wally was relieved; there would be no need for violence today. He nodded to Jeff, a signal to lower his guard. They had neutralized the danger through isolation, not force. Together they would help these broken men, keeping their secrets safe.

TENDING TO THE WEAKENED Harry and Jack, Jeff and Wally offered sustenance in the form of food and water. Despite their initial wariness, the two men, driven by desperation, accepted the assistance provided.

Wally, empowered by microbes, could sense that the fight had gone out of them after being trapped for days in the abandoned bunker. Their anger had faded to resignation and a grudging appreciation for the basic provisions.

Jeff kept a cautious eye on the two as Wally checked them for injuries. Dehydration was the most pressing issue, but they also showed signs of exhaustion and minor scrapes and bruises from their ordeal. Wally was relieved to find they were in reasonably stable condition.

The unlikely foursome sat together in the bunker, the tension slowly dissipating. Harry and Jack ate and drank silently at first, wary of their rescuers. But as their strength returned, tentative conversation began, focusing on the practicalities of getting them off the island.

Jeff made it clear that they would only assist in leaving safely and insisted no more trespassing would be tolerated. Harry and Jack reluctantly agreed, too worn out to consider anything beyond a hot meal and a way home.

Wally reflected that a cycle of conflict seemed to be ending. Perhaps they could depart in peace, with the island's secrets protected. There was still much to resolve, but the immediate danger had passed. For now, the priority was regaining enough strength to leave Bird Island behind.

WALLY, UNDER THE INFLUENCE of the microbes, watched carefully as Harry and Jack eagerly consumed the provisions he and Jeff had brought them. The men were clearly weakened and desperate after being trapped in the bunker for days without food or water.

Once they had their fill and rested briefly to regain some strength, Wally asked Harry bluntly, "Did someone send you here?" Harry shook his head, avoiding Wally's intense gaze.

He pressed further, "Why are you here then?" Harry mumbled something vague about treasure hunting. Wally was unconvinced but didn't push further.

He turned to Jeff and said firmly, "Watch him closely, take no chances." Jeff nodded, keeping his hand near his holstered pistol.

Wally then easily picked up Jack, who was barely conscious and carried him outside. After ensuring no one was watching, he planted a small tracking device inside Jack's boot and another on the outboard motor of their skiff anchored on the western shore.

He gently placed Jack down in the skiff and returned to the bunker for Harry and Jeff. With no effort at all, he slung the bulky

Harry over his shoulder and carried him out. Jeff followed closely behind.

At the skiff, Wally deposited Harry next to where Jack sat slumped. He then stared intensely at both men and said in a low, threatening tone, "Don't come back here again." The weakened men nodded silently, understanding the seriousness of his warning.

Wally and Jeff then turned and headed back into the island's dense foliage, confident that the tracking devices would alert them if the men returned against his orders.

WALLY STOOD ON THE shore of Bird Island, feeling the effects of the microbe-enhanced treats he had consumed. His senses were heightened - he could see farther, hear more acutely, and move with unmatched speed and dexterity. Beside him, Jeff waited patiently, unaware of the extraordinary transformation his young friend had undergone.

"Let's head back," Wally said, his voice brimming with energy. Jeff nodded in agreement. They made their way through the brush to where Jeff's seaplane was anchored just offshore. With Jeff at the controls, they were soon soaring over the glistening waters of the bay, the island shrinking below them.

After landing smoothly at Jeff's homestead, Wally turned to his companion. "We should double-check that Jack and Harry left. Let's take my new plane this time - you can fly it." Jeff's eyes lit up at the offer.

Soon they were cruising over the bay in Wally's slick new ICON A5, Jeff marveling at the responsiveness of the controls. Wally scanned the island below, his enhanced vision piercing its forests and shorelines for any sign of the nefarious men. But the island appeared deserted, only birds and small creatures disturbing its tranquility.

Satisfied that their adversaries were gone, Jeff banked the plane gracefully back towards home. He glanced over at Wally with a smile. "She handles like a dream!" Wally nodded, keeping his transformation secret as the shores of the mainland came into view. The island's secrets would remain protected for now thanks to his augmented abilities, though Wally knew vigilance would be needed to keep hidden what he had discovered in that mysterious bunker.

AS THE SLEEK WHITE ICON A5 seaplane glided smoothly across the water's surface, veteran pilot Jeff executed a flawless landing alongside his dock. The ease and precision of his maneuvers reflected decades of aviation experience. As the plane drifted to a gentle stop, Jeff cut the engine and turned to his passenger, Wally, with a satisfied smile.

"Nice flying, Jeff. Couldn't have done it better myself," Wally said appreciatively as he unbuckled his harness.

Jeff waved off the compliment. "It's a pleasure to take this beauty out for a spin. She handles like a dream."

The two friends climbed out onto the weathered wooden dock. Wally firmly grasped Jeff's hand and shook it. "Thanks again for everything you've done to help protect the island," he said sincerely, thinking of their recent efforts uncovering secrets and fending off intruders.

In an uncharacteristic display of emotion, Wally suddenly pulled Jeff into a big bear hug. Jeff patted Wally's back in surprise but soon returned the heartfelt embrace.

After the brief but poignant moment, Wally stepped back abruptly. Without another word, he turned, hopped back into the pilot's seat of the seaplane, and started the engine. Jeff watched as his young friend piloted the A5 away from the dock and taxied across the bay, swiftly gaining speed and lifting off into the clear blue sky. Wally was heading home, no doubt to immerse himself in work.

Jeff stood alone on the dock for a while, pondering the future adventures he and Wally would share protecting the mysteries of Bird Island. The memories of dangers faced and secrets uncovered bound them together. Jeff knew their mission was far from over.

WALLY LANDED HIS SLEEK white and blue ICON A5 at the local airport, taxiing smoothly to his newly rented hangar. The flight had gone flawlessly, as Wally was finding piloting the responsive aircraft came naturally to him. As he rolled the plane into the hangar, he took a moment to tidy up and do a quick post-flight inspection.

Climbing down from the cockpit, Wally took in a deep breath of the crisp evening air. It was good to be back home after his recent adventures. He slid open the door of his new Hyundai Santa Fe and tossed his bag inside, then paused to admire his plane one last time before closing up the hangar.

Friday night bowling with his buddies Richie and Pug was a standing tradition, and Wally was looking forward to catching up with them. He pulled out his phone and dialed Richie as he started up the SUV.

"Hey man, just got back into town. Still up for bowling tonight?" Wally asked after Richie picked up. The conversation was brief but enthusiastic on both ends. They made plans to meet up at the alley in an hour.

Wally grinned as he ended the call, pulling out of the airport parking lot. It would be great to bowl a few games and swap stories with his friends, especially after all his recent solitary adventures. He cruised along the familiar roads leading home, windows down, relaxing into the seat. Life was good.

Chapter 16
Strikes, Spares, and Secrets

Wally entered the bowling alley, feeling the effects of the microbe-laced treat he had consumed earlier. Though his senses were heightened, he knew he had to restrain his abilities to avoid arousing suspicion from his friends Pug and Richie.

As they laced up their bowling shoes, Wally felt a pang of nostalgia for their carefree younger days. He cherished these rare moments when they could get together, free from adult responsibilities.

The friends took their places at the lane. Wally took a breath and bowled a mediocre first frame, holding back his enhanced strength and coordination. Pug ribbed him good-naturedly as he stepped up to bowl.

Over chili cheese fries and cokes, the conversation flowed freely. For a moment, it felt just like old times hanging out as kids without a care in the world. Wally wished he could stay suspended in this feeling forever, but he knew it was only temporary.

The microbe was wearing off now. Wally bowled a turkey in the next frame before deliberately throwing a gutter ball, trying to avoid arousing suspicion. He laughed off his "bad" throw while Pug celebrated his spare.

As the evening wound down, Wally felt a twinge of melancholy. He cherished these precious moments with his oldest friends, but he knew that he could never again be as carefree as they were. His secret responsibilities weighed heavily upon him.

Wally gave Pug and Richie each a brotherly hug before they parted ways in the parking lot. He promised he'd try to get together again soon, though he knew such reunions would be few and far between now.

Driving home in the darkness, Wally's thoughts turned to Bird Island. He was committed to protecting its secrets, but sometimes he wondered - at what cost? Keeping secrets from Pug and Richie pained him. He longed to unburden himself, yet he knew the dangers of disclosure.

He felt the weight of this solitary mission. At times, the isolation was almost too much to bear. But then he thought of Jeff and Old Man Barnes, his new comrades-in-arms. At least he didn't have to shoulder the entire burden alone.

Pulling into his driveway, Wally regarded his modest house. So different from his carefree childhood home. As an adult, the responsibilities of bills and mortgage payments now fell squarely on his shoulders. How he sometimes longed for the simple comforts of home.

Yet he also felt immense pride in his accomplishments. His successful business, his planes, his licenses and ratings...all achieved with his abilities. Though the microbes unlocked his potential, the work was his own. He had proven his self-reliance.

As he prepared for bed, his mind turned again to the future. Would Bird Island consume his life indefinitely? Or could there come a day when he would pass the torch, no longer bound to this secret crusade?

He did not yet have an answer. For now, the island's defense still required his singular abilities. Until another guardian could rise, he must remain vigilant. This was his purpose, his cross to bear.

Wally fell into a fitful sleep, his dreams filled with visions of seaplanes, bunkers, and friends long gone. Though tinged with melancholy, he awoke with steely resolve. Whatever challenges lay ahead for the island's guardian, he would face them without hesitation. The microbes chose him, and he would not fail in his charge.

WALLY RETURNED HOME after spending the evening bowling with his friends. It was a little after 9 PM when he sat down at his computer and decided to check the tracking device he had discreetly placed on Jack Sparrow before leaving Bird Island.

Accessing the data on his phone, Wally observed that the beacon was emitting a steady signal from the southeast end of the island, near the location of the old military bunker. This indicated that Jack was likely still exploring the bunker's secrets, unaware that Wally was monitoring his movements.

Shifting his gaze to the signal from the tracking device on Jack's skiff, Wally noted that the boat was still anchored just off the island's shoreline, swaying gently in the water. It seemed Jack had not ventured far after initially landing on the island, with his skiff awaiting his return in the shallow bay.

He contemplated these facts, his keen intellect piecing together the clues. For now, Jack remained occupied with the island while his boat stood ready for a quick escape. But Wally knew he and Jack were not the only ones interested in uncovering Bird Island's hidden troves. Their next encounter was unlikely to be friendly.

As he tracked his adversary's movements, Wally considered his next steps. Jack's continued presence on the island posed a threat that would need to be addressed. Wally realized his mission to protect the island's secrets would soon lead to another tense confrontation with Jack, and most likely his partner Harry as well.

WITH A FIRM GRIP ON his backpack, Wally rifled through its contents until he found the cookies. Each one held a different kind of microorganism, except for the violet one. That was special and reserved for later. One by one, he devoured the treats, his taste buds dancing at the sugary sweetness. With each bite, the promise of augmented abilities thrummed in his veins.

His gear was soon packed, and stowed away in neat compartments within his bag. With one last look at his surroundings, he locked his door and set off for the local airport. The early morning darkness shrouded the town in quiet serenity as Wally navigated the empty streets.

At the hangar, his A5 sat gleaming under the overhead lights. He climbed aboard, relishing in the familiar feel of the controls beneath his fingertips. His heart pounded with excitement and a touch of fear as he powered up the aircraft. Before long, the A5 was soaring through the predawn sky, leaving behind a sleeping world oblivious to its secrets.

The lights of Chinquapin twinkled in the distance like far-off stars as Wally dialed Jeff's number. His voice echoed in the quiet cabin as he explained his predicament. The last words that left his lips were etched with an underlying tension that mirrored his worried thoughts: "If you don't hear from me by 10 this morning, please come and find me." The call ended with a click, leaving Wally alone with the humming of his aircraft and his thoughts as he neared Bird Island.

WALLY WAS UNDER THE influence of the microorganisms he had consumed, granting him enhanced abilities as he embarked on his solo mission to Bird Island. With his vision augmented, he quickly located Jack's skiff close to shore on the southeast end of the island. Moving with precision and speed, he climbed aboard and made another small cut in the fuel line next to the fuel tank, knowing the electric fuel pump would only cause a leak if the boat was underway.

Wally then planted a flashbang grenade with a timer and set it to detonate in two hours. He wanted a distraction to draw out anyone inside the bunker. Opening his backpack, he extracted a violet-colored cookie laced with the microorganism AXI-218 and swiftly ate it. As the cookie took effect, his hearing became incredibly sensitive, allowing him to detect even minute sounds from a great distance.

Empowered by his enhanced senses, Wally walked directly to bunker entrance E3 and pressed his ear against the weathered steel door. He filtered through the cacophony of ambient island noises, focusing his hearing into the bunker's depths. Muffled voices echoed from deep within, too indistinct to ascertain exact words or numbers. But the hushed tones hinted at secrecy and stealth, putting Wally on high alert. Gripped with a sense of urgency, he began surveying the area for signs of recent activity, intent on uncovering who or what lay inside the bunker's ominous confines. Wally was determined to protect the island's secrets at any cost.

IN THE DEEP RECESSES of his mind, Wally dredged up the image of the bunker near his Wallylab, a haphazard cache of supplies stored within its concrete belly. His eyes, previously consumed by the dense undergrowth of Bird Island, now flickered with renewed determination. The idea sparked in his mind, a plan unfolding like a meticulously designed blueprint.

With a decisive stride, Wally disappeared into the bunker's gaping maw. He moved with the ease of familiarity, his hands rifling through piles of forgotten materials with a focused intensity. Rusty coils of wire, sturdy planks, long forgotten spikes – the detritus of the bunker was a treasure trove for his plan.

Emerging from the bunker's shadowy confines, he began to assemble his traps. Each was a feat of practical ingenuity: three lengthy spikes serving as firm anchors in the soft island soil, an attached tripwire primed to release a potent spring-loaded arm. This arm was designed to swing with merciless precision upon activation, ready to ensnare an unsuspecting trespasser.

His traps were no mere snares or pits; they were silent sentinels armed with force and precision. Upon activation, they would lash out at knee height, swift and relentless as a striking snake. They were designed not to kill but incapacitate - an unseen guard against intruders on his island fortress.

Wally worked tirelessly under the indifferent island sun, constructing seven of these silent protectors. Each one he nestled into likely footpaths and thoroughfares around the bunker, their presence as unassuming as any other part of the wild landscape.

As he positioned the final trap in alignment with the distant skiff anchored offshore, Wally wiped beads of sweat from his brow. Forty-five minutes had passed since he embarked on this defensive mission - forty-five minutes that may very well safeguard Bird Island's secrets from unwelcome prying eyes.

WALLY MOVED THROUGH the abandoned bunker with heightened senses, recalling his earlier discovery of a cache of military smoke bombs stored away in a forgotten locker. He swiftly navigated the winding corridors until he reached the small storage room. Crouching down, Wally opened the metal locker and gathered up as many of the old smoke bombs as he could carry. Their once bright color had faded after decades left untouched in the darkness, but Wally was certain they could still serve their intended purpose.

With his cargo of smoke bombs secured, Wally focused his enhanced hearing and tracked the muffled voices of the intruders, Jack and Harry. Moving silently through the bunker, he tracked them to the north corridor, only fifty yards from the exit they desperately sought. Wally carefully set the smoke bombs on the floor, pulling their pins in rapid succession as he retreated back down the hall.

Thick plumes of colored smoke soon billowed through the passageway, obscuring Jack and Harry's vision and choking the confined air. Coughing and blinded, the panicked men stumbled in the haze, unable to find their way out. Seizing the opportunity, Wally rushed past them, gathering up their electric lanterns and flashlights. Now without light or visibility, Jack and Harry were left disoriented and helpless in the smoke-filled tunnel. Wally secured their only light sources, leaving the intruders trapped in darkness and buying himself time to decide their fate.

AS WALLY REENTERS THE bunker, the heavy door shuts with a resonant thud, echoing through the musty air. He leans against the cool metal, and the sound slowly fades, surrendering to the subterranean silence. Standing still, he tunes his ears to the environment, heightened senses provided by the microorganisms coursing through his body.

In the distance, he hears the suppressed coughing of Jack and Harry as they struggle to clear their lungs of the irritating smoke residue. Their raspy breaths grow steadier but retain a trace of distress. Shuffling feet scrape over concrete, the slow, weary steps of men navigating in pitch darkness, searching for any hint of an exit or illumination.

Suddenly, a soft clink—a sound of metal hitting the concrete floor—suggests a fruitless search through pockets for any lost equipment that may provide light. The clinking gives way to subdued murmurs of frustration. Wally detects the edge of fear in their voices as they communicate in hushed tones, likely speculating about their next move or the possibility of rescue.

A faint echo from further within the bunker hints at its hollow expanses—distant drips of water from condensation hint at the bunker's age and the relentless nature of time.

With no sounds of immediate escape efforts, Wally understands that Jack and Harry remain disoriented. Their attempts at navigation have likely brought them in circles, reinforcing their trap. Wally's keen senses allow him to feel the vibrations of their movements through the concrete floor, painting a silent picture of their confusion.

In the quietude, Wally's internal debate about their fate consumes him for a moment. Then, he shakes away the introspection, focusing once more on the auditory clues surrounding him, prepared to act on the responsibility his secret knowledge demands.

WALLY MOVED CLOSER to the disoriented men, Jack and Harry, who were coughing and stumbling blindly in the darkness of the abandoned bunker. Under the influence of special microorganisms that enhanced his senses, Wally could keenly perceive the men's distress and confusion as they fruitlessly searched for a way out or source of light.

Stepping out of the main walkway to ensure his safety, Wally said in a loud, stern voice, "I told you not to come back or you would regret it." His warning echoed through the bunker.

Wally then tossed a piece of trash across the room, the sudden sound startling Jack and Harry, who jumped in surprise. "Who's there?" Jack called out nervously into the darkness. Harry whispered harshly for Jack to be quiet. Both men tensed, listening intently for any further sounds that might reveal who had spoken and startled them.

AS HARRY AND JACK STUMBLED blindly through the dark tunnels of the abandoned bunker, their desperation growing with each turn, a silent observer watched their every move. Wally blended into the shadows, tracking the two men effortlessly with his enhanced senses granted by the microbes he had consumed. He noted their ragged breathing and faltering footsteps as they grappled with walls, disoriented without the flashlights and lanterns he had confiscated.

Wally contemplated his next actions carefully. While he felt no malice towards the misguided intruders, he knew the secrets hidden on this island were too valuable to risk falling into the wrong hands. He considered the possibilities ahead - whether to reveal himself and confront the men directly, continue covertly manipulating the environment around them, or take more drastic measures to neutralize the threat entirely. For now, he decided maintaining the upper hand from the shadows was the wisest course.

As Jack and Harry's whispers took on a more panicked edge, Wally soundlessly circled around them, observing every detail. He tracked their movements and listened to their fruitless planning. When he sensed an opportunity, Wally intentionally scraped a metal pipe along the concrete wall, sending an eerie shriek echoing down the passageway. The men startled violently at the sudden noise.

"What the hell was that?" Jack gasped, holding his chest.

Harry's wide eyes darted around the darkness. "This place is haunted or something, man. We need to get out of here!"

Wally remained out of sight, weighing his next actions. He had no intention of allowing these trespassers to uncover the bunker's secrets. But he was also reluctant to inflict harm without necessity. For now, it seemed his ghostly manipulations were sufficient to deter their mission. He would continue strategically influencing their environment - a cacophony of mysterious noises, moving objects, and unseen eyes tracking their every turn. Whatever it took to protect this island and its hidden knowledge.

As the men stumbled ahead, Wally soundlessly pursued, merging with the darkness. His enhanced senses guided him flawlessly through the maze of corridors. He was determined to steer the intruders away from danger and defend the bunker's secrets - one carefully calculated unseen maneuver at a time.

HE STOOD SILENTLY IN the shadows of the abandoned bunker, observing Jack and Harry as they stumbled around in the pitch darkness. His enhanced senses, granted by the special microbes he had consumed, allowed him to see and hear everything with perfect clarity, despite the lack of light. Jack coughed and wiped his eyes, still irritated by the smoke bomb Wally had used earlier to disorient them.

"I can't see a damn thing," Jack grumbled. "We need to find a way out of here."

Harry leaned against the cold concrete wall, trying to get his bearings. "Yeah, if we can just get back to the entrance, we can make a run for the boat."

Wally smiled to himself, knowing that their boat was now out of commission thanks to the sabotage he had done earlier. Still, he decided to stay silent and continue observing for now.

The two men started feeling their way along the walls, hands outstretched in front of them. Wally followed stealthily behind, able to see every movement and expression. After several minutes of aimless wandering, Harry let out a frustrated sigh.

"This is useless, we're just going in circles. We need some kind of light."

Jack paused, considering their options. "Maybe there's something left behind we can use. Let's check the rooms ahead."

As the men resumed their slow, blind search, Wally contemplated his next move. He could easily capture them now in their vulnerable state. But he hesitated, not wanting to reveal his enhanced abilities. Plus, a small part of him felt sympathy for their plight. He decided to wait it out a bit longer and simply keep monitoring them for now. There would be plenty of time to act, with the bunker's secrets secured. For the moment, he was content just to watch and listen from the shadows.

WALLY MOVED SILENTLY through the dark corridors of the abandoned bunker, his senses heightened by the microbes he had consumed earlier. He trailed behind Jack and Harry at a distance as they stumbled blindly ahead, disoriented by the smoke bomb he had set off.

Though initially tempted to confront the men directly, Wally reconsidered. He knew he had to get them off the island without revealing his augmented abilities. With care, he began subtly herding them toward the bunker's entrance nearest their sabotaged skiff by scraping the wall behind them with a piece of metal, creating an unsettling sound that urged them forward.

When the men reacted by moving in the desired direction, Wally would wait and then repeat the noise further ahead once they started to veer off course. In this cautious manner, he steadily funneled them toward the exit. As they approached the door, Wally dropped back, not wanting to be seen when it opened.

Finally reaching the exit, Jack and Harry scrambled to get out, coughing and gasping for fresh air. Temporarily blinded by the sunlight, they stumbled toward the sound of lapping waves, desperate to locate their boat and escape the island. Just as Wally had intended, the men hurried directly to their sabotaged skiff, unaware it could no longer carry them away from the secrets they had been so close to discovering.

JACK AND HARRY, COUGHING and disheveled from their harrowing experience in the smoke-filled bunker, staggered through the exit and into the blinding daylight. Blinking furiously as their eyes adjusted, they leaned on each other for support, their legs shaky from disorientation and fear. Their only thought: to make a swift retreat from the accursed island that had been nothing but a source of dread and confusion.

Guided by the rhythmic sound of water kissing the shore, they stumbled towards the familiar comfort of their skiff, their urgency fuelled by their desperation to leave Bird Island and its hidden terrors behind. A gritty mix of salt and sand crunched under their heavy boots as they trod the short distance to where they remembered mooring their vessel.

The sun beat down on their backs, a stark contrast to the dank chill of the underground labyrinth they had just navigated. They arrived at the shoreline, blinking against the glare off the water, and beheld their skiff swaying idly with the gentle push of the tide against the shore.

Without pause, Harry leapt into the boat, eager to put the island behind him, while Jack secured their meager belongings. Their hands fumbled over the motor, their eagerness growing as they anticipated the soothing hum of the engine. However, as they tried to start it, their growing anxiety turned to dread. The engine coughed and sputtered but would not catch — the skiff, which had been their lifeline, was effectively dead in the water.

Their escape from Bird Island had been thwarted, leaving them stranded, with the ominous sensation that the island was not done with them yet. Harry, with a scowl darkening his face looked at Jack, his eyes reflecting a mixture of fear and anger, as if questioning what more misfortunes awaited them amidst the unknown shadows cast by the treacherous marshland.

WALLY WATCHED FROM a distance as Jack and Harry emerged from the foliage onto the small beach where their skiff was anchored. Even from afar, he could sense their fatigue and desperation. They had clearly been through an ordeal since he last saw them in the bunker.

Jack slumped down in the sand next to the boat while Harry examined the outboard motor. After several minutes of futile tinkering, Harry let out a frustrated yell and kicked the side of the boat. It was clear the engine was not going to start. Defeated, the two men sat in silence on the beach, contemplating their next move.

Eventually, Harry stood up and started pacing up and down the shoreline. "We need to go back and find our gear," he said to Jack. "We're almost out of water. We won't last long without supplies."

Jack shook his head. "No. I'm done, Harry. That place is a death trap. I'm not going back in there again."

Harry's face contorted in anger. He stormed over to Jack and grabbed him by the shirt. "We don't have a choice!" he shouted. "We'll die out here if we don't get food and water!"

Jack shoved him away. "I don't care. Do what you want, but I'm staying right here."

Harry glared at him for a moment, then turned and started marching angrily into the trees. "Useless coward," he muttered over his shoulder.

Wally observed all this from his hidden vantage point. He was conflicted. On the one hand, he wanted these trespassers off the island and unable to access its secrets. But he also didn't wish them harm. As Harry disappeared from view, Wally contemplated his next move. He would have to act soon before the situation escalated further.

HE MOVED SWIFTLY AND silently through the brush, his senses heightened by the special microbes coursing through his system. Despite the darkness, he could see Harry's outline clearly as the man blundered ahead with his makeshift torch. Wally's eyes narrowed as he saw Harry making a beeline for the bunker's E3 entrance.

With his enhanced speed and agility, Wally raced ahead and slipped inside the concrete doorway seconds before Harry arrived. He pulled the heavy steel door shut behind him with a resounding clang that echoed through the empty corridors. Wally grabbed a sturdy metal rod leaning against the wall and wedged it horizontally through the door handle, barring the entrance from outside access.

Satisfied his work was done, Wally exited through a smaller side door leading out the back of the bunker. This hidden exit, marked only with a small "S1" sign, was an old service entrance once used for supplies and maintenance crews. Wally latched it securely and stole away into the brush, circling around to keep an eye on the main entrance.

He took up a concealed position in a stand of cordgrass, watching as Harry arrived moments later. The man's frustration was evident even in the dim firelight as he grasped the handle and heaved with all his strength, cursing when the door wouldn't budge. Harry slammed his fists against the steel in anger, then began scanning the area as if searching for another way in.

Wally remained perfectly still, tracking Harry's every move from the shadows. Though curious about what the man's next steps might be, his priority was defending the bunker and its secrets. For now, the entrance was secure, and he intended to keep it that way.

HE CREPT SILENTLY THROUGH the foliage, following Harry's movements as the man circled the island alone. Though disoriented and exhausted, Harry persisted in his search for resources, driven by desperation.

Wally tracked him carefully, camouflaged in the brush. He knew it was only a matter of time before one of the traps he had set was triggered. Wally had planted them strategically along the island's paths for this very purpose - to stop unwanted visitors without causing permanent harm.

Sure enough, Harry's foot snagged a nearly invisible tripwire strung between two trees. Before he could react, a spring-loaded arm swung out in a wide arc, catching him solidly just below the left knee.

The impact swept Harry's legs out from under him and he crashed to the ground with a shout of pain.

Wally could tell immediately from the unnatural angle of Harry's lower leg that his kneecap had been dislocated. Harry lay writhing in agony, gripping his leg as he stared around wildly trying to comprehend what had happened.

Wally watched impassively, the slightest hint of regret flickering across his face. The trap had served its purpose, incapacitating the intruder, but Wally took no pleasure in the man's suffering. He only wanted to protect the island and its secrets - and sometimes that required difficult measures.

Chapter 17
Trapped by Choices

He approached Jack, who was seated on a fallen log near the shoreline, staring blankly at the broken-down skiff. From his vantage point, Jack seemed less confrontational than Harry, more bewildered by the whole situation. Taking a deep breath to steady his nerves and ready himself for the potential volatility of the conversation, Wally stepped out from the cover of the trees.

"Jack," Wally began, his tone firm but non-threatening, "I know you're not here for the wildlife."

Jack's head snapped up, surprise flashing across his features as he registered Wally's presence. Wally noted the defensive posture and the flash of fear in Jack's eyes, confirming that the man felt out of his depth.

"You look like a man who's had better days," Wally continued, careful to keep his body language neutral. "I'm not here to make things worse for you, but you and Harry came to this island uninvited. I need to know why."

Jack's gaze flickered, torn between wariness and the allure of someone willing to listen. He let out a heavy sigh, the braggadocios facade slipping as he weighed his limited options.

"We were looking for something, alright," Jack admitted grudgingly. "Harry heard rumors about military secrets, stuff left over from the war. They said treasures were buried on Bird Island... and where there's treasure," Jack shrugged, a half-smile playing on his lips, "there's coin to be had."

Wally nodded, taking a cautious step closer. Jack didn't flinch, which Wally took as a good sign.

"Harry thinks all that's worth risking his life for," Wally observed, the hint of an offer in his voice. "Do you?"

Jack's eyes met Wally's. The desperation and hunger for an escape from the recent turn of events shone clear as day. "After what just happened? No treasure is worth being left stranded or worse," Jack confessed, glancing in the direction Harry had gone. "I'm just looking to get out of here in one piece, man."

"That's reasonable," Wally acknowledged. "Help me understand more about what brought you here, and maybe I can help you get off this island."

Jack hesitated for a moment, chewing on his lower lip, then exhaled in resignation. "It was all Harry's plan. Heard from some shifty character at the docks. Mentioned a bunker full of expensive tech, old documents and such. I was just along for the ride... and the payday."

"So, no specific location or item you were looking for?" Wally pressed gently.

"Just wild goose talks," Jack muttered. "Some old military experiment stuff, hidden away from prying eyes. I thought it was a fool's errand from the start."

"You don't strike me as a fool, Jack," Wally said, offering a sincere smile. "Cooperate with me, and I'll see you're taken care of."

Jack looked at Wally, the hard edge of a man used to life's knocks softening. "I got no love for Harry or this island," he said. "You get me out of here, and you won't see me again."

Wally held Jack's gaze, searching for any hint of deceit. Finding none, he nodded slowly. "Alright, stay put. I'll be back for you soon. Try to keep out of trouble until then."

As Wally turned to leave, Jack called out, his voice tinged with genuine relief. "Hey, thanks."

Wally raised his hand in acknowledgment and disappeared back into the trees, his mind already calculating the next steps in this precarious dance of wits and survival.

WALLY APPROACHED HARRY with caution, aware of the man's reputation for being ruthless and devoid of any moral scruples. Harry sat on a cluster of rocks, cradling his injured knee, his face creased with pain but also hardened by anger and frustration.

He cleared his throat to announce his presence. "Harry, we need to talk."

Harry glared up at Wally with a mixture of shock and indignation. "You! What kind of sick game are you playing on this cursed island, huh?" Harry spat out with venom.

Ignoring the provocation, Wally replied evenly, "I'm not playing games. You're the one who came here looking for something. Tell me what you're after."

The mention of a motive seemed to shift Harry's focus from his pain to his drive. "What's it to ya?" snarled Harry. "If I knew the trouble this place would cause, I'd have stayed clear. But information has its price, and I was told there'd be valuables, things to set me up for life."

Wally observed Harry's mixture of greed and desperation—the curl of his lip as he spoke of 'valuables' and the grit in his eyes from the promise of wealth. "Valuables can mean many things. Documents? Artifacts?" Wally probed, trying to keep the conversation grounded.

Harry's gaze faltered, and he shifted, wincing as he moved his bad leg. "Military stuff, classified things. Everyone knows there's unused bunkers here with leftovers from World War II." Harry's tone had an edge of caution to it, as if fearing he had said too much.

"I can help you get off this island," Wally offered, noting Harry's momentary lapse in hostility.

"And why would you do that?" Harry asked suspiciously.

"Because," Wally said, taking a step forward, which caused Harry to stiffen, "continuing this back and forth isn't going to end well for either of us. You give me your word that you'll leave for good, and I'll make sure you make it back to the mainland safely."

Harry looked at Wally, a calculating glint in his eye. "My word?" he sneered. "Sure, you'll get my word. But first, how do I know you're not gonna tie me up and leave me for the coyotes?"

There was a silence as Wally contemplated his options. Finally, he spoke, "I'm not out to hurt you, Harry. I'm protecting this island. If that means getting you safely away from it, then so be it."

Harry weighed Wally's words, searching for a sign of duplicity. Eventually, with a deep, pained sigh, he nodded. "Alright, you've got a deal." Harry extended his hand, grimacing from the physical pain and the pain of his bruised ego.

Wally accepted the handshake, knowing that trust was far from established but that a temporary truce had been brokered. "Rest up," he said. "I'll be back to check on you soon."

Turning away from the injured man, Wally retraced his steps through the dense undergrowth, pondering the fragile alliance and preparing for any outcome, fully aware that men like Harry were unpredictable at best.

WALLY MOVED SILENTLY through the dark corridors of the bunker, his senses heightened by the microbes flowing through his system. He had offered to help Harry leave the island in exchange for his word to never return. But Wally knew better than to trust the ruthless man's promise.

Earlier, when disabling Harry, Wally had retrieved the pistol that Harry carried, unloading it and sticking it into his own jacket pocket for safekeeping. Now, as he went to check on the injured Harry, Wally deliberately turned in such a way that caused the pistol to slip out of his pocket, falling to the ground next to where Harry sat propped up against a rock.

He paused, watching. He was curious what Harry would do when presented with the opportunity.

Harry's eyes widened as the pistol clattered on the hard floor near him. Ignoring the pain in his injured leg, he lunged for the weapon with unexpected speed and aggression. Gripping the pistol in both hands, Harry swiveled the barrel towards Wally, his face contorting in anger.

"Don't move, or I'll shoot!" Harry bellowed. Wally stood motionless, having expected this reaction. Harry's heavy breathing echoed in the empty space as his eyes darted around, looking for an escape route while keeping the pistol aimed at Wally's chest.

He stayed calm, realizing Harry did not know the pistol was unloaded. He planned to use Harry's assumption to maintain control of the situation, waiting for the right moment to reveal the uselessness of Harry's confiscated weapon.

HARRY, STILL REELING from the sudden and forceful turn of events, feels a rush of adrenaline as Wally snatches the pistol from his grip with ease. Before he can process what's happening, he's hoisted up and slung over Wally's shoulder, his world tilting vertiginously. Every jostle sends shots of pain radiating from his injured leg, and panic sets in as he's carried deeper into the bowels of the bunker.

The air grows colder and the echo of their footsteps against the concrete merges with Harry's labored breathing. The darkness envelops him; it's a suffocating blanket, devoid of light, robbing him of his sense of time and place. Desperation laces his thoughts as he's unceremoniously tossed over a storage unit in what feels like an abandoned part of the bunker.

Landing hard, Harry grapples with the realization of his confinement. Isolation presses in on him, punctuated only by Wally's chilling words about the multiple entrances—of which only one offers the faintest hope of escape. His mind races, flipping between the urgency to escape and the hopeless understanding of his physical limitations.

With Wally's departure, Harry is left with a growing fear, wrestling with the mental torment of his situation. Confusion about which entrance might be his way out gives way to despair, as he contemplates the maddening possibility of choosing wrong and wasting what little strength he has left. Hunger and thirst loom as future adversaries, but for now, his greatest struggle is with the debilitating uncertainty and dread that comes with being utterly alone in the dark, encased within the silent, impenetrable walls of the bunker.

WALLY, HIS SENSES KEENLY alert, paused at the brink of the bunker's threshold, the one that remained defiantly unlocked amidst the myriad passageways and protected entries within the concrete labyrinth. He harbored six flashbangs—loud, blinding devices designed to disorient. These he methodically set, arming each with a timer meticulously calculated to detonate 12 hours apart, beginning precisely 12 hours from the moment he synced their mechanisms.

The first device, he placed at his feet, just inside the entrance. He advanced a few paces towards the second location, placing the flashbang with equal precision. He repeated this action four more times, each placement deliberate, the positioning strategic throughout the corridor leading inwards.

These beacon-like explosions, he hoped, would serve as auditory and visual lighthouses for Harry, should he find himself ensnared in the bunker's shadowy embrace. With each set to erupt in a sequence spanning up to three days, they were Wally's attempt to slice through the darkness with intervals of light and sound, offering Harry, if luck was on his side, a thread of guidance to sustain him through 72 potential hours of isolation. Once his task was complete, Wally withdrew, the steel door to the bunker silently observing his departure into the island's wilderness.

THE MIDDAY SUN CAST long, dancing shadows across Bird Island as Wally, his senses sharpened by the influence of the microorganisms, made his way back to the beach. Jack was still there, a solitary figure slumped beside the broken-down skiff. The air hung heavy with the salt of the sea and a faint sense of trepidation.

"Wally!" Jack's voice carried across the sand, relief bleeding into his tone. "Where's Harry?"

He shrugged, his gaze steady on Jack. "He's taken a shine to the bunker. Decided to stay awhile longer."

Jack's eyes widened, but he didn't argue. Wally extended a hand to Jack, helping him to his feet. He was light, almost frail under Wally's firm grip. With an arm around Jack for support, they made their way to the skiff. Wally helped Jack board with practiced ease before turning his attention to the anchor.

It was heavy in his hands but felt weightless under his enhanced strength. He lifted it effortlessly and dropped it into storage with a satisfying thud that echoed through the silence.

Leaving Jack on board, Wally pushed the skiff away from shore. His feet sunk into the soft sand as he walked it out into the water until it was free floating. He pointed it south, letting it catch the gentle sea breeze that began to pick up.

"The wind will push you across the bay to land," he said, turning back to look at Jack who sat quietly in the skiff. "You should be there by dark."

Jack nodded slowly, accepting Wally's instructions without protest. Wally continued, "On board, you'll find a gallon of water. Once you hit land, walk east... it's about a three-hour walk to find help."

Wally paused for a moment before adding in a stern voice that brooked no argument, "Don't come back. Don't wait for Harry."

And with that, he turned away from the skiff, leaving Jack to his journey and the promise of a long walk ahead. The sun began its descent, casting long shadows across the beach as Wally disappeared into the island's wilderness, leaving behind only footprints in the sand.

WALLY STOOD AT THE edge of the island, looking out over the calm bay waters as he dialed Jeff's number.

"Hey Jeff, it's Wally. Just wanted to give you an update on the situation here," he said into the phone. He went on to describe finding Jack and Harry, trapping them in the bunker, and how he had ultimately set Jack free while leaving Harry behind.

"I'm going to head home for now to get some work done, but I'll be back in a couple days to check on Harry and make sure he's still contained. I left some of the traps set around the island for now as a precaution."

After finishing his call with Jeff, Wally did one last sweep of the perimeter before climbing into his sleek ICON A5 aircraft. He went through his preflight checklist methodically, still feeling the lingering effects of the microbe-enhanced cookies he had consumed earlier. Soon he was lifting off from the island's shoreline, pointing the nose of the plane homeward.

As he gained altitude, Wally glanced back at the island retreating into the distance. He was beginning to feel the fatigue setting in from the exertion of the past days. He looked forward to being back home again, resting and catching up on work. The mysteries of Bird Island still called to him, but for now, it was time for a brief respite. He settled in for the flight home, content with how he had handled the latest threat to the island's secrets. There would be time later to unravel more of its hidden truths.

WALLY WOKE LONG BEFORE daybreak, knowing it would be hard to focus on Bake-RiteZ today. His thoughts were preoccupied with the events unfolding on Bird Island and the two men he had trapped in the old bunker there.

He grabbed his backpack and took out the specially prepared cookies - orange, blue, and red. He had imbued each cookie with different microorganisms that granted him unique abilities. Wally put the violet cookie, which would give him enhanced hearing, in his coat pocket and ate the others.

Soon Wally did a quick pre-flight check on his plane and was airborne, heading for Bird Island. He might as well check on Harry, who was injured and still trapped in the bunker.

As he approached Bird Island, Wally gave Jeff a call on the radio, letting his friend know he had arrived. Wally asked Jeff to check on him if he had not called back by 10 AM.

There was a steady breeze from the northwest that morning, so the bay's waters would be a little choppy. Wally kept that in mind as he scanned the island while circling above. He wanted to ensure there were no signs of Jack returning before he landed. Satisfied that the coast was clear, Wally descended and landed his seaplane in a sheltered lagoon, tying it securely to a tree on shore. He headed inland, ready to deal with Harry and protect the bunker's secrets. The microorganisms he had consumed coursed through his system, enhancing his senses and abilities for whatever lay ahead. He paused to nibble on the last cookie, the violet one.

WALLY APPROACHES THE bunker at entrance E3 and enters. He pauses to listen, his enhanced hearing picking up the sounds within. Wally's heartbeat became part of the soundscape, a steady drum affirming life in a place surrounded by echoes of the past. It was a rhythm soon joined by another—a distant cadence. He could hear the erratic tapping of desperate footsteps, Harry's no doubt, seeking an escape or salvation within the labyrinth. The faint sound of strained breathing, a mixture of fear and exertion, painted a stark picture of Harry's condition without the need for visuals.

He then sets off slowly in Harry's direction, conflicted about simply observing the man's suffering versus intervening. While Wally's objective was to protect the bunker's secrets, leaving another human being to slowly perish went against his core values. Yet Harry had proven ruthless and untrustworthy, justifying caution. Wally crept forward, relying on his enhanced senses to follow Harry's movements through the maze of corridors and rooms. He trailed the echoes of frantic footsteps and raspy breaths, drawing incrementally closer to the lost man.

WALLY PEERED AROUND the storage cabinet, his enhanced vision allowing him to see Harry clearly despite the pitch-blackness that engulfed the bunker. Harry was disheveled, his clothes filthy and torn in places from his struggle through the dark corridors. One leg dragged limply behind him as he leaned heavily against the cold concrete wall, trying to catch his breath.

His face was etched with pain and exhaustion, eyes bloodshot from lack of sleep. Wally watched as Harry paused and cocked his head, as if trying to get his bearings. He appeared to be debating which direction to go next, wavering unsteadily on his feet.

After a few moments of hesitation, Harry pushed off from the wall and began limping forward again, one hand dragging along the rough surface for support. He was cradling his injured leg with his other arm, barely putting any weight on it. Wally could see the awkward angle of Harry's knee, evidence of the damage from the trap Wally had laid.

Harry paused again, then turned left down another passageway. This one was cluttered with debris and piping, making the going even more treacherous. Harry grimaced as he stumbled over an old bucket, cursing under his breath. He proceeded slowly, testing each step before committing his weight.

He continued to shadow Harry from a distance, watching as the injured man navigated the maze of corridors. Harry's breathing grew more labored, his limp more pronounced with each faltering step. He stopped periodically to listen for any signs that he was not alone in the bunker.

MISERABLE HE WAS, BROKEN he was not, it was not time to rescue Harry, Wally turned to leave the bunker. He had seen enough of Harry's struggle through the dark maze of corridors to know that the man still possessed some inner fortitude despite his desperate situation. Though injured and fatigued, Harry continued to persevere through sheer willpower. Wally realized that a rescue now might only breed further resentment and retaliation. More time was needed for Harry's defiance to give way to compliance.

As the A5 lifted above the bay, Wally turned towards Jeff's homestead, he had loaded in computer equipment just in case and planned on spending the day set up in Jeff's hangar working. Jeff had graciously offered the use of his hangar and tools if needed. Wally looked forward to a productive day focused on his projects, taking advantage of the temporary respite from the island's disturbances. The computer equipment he brought would allow him to monitor his networks and troubleshoot any issues with his growing client base. Though never fully detached from his responsibilities as guardian of the island, a day immersed in his true passion would provide balance and rejuvenation.

He would check on Harry just before day end. Nightfall seemed an appropriate time to observe the intruder again when Harry's isolation and exhaustion might leave him more receptive to reason. Wally planned to return under cover of darkness, relying on his enhanced night vision to evaluate Harry's condition and mentality. Perhaps after a day of solitude and reflection, they could reach an understanding that ensured Harry's safe passage off the island, while also guaranteeing the secrets buried within remained undisturbed. If any remnants of defiance lingered, Wally would allow the passage of time to erode them further.

WALLY SAT IN JEFF'S hangar, focused on monitoring the Bake-Ritez cloud network data transfer on his laptop. The steady clicking of computer keys filled the space as code streamed across the screen. Meanwhile, Jeff worked diligently nearby, replacing the rubber molding around the Cessna passenger door. He carefully removed the old, cracked rubber and began fitting the new molding into place, smoothing it out and checking for any gaps.

In the background, a radio played the local news station. As Jeff worked, a report came across about a disturbing discovery - a Mexican shrimper had dredged up a body in his net. According to the news anchor, it was an unidentified male in his mid-50s who appeared to be Russian.

Upon hearing this report, Wally looked up from his laptop screen. "Well Jeff," he remarked, "now we know what happened to Alexei."

Jeff paused his work on the plane and turned towards Wally with a solemn nod. "I reckon you're right about that," he said. The fate of Alexei, who they had encountered under tense circumstances on Bird Island, had been unknown to them until now. This report seemed to confirm their suspicions that the Russian had met an untimely end out in the bay.

Both men fell silent for a moment, reflecting on this grim development. Though not friends, there was a twinge of sadness at the loss of life and the mystery surrounding it. Jeff eventually broke the silence, muttering "shame" under his breath before returning to his work on the Cessna. Wally gazed out the hangar door at the shimmering water of the bay in the distance, contemplating the news of Alexei's demise.

JEFF AND WALLY SPENT the afternoon at their favorite burger place, chatting casually about Wally's new ICON A5 aircraft and its excellent handling and speed. As the sun began to dip low in the sky, they wrapped up their meal and drove back to Jeff's hangar, where Wally gathered up his computer equipment and loaded it into his plane, preparing for another trip out to Bird Island.

Before climbing into the cockpit, Wally turned to Jeff and asked him to call out to the island and check on him if he hadn't heard from Wally by 10 PM tonight. Jeff nodded, understanding the potential risks of Wally's solo missions to the remote island.

With a quick handshake, Wally climbed aboard his sleek sport plane and went through his preflight checklist with practiced ease. In minutes he was taxiing down the runway and lifting off into the painted sky, angling southeast toward the coastline.

As the lights of shore faded behind him, Wally settled in for the flight, his mind turning toward the island ahead and the injured man he had left trapped deep in its abandoned bunker days before. Wally wondered how much progress Harry had made through the dark maze of corridors and rooms, driven onward by desperation and the faint echoes of the timed explosives Wally had left to sustain him.

There was no telling in what state Wally would find the man when he arrived. But he knew his enhanced abilities from the microbe-laced cookies would give him the advantage if Harry was ready to turn against him. Wally touched the pocket where the remaining cookies waited, feeling the weight of his secret abilities even as he relied on them more with each passing day.

The sun slipped below the horizon as Wally flew onward, a small plane cutting across the growing night, headed toward an island of mysteries known only to him.

WALLY APPROACHED THE inconspicuous bunker entrance marked E5, obscured by vines and weathered concrete. He paused before the rusted steel door and consumed the remainder of the violet-hued cookie he had brought, feeling the enhanced auditory perception spread through his body.

Descending into the darkness, Wally reached the bottom step and stopped, allowing his heightened senses to take hold. Soon, he picked up faint sounds echoing through the bunker's corridors - the scuffling of shoes on concrete, muffled curses, and utterances of revenge.

He determined it was still not yet time to rescue Harry. His adversary was not ready to comply or leave the island willingly. Silently, Wally retreated from the depths of the bunker and slipped away into the island wilderness.

Soon he was airborne, piloting his aircraft away from Bird Island and heading back home. As the lights of town came into view, Wally called his friend Jeff Mitchell and gave him an update on the situation with Harry, whom they had trapped in the abandoned bunker. Jeff acknowledged the report, and they agreed to confer again soon.

Wally looked forward to spending the night in the comfort of his own bed back on the mainland, resting up for the challenges that still lay ahead in protecting the secrets of Bird Island.

Chapter 18
Bridging Technology and Nature

Wally had just finished cleaning up the breakfast leftovers when the phone rang. It was Frank calling to confirm their meeting with a new client at 10 AM that morning. Wally acknowledged that he would be there. Other than an occasional meeting or face-to-face contact, Frank had taken this load off of Wally. He could not handle many large clients at a time, therefore he was careful about the projects he took on, making sure they did not have hidden problems that would chew up time, and that the client would receive a high-value return from Wally's software.

After hanging up with Frank, Wally tidied up the kitchen and glanced at the clock. He still had a couple of hours before the meeting, just enough time to go over his notes and prepare. Wally appreciated having Frank handle most of the client interactions. It freed Wally up to focus on the work he loved - designing efficient systems and writing clean code. He knew Frank was meticulous about vetting potential clients to ensure a good fit.

He gathered his laptop bag and headed out the door. As he drove to the office, he thought about the upcoming meeting. He was looking forward to diving into a new project, confident that Frank had done his due diligence. Wally's skills were in high demand, but he was selective about taking on clients. His goal was to deliver robust solutions that made a real difference for businesses, not just pad his wallet. For Wally, it was about the satisfaction of a job well done.

THE FINAL RAYS OF THE setting sun painted the sky with hues of gold and crimson as Wally, tucked away in his office, put the finishing touches on a new client's contract. His eyes, sharpened by countless hours spent scrutinizing code and paperwork, scanned the document one last time. Just as he was about to sign off for the day, a flicker on one of his surveillance monitors caught his attention.

Bird Island. A monitor had tripped.

His heart pounded in his chest like a drum echoing through a silent night. Could it be? Had Harry somehow managed to escape the bunker?

Without wasting a second, Wally reached for his phone and dialed Jeff's number. As soon as Jeff picked up, Wally relayed the news.

"Hold tight," Jeff instructed him over the phone. "I'll do a flyover and call you back in about an hour."

With that, Wally hung up the phone and sprung into action. He swiftly sorted through the papers strewn across his desk, filing them away with mechanical precision. He then changed into his outdoor gear, packed up his backpack with essentials, and headed towards his hangar.

Wally's foot had barely touched the cold concrete floor of his hangar when his phone buzzed again. It was Jeff.

"Harry's loose," Jeff informed him urgently. "I saw him sitting on the southeast shore, not far from where the skiff had been anchored."

"Thanks for calling," Wally replied curtly, feeling an icy shiver run down his spine at the news. "I'm on my way. If you don't hear back from me in four hours... please find me."

As he ended the call, Wally stared at his plane – a metallic beast resting in the dim light of his hangar – ready to whisk him away to Bird Island once again. He took a deep breath, feeling the weight of the task ahead. Harry was loose, and Wally was the only one who could ensure the secrets of Bird Island remained hidden.

With a final glance at his phone, Wally climbed into his plane, bracing himself for what was to come.

WALLY'S A5 SEAPLANE hummed a steady rhythm as it sliced through the air, heading towards Bird Island. Below, the waters of East Matagorda Bay churned restlessly, their waves glinting in the afternoon sun. His gaze scanned the terrain, eyes searching for any signs of movement or irregularity.

His hand slipped into his pocket, retrieving four small cookies, each one laced with a different microorganism. He chewed thoughtfully on the first one, its red hue corresponding to CLF-532, known for its endurance-enhancing properties. He then consumed the orange cookie imbued with VAM-345. A faint glow appeared before his eyes, illuminating details he would have otherwise missed.

Next came the blue cookie infused with BRV-076. Instantly, memories flooded his mind in vivid detail - Harry's face, the layout of the island, every leaf and rock in his path. Finally, he swallowed the violet cookie laced with AXI-218. The hum of the plane's engine sharpened, the distant crash of waves grew louder; his auditory perception amplified to an uncanny degree.

Despite his enhanced abilities, Harry remained elusive. The island sprawled beneath him like a natural fortress, its secrets tucked away beneath thick foliage and stubborn earth. Wally knew he had to tread lightly - for all its tranquility, Bird Island was not to be underestimated.

With practiced ease, Wally maneuvered the plane towards a gentle water landing just south of the E3 entrance. The A5 skimmed across the surface before settling into a calm float, its engine sputtering to silence.

Wally unfastened his seatbelt and stepped onto the plane's float. He paused for a moment to take in his surroundings - the gentle sway of cordgrass in the breeze, a coyote darting into the underbrush. He could hear Harry's desperate breaths echoing in his mind, a chilling reminder of the task at hand.

Drawing a deep breath, Wally prepared to plunge into the island's heart on foot. His senses buzzed with heightened awareness, each cookie amplifying his abilities in a unique way. The secrets of Bird Island lay before him, but so did Harry - a threat that needed to be neutralized. Wally's resolve hardened as he stepped onto the island, ready to confront whatever lay ahead.

WALLY MOVED STEADILY through the dense foliage of Bird Island, pausing every so often to listen intently for any sounds that might reveal Harry's location. But the island remained eerily quiet, with only the rustling of leaves and the calls of distant gulls breaking the silence.

He was unaware that luck was not on Harry's side today. In his desperate attempt to escape the island, Harry stumbled directly into another one of the ingenious traps that Wally had set around the perimeter. When it triggered, the long wooden arm of the trap whipped around with force, striking Harry's already injured leg and shattering the makeshift splint. He cried out in agony as the blow also fractured his other leg just below the knee.

Harry had crumpled to the ground, his legs useless and wracked with pain. Driven by pure adrenaline and instinct, he had dragged himself into the cover of the tall grass before passing out from the trauma. There he lay hidden, unconscious and helpless, as Wally continued his methodical search of the island's interior.

He was meticulous in his exploration. He moved steadily but cautiously, all his heightened senses engaged. The special microbe-enhanced cookies he had consumed allowed him to perceive details that would be impossible for an ordinary man. But so far, even Wally's augmented hearing could not detect any trace of Harry.

AS HARRY BEGINS TO regain consciousness, his moans and groans become audible. It was not long before Wally picks up on the sound with his enhanced hearing and finds Harry lying unconscious in the tall grass. Wally carefully lifts Harry and carries him to a clump of live oak trees nearby, clearing a space on the ground. He builds a small fire using kindling and logs from the surrounding area, providing warmth and light as the sun begins to set.

Wally makes Harry as comfortable as possible, giving him sips of water and bits of food from his pack to help him regain some strength. Harry remains only semi-conscious, drifting in and out, but manages to ingest some of the offered sustenance.

Once Harry appears stable, Wally sits down on a log and ponders what to do next with this intruder who poses a threat to the secrets of Bird Island. Wally knows he cannot allow Harry to roam free or leave the island with any knowledge of its hidden bunkers and mysterious contents. However, he debates whether permanently trapping Harry here is ethical or if he deserves a second chance under strict conditions. Weighing his options, Wally stokes the fire and keeps a close watch over Harry as night falls and the choices ahead weigh heavily on his mind.

WALLY HATCHED A PLAN as he searched Bird Island, which was not only home to a historic military bunker but also a federal wildlife sanctuary. He combed the shores and marshes, looking for specific items that would help implicate Harry as a criminal.

First, Wally gathered feathers shed by seabirds and raptors like bald eagles and ospreys. He carefully collected them until he had almost enough to execute his scheme. Then he hit the jackpot - a nest of endangered whooping crane eggs. Wally quickly secured a padded container to protect the fragile eggs and placed them gently inside.

Next, Wally entered the abandoned bunker. He located several artifacts from the bunker's military past, including a folder marked "Top Secret." Wally packed these items into a vintage military duffle bag along with the feathers and precious eggs.

By planting the eggs and feathers on Harry, as well as the stolen artifacts, Wally intended to frame him as both a wildlife poacher and artifact smuggler. The authorities would come down hard on someone disturbing an endangered species and looting from a historical site. Wally felt this was the only way to permanently stop Harry from returning and revealing the bunker's secrets. Once the authorities arrived, Harry would be arrested and unable to threaten the safety of the island ever again.

WALLY RETURNED TO WHERE Harry now slept under the live oak trees. He quietly added enough wood to the fire to last most of the night, ensuring Harry would stay warm. Then, Wally methodically removed all of the traps he had set around the island, disarming each one to prevent any further injuries.

With the island now cleared of his defenses, Wally headed back to his seaplane. He started up the engine and took to the sky, leaving Bird Island behind. Once airborne, Wally called his friend Jeff Mitchell and informed him of everything that had transpired with Harry. He asked Jeff to call the local Game Warden and report seeing a fire and strange activity on Bird Island. This would prompt an investigation that would likely implicate Harry in illegal activities and prevent his return.

Satisfied with the actions taken, Wally turned the seaplane towards home. He was ready to put this incident behind him and hoped Harry would finally face consequences for trespassing on the island. Though conflicted about leaving the injured man, Wally knew reporting him was necessary to protect the secrets of Bird Island. As the island faded from view, Wally looked ahead to being back home and resuming his normal life, the island's mysteries secure once more.

AS THE SUN BEGAN TO rise on Bird Island, casting a warmth across the dew-kissed marshes, a pair of local game wardens made their way through the dense foliage. The air was filled with the melodic calls of coastal birds greeting the new day. Moving with purpose, the wardens, clad in their distinctive olive uniforms and sturdy boots, navigated the landscape under the expansive canopy of live oak trees that stood as silent witnesses to the island's storied past.

The golden rays of daylight filtered through the thick branches, painting the ground with patterns of light and shadow. On one such spot of light laid a surprising scene that halted the wardens' progression. There, strewn beneath the knotted live oaks, lay a haphazard collection of items: a pile of feathers from various birds of the region, amongst them the distinctive white and black plumage belonging to the majestic, yet endangered, whooping cranes.

Beside the feathers, cradled in a makeshift padded container, lay a clutch of whooping crane eggs, so rare and protected they shimmered like pearls of the utmost value. The wardens noted the location of the precious eggs with a blend of surprise and concern, understanding immediately the legal implications of such a discovery.

A vintage military duffle bag sat conspicuously alongside, its weathered canvas unfolding to reveal its contents. The reveal of aged documents labeled "Top Secret," along with an assortment of military artifacts, intensified the gravity of the situation. Every trained muscle in the wardens' bodies tensed, knowing full well that both the law and the sanctuary of Bird Island had been grossly violated.

Nearer to the live oaks' trunks rested Harry, a prone figure who was now stirring awake amid the sound of encroaching footsteps. Confusion clouded his features as the wardens approached, radios crackling with the chatter of pending enforcement action. The authorities knew these trees well, their sprawling roots a familiar foundation that had grounded countless patrols. But this morning, they bore silent testament to an unfortunate act of greed and desperation.

With meticulous professionalism, the game wardens began documenting the scene, photographing the items and securing the area. The charges were evident and severe: poaching and unauthorized possession of endangered species, theft of protected historical artifacts, not to mention potential violation of federal sanctuary laws.

Harry, pinned under the game wardens' scrutiny, found himself entangled in a web of incrimination, unable to dispel the circumstances that enveloped him as tightly as the island's morning fog. As the wardens awaited backup, the chorus of feathered inhabitants resumed their songs, the natural chorus continuing despite the human transgressions that had sought to disrupt their sanctuary.

WALLY HAD SPENT MANY sleepless nights wondering about the fate of Harry after leaving him injured on Bird Island. Though it pained him to abandon the ruthless man in such a state, he knew it was necessary to protect the island's secrets.

So when Jeff called that morning to relay news from the game warden who had investigated Harry's illegal activities on the island, Wally was anxious to learn what had transpired.

Jeff explained that the game warden had found Harry barely conscious amongst the remnants of endangered bird eggs and feathers that Wally had planted to implicate him. Harry had apparently provided only garbled, incoherent responses when questioned about the prohibited poaching.

With no ID or means to identify himself, Harry was transported to a secure psychiatric facility on the mainland. The doctors diagnosed him with delirium and psychosis, likely from dehydration, hunger, and the trauma of his ordeal alone on the island. Harry was receiving treatment but continued to ramble about supernatural events, hidden bunkers, and a mysterious boy with superhuman abilities.

Of course, the authorities dismissed these nonsensical claims. But it was clear Harry posed no further threat, as his harrowing experience had left him a broken, incapacitated man.

Wally took a deep breath upon hearing the news, conflicted about Harry's fate but relieved that the island's secrets remained protected. Perhaps now his vigilant defense of Bird Island could subside, and he could start to regain normalcy in his own life.

WALLY SLUMPED IN HIS chair, a weariness creeping into his bones that no amount of caffeine could banish. His world had been whittled down to lines of code and endless troubleshooting, an endless loop of work that was beginning to blur together. The passion that had once ignited him was flickering, struggling against the monotony.

His gaze fell on a photograph pinned to the wall, a splash of color amidst the clutter of notes and diagrams. It was a picture of his mother, her face wreathed in a warm smile as she cradled a vibrant Don Egolf Redbud in her hands. The memory of her love for plants tugged at him, a whisper from the past reminding him of another life he could live.

The ESP-628 beckoned him, its potential untapped and inviting. Could it really enhance plant growth? Would it cut short the ten long years he would otherwise have to wait for a Redbud to mature? It was a gamble, but one he was willing to take.

With newfound determination, Wally set aside his work and rose from his chair. His fingers tapped out a quick message on his phone, reserving a Redbud for pickup at the local nursery. That done, he strode towards his garden shed, mirroring the design of his mother's down to the smallest detail.

Inside the shed, Wally gathered what he needed with practiced ease: A sample of ESP-628, a pair of gloves, and an old spade. His heart pounded with anticipation as he looked at the tools laid out before him. For the first time in weeks, Wally felt alive.

Outside, under the vast expanse of Texas sky, Wally began to work. He was taking a risk with ESP-628, stepping away from the safety of familiar code and algorithms. But if it meant breathing life into his Redbud and reclaiming a piece of his mother's legacy, it was a risk he was willing to take.

He may not have to wait 10 years for a mature Redbud. The thought was both exhilarating and terrifying, and Wally couldn't wait to see what would happen next.

THE DAYS PASSED IN a whirlwind of code and innovation. Wally was knee-deep in the intricacies of machine automation for Bake_Ritez's cloud system, a project that set his heart pounding with excitement. It was more than just a lucrative opportunity; it was a challenge, a puzzle to be solved, a chance to flex his coding muscles in ways he hadn't in months.

Work consumed him, his world narrowing down to the hum of his computer and the tap-tap-tap of keys under his fingertips. So engrossed was he in his work that the Redbud tree he'd ordered slipped from his mind entirely. It wasn't until the shrill ring of the phone jarred him from his coding trance that he remembered.

Excitement bubbling within him, Wally constructed a miniature greenhouse at the side of his boat storage shed. His hands worked with practiced efficiency, securing the framework and covering it with transparent plastic sheets. The space was small but sufficient for what he had planned - a sanctuary for his Don Egolf Redbud.

His greenhouse ready, Wally fetched his tree. Its slender branches reached skyward, leaves quivering in anticipation of their new home. Wally nestled it into the fertile soil within the greenhouse, ensuring it was securely rooted.

His tree cared for, Wally turned his attention to an experiment he'd been nursing on the side - Microorganism ESP-628. The test batch bubbled promisingly, like a witch's brew in an old fairy tale.

From the kitchen, Wally rolled out enough dough for a dozen cookies, each laced with the microorganism-filled concoction. The oven hummed as it preheated, swallowing up the cookies as Wally slid them onto its heated racks.

The oven timer dinged and Wally pulled out a tray of warm cookies. Their scent filled his nostrils as he bit into one, the remainder tucked into his pocket for later. The rest were sealed in shrink wrap, waiting for their turn to be consumed.

With the first cookie of ESP-628 safely ingested, Wally decided to take it slow, savoring each bite just in case. He didn't know what to expect from the microorganism-infused treat, but he was eager to find out.

OVER THE NEXT TWO WEEKS, Wally was caught up in an endless chain of new requirements and changes at Bake-RiteZ. All had been quiet on Bird Island, with no activity showing up on Wally's surveillance monitors.

Suddenly Wally remembered - the redbud tree! He hurriedly went to the shed to check on it. Inside, he was amazed to see that the young redbud, which had been a spindly sapling just days before, had grown into a small but healthy young tree. Its stems and branches were covered in shiny green leaves, and the beginnings of vibrant pink flower buds were just starting to emerge.

Wally realized that the experimental microorganism ESP-628 must have worked - it had clearly accelerated the redbud's growth at an incredible rate. He carefully inspected the plant, looking for any abnormalities or signs of instability, but it seemed perfectly healthy, just far more mature than expected. Running his hands over the smooth bark and delicate leaves, Wally smiled, both proud of the success of ESP-628 and happy to see his mother's favorite tree thriving. This unique redbud would be a living legacy, a secret sign of Wally's accomplishments.

After ensuring the redbud's soil and water were optimal, Wally closed up the shed, making a mental note to continue monitoring the plant's progress. For now, it seemed the microorganism had only positive effects, but Wally knew looks could be deceiving. He would have to remain vigilant, even as demands from Bake-RiteZ continued. Wally took one last glance at the flourishing redbud before returning to his work, content that both the tree and Bird Island's secrets remained safely under his protection.

Chapter 19
The Legacy Lives On

He walked slowly around SeaWings, he had named her a few days back as he tired of referring to her as the A5. Previously Wally had asked his dad to meet him at the airport for a quick lunch and he had just arrived. As Wally walked into the small bar where they served mostly burgers and sandwiches, his dad was already seated. After a lite lunch, Wally stands and says, "Come on dad, I want to show you something, I hope you enjoy it." Wally leads his dad to the hanger where SeaWings waits. Wally looks at his dad and says, "Hop in, lets take her up, we can make it a short ride or a longer one, your choice".

Wally's dad looked at the sleek white and blue seaplane with surprise and admiration. "She's a real beauty," he said, running his hand along the wing. Though initially hesitant, his excitement grew as Wally enthusiastically described the plane's capabilities. "Alright, let's take her up," he finally said, settling into the cockpit next to his son. "How about we head up the coast a ways so I can really see what this bird can do?" Wally smiled, thrilled to share his passion for flying with his dad, as they buckled in and prepared for takeoff. With a roar of the engine, SeaWings lifted gracefully into the sky, ready to grant Wally's dad an exhilarating first flight.

WALLY MADE A QUICK check making sure his backpack was in the rear, just in case. He then took a southwest heading in his seaplane SeaWings, with his father in the passenger seat.

As they flew over the shimmering blue waters of the Gulf, Wally gave his dad a complete update about the events that had taken place on Bird Island over the past few days. He told him about discovering the abandoned bunker, encountering intruders like Jack and Harry, and using special abilities gained from microorganisms to defend the island's secrets.

He was amazed and proud that his son had taken on such a big responsibility to protect the island at his young age.

Before making a water landing near Bird Island, Wally did a quick flyover just to make sure the island had no uninvited visitors. Seeing it was deserted, he smoothly landed SeaWings in a secluded lagoon.

Father and son took a brief walk on the island, with Wally pointing out landmarks from his adventures. Too soon, it was time to head back. As quickly as they sat down, Wally lifted off making a slow circle over Jeff's home and then turned for home.

Soon they were taxiing up to the hangar. Wally's father smiled, clearly impressed by his son's skill as a pilot. He told Wally how proud he was, and that he would support him on his mission to guard the secrets of Bird Island, as unbelievable as they still seemed. Wally felt relieved and thankful for his father's trust.

WALLY LEANED BACK IN his desk chair and admired the complex code on his computer screen. After weeks of intense focus, he had finally implemented the fuzzy logic automation module into the Bake-Ritez cloud system. The flexible rules and machine learning capabilities would allow the software to handle nuanced business scenarios without constant human oversight.

He clicked "Run Diagnostics" and watched as the code processed test data flawlessly. A smile crossed his face, knowing this breakthrough would impress his clients and open up new opportunities for his company, Flex-Code. Beyond that, it represented the leading edge of cloud software capabilities. Wally's passion and talent for elegant coding solutions shone through.

With the Bake-Ritez project winding down, Wally suddenly found himself with free time on his hands. It was a welcome change of pace after being consumed by work for so long. He realized he had been neglecting other areas of his life and looked forward to reconnecting with friends and family.

He glanced at the calendar and remembered that today was his mom's birthday. An idea popped into his head - he would give her the redbud tree he had been nurturing with the experimental microorganism ESP-628. In just a few weeks under his care, the tree had grown from a sapling to over six feet tall, with vibrant magenta flowers starting to bloom.

He carefully transported the redbud to his trailer and drove to his childhood home. When his mom saw the tree, a huge smile lit up her face. She was so impressed that her son had raised it himself. Wally helped plant the redbud in the backyard, where its blossoms would remind his mom of his love and care for her.

As Wally embraced his mom and wished her a happy birthday, he felt content. With his software project successful and Bird Island secure for now, he could relax and focus on the personal connections that mattered most. Life was becoming fun again.

AS THE SUN BEGAN TO set, casting a warm glow over the vibrant redbud blossoms, Wally stood beside his mother, soaking in the tranquility of their family garden. Reflecting on the successful completion of his project and the recent adventures on Bird Island, he sensed a stirring wind of change—whispers of mysteries yet to unravel and threats that loomed in the shadows. For now, though, those were concerns for another day. With his mother's laughter mingling with the rustle of leaves, Wally smiled, knowing that no matter what the future held, he was ready. The Guardian of Bird Island would rise to meet it, with SeaWings at his command and the uncharted secrets of the island beckoning him to new horizons. Behind the serenity of the blooming redbud—a symbol of life's resilience and renewal—the story of Wally and Bird Island was only beginning.

About the Author

Wallace Berry was born in Little Rock, Arkansas, as World War II began, and his upbringing took place on a farm in the Arkansas countryside. His childhood was steeped in the rustic simplicity of farm life, absent of modern conveniences such as electricity, indoor plumbing, relying on wood stoves for warmth, and lanterns for light. This immersion in a world where nature and necessity dictated daily life deeply rooted in him a love for the wilderness. His adventures in the surrounding forests and the hands-on experiences of early rural living profoundly shaped his appreciation for nature and a life outdoors. As he grew older, Wallace chose the Texas Gulf Coast as his place of residence, carrying with him the values and passions developed during his formative years.